DANGEROUS LOVER

Crime and Passion, Book 3

Mary Lancaster

ARE YOU SIGNED UP FOR DRAGONBLADE'S BLOG?

You'll get the latest news and information on exclusive giveaways, exclusive excerpts, coming releases, sales, free books, cover reveals and more.

Check out our complete list of authors, too!

No spam, no junk. That's a promise!

Sign Up Here

www.dragonbladepublishing.com

Dearest Reader;

Thank you for your support of a small press. At Dragonblade Publishing, we strive to bring you the highest quality Historical Romance from the some of the best authors in the business. Without your support, there is no 'us', so we sincerely hope you adore these stories and find some new favorite authors along the way.

Happy Reading!

CEO, Dragonblade Publishing

Additional Dragonblade books by Author Mary Lancaster

Crime & Passion Series
Mysterious Lover
Letters to a Lover
Dangerous Lover

The Husband Dilemma Series
How to Fool a Duke

Season of Scandal Series
Pursued by the Rake
Abandoned to the Prodigal
Married to the Rogue
Unmasked by her Lover

Imperial Season Series
Vienna Waltz
Vienna Woods
Vienna Dawn

Blackhaven Brides Series
The Wicked Baron
The Wicked Lady
The Wicked Rebel
The Wicked Husband
The Wicked Marquis
The Wicked Governess
The Wicked Spy
The Wicked Gypsy
The Wicked Wife

Wicked Christmas (A Novella)
The Wicked Waif
The Wicked Heir
The Wicked Captain
The Wicked Sister

Unmarriageable Series
The Deserted Heart
The Sinister Heart
The Vulgar Heart
The Broken Heart
The Weary Heart
The Secret Heart
Christmas Heart

The Lyon's Den Connected World
Fed to the Lyon

Also from Mary Lancaster
Madeleine

CHAPTER ONE

THE HOUSE LOOMED out of the fog, indistinct yet alarming. Since it was surrounded by a high wall, Alexandra could make out only the upper stories until she came to a tall, wrought iron gate. Through the bars, it looked dauntingly old and uninviting. Neither did the air around it smell very pleasant. It was too close to the river.

Well, I have lived in worse places, and the salary is excellent. Taking a deep breath, she lifted the gate latch and walked into the garden. She closed the gate behind her and walked briskly up the path, which was clear of weeds and moss, though overhung by large trees and thick bushes. Ignoring the prickle up her spine, she stepped onto the porch and lifted the brass knocker.

Decent employers did not have to live in Mayfair or Belgravia, she reminded herself. Though it was surely odd to find a baronet living in this part of London, that was not her concern. Even so, when the door opened to reveal a smartly dressed maidservant, she was distinctly relieved.

"Alexandra Battle," she introduced herself. "I believe I am expected."

"Oh, yes, Miss Battle, come in out the nasty, damp fog," the girl invited. "Mrs. Dart is waiting for you. James, t'will you tell Mrs. Dart that the governess has arrived."

The large manservant so addressed was not in livery and was hurrying toward the back of the house, but he raised one hand in acknowledgement.

"Perhaps you'd like to wait in here, Miss." The maid led her across a surprisingly cramped but tall entrance hall. There was a lot of dark wood with ornamental carving, and light tricking down the staircase. And a small, human figure skulking in the shadows beneath.

Alexandra pretended not to see the small figure—after all, it was natural for a child to be curious about her new governess—and merely followed the maid into a rather bare chamber. Here, an ancient wooden settle with cushions and a small round table seemed to be the only furnishings. At least the room appeared to be clean, as far as she could tell, for there was little light coming in the window.

The maid bustled off and Alexandra, still in her hat and cape, sat on the unforgiving settle. The door had been left ajar, and a moment later, a small girl materialized in the space. Beneath a wealth of dark, well-brushed hair, a pair of wide, serious brown eyes regarded her with more than a hint of foreboding.

"Good morning," Alexandra said. "Are you, by chance, Evelina?"

The girl nodded and took a step further inside.

"How do you do?"

Whatever the child might have answered to this, remained unclear, for Mrs. Dart, the motherly, middle-aged housekeeper rustled into the room and took Evelina by the hand.

"So glad you found us, Miss Battle. I was worried about you seeing the correct house in this fog."

"I imagine it must stand out in any other weather," Alexandra said, rising to greet the housekeeper. They had met before, in a teashop in the Strand, where Mrs. Dart had interviewed her for the position. In fact, it was Mrs. Dart's agreeable character and obvious respectability that had induced Alexandra to accept the position, for she found it odd not to meet the employers themselves. But then, since Mrs. Dart had only ever referred to Sir Nicholas Swan and never to Lady Swan, she assumed the mother was sadly deceased and the housekeeper more adept than a mere male at engaging governesses.

"This is Evelina," Mrs. Dart said, tugging the little girl forward. "Evelina, this kind lady is your governess, Miss Battle. You must mind her as if she were your papa."

For the first time, a smile lit up Evelina's face. She actually laughed. "But she is nothing like Papa!"

"Of course, I am not," Alexandra agreed, smiling back and holding out her hand. "But I'm sure we shall get on famously just the same."

The girl curtseyed in a wobbly kind of way, then approached close enough for Alexandra to take her hand in a gentle shake. Evelina seemed slightly surprised but not displeased. She still had a shy smile in her eyes.

"Perhaps," Alexandra suggested. "You could show me your schoolroom?"

"Oh yes," Evelina said enthusiastically. Her little fingers gripped Alexandra's and began tugging her toward the door. "Everyone has been cleaning it out, so that is *huge* now and it sparkles!"

"A sparkling schoolroom," Alexandra marveled. "I have never seen one of those before. Lead on!"

Mrs. Dart cast an indulgent smile at the child and said, "I'll come and find you later, Miss Battle, to explain living arrangements and so on."

"Thank you," Alexandra said, allowing herself to be tugged from the room and across the dark hall to the stairs. The steps crunched underfoot, as though they had not been swept for some time. The bannister was dusty, and Alexandra spotted more than one cobweb. "How long have you lived here, Evelina?"

"Not long," said the child.

From the first-floor landing, Alexandra glimpsed a large, empty hall straight ahead and several closed doors on either side. Evelina drew her on up to the next floor and turned right along a long, narrow passage. More wood and dust, closed doors and cobwebs, until finally an open door revealed what seemed like a flood of light. Evelina smiled proudly and led her inside.

In fact, it was not a huge room, but it had space to teach several children, and it was brighter than the downstairs rooms, as though it was too high up for the fog to penetrate.

Two new looking wooden desks had been placed close to the fireplace. One small one for Evelina, and, facing it, a larger one clearly meant for a teacher. On each lay a row of pens and pencils beside the ink wells. A bookcase to one side contained a few well-used books, new notebooks, and loose paper.

"This is a very pleasant room," Alexandra agreed, taking off her hat and wrap, and hanging them on the hooks on the back of the door. "I think we shall have a lot of fun here."

She pulled a notebook from the shelf and set it on the smaller desk. "Can you write your name on the book?"

Apparently she could. In a round, childish hand, she wrote *Evelina Swan*.

"And how old are you, Evelina?"

"Six."

"Can you write your birthday?"

She wrote *21ˢᵗ March 1845*.

"Well done. Can you write your address, too?"

She wrote, *New Hungerford House, Craven Lane, London.*

"Excellent," Alexandra approved and won a smile. "You have not always lived in London, though, have you? Where did you live before?"

"Palazzo Fabrizio, Venezia," she replied promptly.

"That sounds very grand," Alexandra said in Italian. "I believe I was chosen to be your governess because I, too, speak Italian."

"Did you live in Venice?" Evelina asked eagerly.

"No, in Rome and Florence, for a little, though I visited Venice once or twice. It is a beautiful city."

Evelina beamed. "There is a river here, too, and boats, but not like in Venice."

"No, not like Venice," Alexandra agreed. "Do you have watercolor paints, Evelina?"

"Oh yes. Not here, though—should I fetch them?"

"Yes, please."

Evelina trotted off through an inner door, to what seemed to be a playroom, for here were the toys and storybooks that Alexandra had hoped to see. Two more doors led off this playroom, but she held back her curiosity, for Evelina had found her box of paints, and Alexandra set her to paint a picture of her old house in Venice and then her new house in London.

"Then we can put them both on the wall, and I think that will make the schoolroom even more agreeable."

Evelina set to with perfect good nature. At their interview in the tearoom, Mrs. Dart had warned Alexandra that her charge was subject to wild temper tantrums, but there were no signs of those so far.

"Do you feel capable of dealing with such incidents firmly but without violence?" Mrs. Dart had asked.

"Violence?" Alexandra had said, startled. "The child is six years old!"

"And in a temper, she seems to have a strength three times that," Mrs. Dart had said dryly. "She can be a difficult child. Nevertheless, if you lift a hand to her, it would mean instant dismissal. Her father will not tolerate it."

"Neither shall I. There are other ways to discipline a child."

"Sir Nicholas would be glad to hear you say so." She had hesitated, then added, "Sir Nicholas does not want her locked in her room either."

"How does Sir Nicholas deal with these tantrums?" she had asked.

Again, Mrs. Dart had hesitated. "The only time I saw her do so with him, he held her until the screaming stopped. Which it quickly did."

Alexandra had refrained from comment. After all, she needed the position.

While Evelina was occupied, Alexandra took out the books she carried to each new position and set them on her desk. Then she wandered into the playroom, which she had already seen. As she had expected, one of the doors off it led to what was clearly Evelina's bedroom. The furniture was elegant and small, as if it had been specially made for a child—probably in Italy. And on the dressing table was an ornate double frame containing two miniature portraits.

Alexandra couldn't resist moving forward and picking up the frame. On the left was an accomplished painting of an incredibly beautiful woman, raven haired and hazel eyed. There was something tempestuous in the brilliance of those eyes, in the way she held her head, as though in mid-toss. Her luscious lips drooped faintly with discontent. Was this Evelina's dead mother?

If so, then the dark, scowling man in the other picture must be her father, the elusive Sir Nicholas. He was not handsome, precisely. He was altogether too swarthy for that, his long, thin nose and prominent cheek bones too sharp, his brows too thick. The tilt of his head spoke of impatience and arrogance. In all, it was a face of uncompromising strength, but it was the compelling eyes that snatched her breath. Dark and restless and demanding—and God help you if you didn't obey.

From her initial conversation with Mrs. Dart, she had imagined a rather weak, negligent young parent, overindulgent and careless by turn. But he looked older than she had imagined, closer to forty than thirty. And there was neither weakness nor affection in that face.

She could well understand why Mrs. Dart and the rest of the household went out of their way to make sure he was obeyed to the letter.

I don't like you, she thought grimly. *But I will endeavor never to get on the wrong side of you.*

Alexandra replaced the frame and left, closing the door on the bedroom. She tried the next door, which led to another, smaller chamber, clearly occupied, but very neat.

"The nurserymaid sleeps here," Mrs. Dart said, startling Alexandra by suddenly appearing at the chamber's other door which led into the passage. "This is Anna. She's Italian but speaks English increasingly well."

The nurserymaid, a dark-haired woman of perhaps thirty years, stared at Alexandra without welcome.

"Excuse me," Alexandra said politely. "I didn't mean to intrude. I was just exploring."

Anna nodded once, though her expression grew no warmer. The three of them passed into the playroom once more, from where they could see Evelina happily painting.

"She will get paint everywhere," Anna observed.

"Then we shall clean it up," Alexandra said pleasantly. "Perhaps, you could find her a smock to protect her clothes?"

"And stay with her while I show Miss Battle her own chamber," Mrs. Dart added.

Before she went to fetch her bag from the schoolroom, Alexandra glanced at the third door leading off the playroom.

"Oh, it's empty," Mrs. Dart said, throwing it wide.

It wasn't quite empty. Some excess and probably old cushions had been abandoned there. Alexandra smiled.

"We could make it up for you," Mrs. Dart said doubtfully. "But I thought you would prefer a room apart from the schoolroom, especially with Anna already sleeping so close to Evelina."

"Of course." Alexandra closed the door, fetched her bag from the schoolroom, where she paused to admire Evelina's painting and tell the child she would return momentarily, and then followed Mrs. Dart out into the passage.

"I've put you just along here, closer to the staircase," the house-

7

keeper said, marching along the bare floor. "I think it is a pleasant room, now that it is cleaned and aired. You must forgive the state of much of the rest of the house. We are working on it, but it is a large undertaking. The house was not lived in for decades before Sir Nicholas took it into his head to move in. Everyone thought he would sell it, ancient, inconvenient, and badly located as it is."

"Perhaps he lived here in childhood?" Alexandra guessed.

"He most assuredly did not," Mrs. Dart retorted, clearly affronted by the very idea. "He lived at the Grange and in Brook Street."

"Oh. Then this is not an old family property?" Alexandra asked in surprise.

Mrs. Dart sniffed. "Family property, yes, family home, no. I wasn't aware of its existence until Sir Nicholas chose to live here rather than eject his brother from Brook Street where, frankly, Mr. Ralph has no right to be as the younger son. Here is your chamber."

It was indeed a pleasant room, bigger and much more comfortable than she had expected. The furnishings were old but functional, the bed large, and the curtains heavy and clean. The fog appeared to be lifting, for a definite beam of sunshine penetrated the window.

"This is wonderful," Alexandra said gratefully.

"It should be peaceful," Mrs. Dart said. "There is nothing but the nursery on this part of the floor. At the far end is a servants' stair, but I'm the only one who uses it, since my room is off the half-landing. The servants use the stairs on the other side, where Sir Nicholas has his rooms. Would you like one of the maids to unpack for you?"

Alexandra laid her bag on the bed. "No, thank you. It won't take me long."

"Sir Nicholas tends to eat out, but he has suggested you use the dining room and dine with Evelina. I know it is not usual," she added hastily, "but as I think I told you when we first met, there is no lady of the house, and you will not wish to take all your meals in the school-room, or alone. And I think the child will be glad of the company."

"I am quite happy to do as Sir Nicholas thinks fit," Alexandra said calmly. "It will probably be good for Evelina to get used to dining formally. Where has she been eating?"

"In the schoolroom, usually, sometimes with Anna. Occasionally in the dining room with her father, but he is a busy man and not often at home."

Alexandra was gaining an impression of Sir Nicholas as a careless parent, spoiling his difficult child, while laying down the law for everyone else to abide by.

"Can I ask how long it is since Lady Swan passed away?"

Mrs. Dart blinked. "Lady Swan? Why, it must be some fifteen—" She broke off. "Ah, you mean Evelina's mother. She was not Lady Swan. Sir Nicholas has never been married. But," she added, while Alexandra wished she had not been naïve enough to ask, "he is fond of the child and gives her his name. Though it won't change the stigma the poor thing will face as she grows up. I hope it makes no difference to *you*?"

"Of course not. I only asked to better understand the stage of Evelina's grief."

"I believe it was recent. A few months only, less than a year. Consumption. She was a performer, a singer or some such." Mrs. Dart sniffed, signaling contempt for the dead mother, if not for her innocent child.

》》》《《《

THE DINING ROOM was not dauntingly huge like some she had faced. In fact, it was a pleasant, cozy room. The furniture may have been a hundred years old, but the chairs were newly upholstered and comfortable. Alexandra and Evelina sat at one end of the table, and were served by a maid and a footman, which Evelina seemed to take for granted.

Somewhere during the day, Evelina had lost her shyness, responding naturally to every conversation Alexandra initiated, and chattering happily about her own life.

Once, she asked, "Have you always been a governess?"

"For the last six years."

"Then you have taught lots of children?"

"A few."

"Did you like them?"

"Most of them," Alexandra replied truthfully.

Something seemed to strike Evelina, and she laid down her fork. "You are English. Why were you in Italy?"

"Because my father went there. He was a musician and traveled about the continent, playing the piano for noblemen and theatre audiences." *On good days…*

Evelina's eyes widened. "Like Mama! Only Mama sang. Perhaps your father played for her!"

"Perhaps he did."

"Don't you remember? I shall have to ask Papa."

Alexandra bit back the panicked *Please don't do that*, and instead changed the subject. After all, even if Evelina remembered to ask, the chances of her father paying any attention to either question or answer were remote. Alexandra was only the governess.

As they finished dinner, Anna, the nurserymaid, came to take Evelina away and, presumably, put her to bed, for the child called, "Good night, Miss Battle!" as she trotted off.

Alexandra sat back, thoughtfully, wondering if and when more arduous duties, such as mending, might come her way. So far, she appeared to have landed on her feet in this position, however irregular the family.

The same maid who had admitted her to the house that morning, came bustling in with an empty tray to clear up. Alexandra made to stand.

"No, no, stay where you are, Miss," the girl said cheerfully. "I won't be a minute, and no one will bother you here. The master isn't home. He isn't, usually."

Governesses did not gossip with the servants, but she allowed herself to say neutrally, "Evelina seems to be alone a great deal. She must miss her mother."

The maid piled plates and cutlery on to the tray, separating the cutlery. "I suppose she must, but she seems happy enough, as long as you don't get on the wrong side of her. I think she had a difficult life in Italy, what with a mother like that."

"And her father," Alexandra felt compelled to point out.

"Oh, he didn't live with them from what I can gather. He was a bit of a wild one in his youth, Sir Nicholas. I'm Clara, by the way, all-purpose housemaid, so if you need anything, just ask." Clara reached for the serving dishes.

"Thank you." Judging by his portrait in Evelina's room, he had not been so very young when his daughter was born. Which was none of her business, or the maid's. So, despite inevitable curiosity, Alexandra kept her next inquiry impersonal. Or thought she did. "Was it business that took Sir Nicholas to Italy in the first place?"

Clara grinned. "No, he was only eighteen, bless him, and he ran off with a married lady!"

"Evelina's mother was married to someone else?" Alexandra asked, startled.

"Bless you, Miss, I don't know anything about that. Sir Nicholas didn't run off with *her*. She was Italian. He ran off with Lady..." She glanced around nervously. "Well, I'd better not say. But, I heard he tired of her quickly, abandoned her, and took up with Evelina's mother instead. Can't blame him, really—she was beautiful, whatever else she was."

Abandoning the woman whose life one had ruined did not sit well with Alexandra, but who was she to cast blame?

"The family never spoke of him after he left," Clara confided. "And even when old Sir Bennet died, it was Mr. Ralph who took over the townhouse. We all began to think Sir Nicholas must be dead. And then he appears without warning in Sussex with little Evelina, turns everything upside down, puts in a new steward, and takes Mrs. Dart and me and several others up to London to live in this funny house. While Mr. Ralph," she finished darkly, "lords it up in Mayfair."

She hefted up the loaded tray and made for the door. "Mind you, wouldn't want to be in Mr. Ralph's shoes if Sir Nicholas comes calling!"

Alexandra was left feeling glad she was merely the governess. She must ensure that this positive tirade of scandal, gossip and, it seemed, family feuds, did not distress Evelina.

CHAPTER TWO

WITH THE INEVITABLE difficulties and anxieties that came with the first day in a new post, Alexandra retired early that evening. In her warm, comfortable room, she all but flopped into bed and fell immediately asleep.

However, it was not an undisturbed sleep. Dreams involving giant cobwebs and furious children who looked like the angelic Evelina—or sometimes her beautiful mother—disturbed her. Sometimes, she was stepping over rubble with Evelina or one of her previous pupils. Sometimes she was playing the pianoforte among the cobwebs. Sometimes her father was. And once, the threatening, saturnine figure of her employer stood among the shadows, waiting for the mistake that would ruin her position and her life. When she swung away, he was suddenly before her, large and frightening. And yet in the midst of the fear, she felt the sweet, heavy tug of desire, and seeing it, he began to smile just as she jerked into wakefulness.

Twice more, she woke, once to distant voices—male voices, so perhaps the elusive Sir Nicholas had come home at last. She fell asleep again, almost at once, only to be wakened again by strange, bumping noises. Had she been susceptible to the gothic romances she loved to read, she could have imagined it was clanking chains. However, the bumping seemed far too rhythmic for that. Unless the chained one was dancing or drumming, she could not believe in such a scene.

She thought of getting up and creeping through the old house to the source of the noise, and in truth, it intrigued her. She tried pulling the pillows over her ears, but the noise persisted.

She sat up.

She was the new governess. She had not been in the house twenty-four hours. Did that mean curiosity was more or less forgivable? She should at least go as far as the schoolroom and make sure Evelina was neither disturbed nor causing the racket in the first place.

The fact that Anna, the nurserymaid, was closer did not seem terribly relevant as she rose from bed and padded across the cool floor to find her dressing gown. It was old and worn and no longer very warm for winter, but it was quite adequate on a warm July night like this.

Lighting her night candle, she picked it up and went out into the dark corridor. She walked quickly toward the schoolroom, though by the time she got there, she realized she could no longer hear the muffled clanking. When she opened the schoolroom door, all was dark and silent. So she closed it as softly as she could and, with a shrug, padded back the way she'd come. At her own closed door, she hesitated, then moved past it toward the stairs, for it suddenly struck her that the sound could have come from the room below, which would explain why it was less easily heard elsewhere.

Pausing at the head of the staircase, she saw no lights downstairs, heard no voices. No doubt it was inevitable that curiosity got the better of good sense, for she had been itching to explore the house properly since she got here. She just hadn't planned on doing so in the middle of the night.

However, at least if everyone was in bed, she was unlikely to disturb anyone at work or run into the unpleasant master of the house. Probably. And if she did encounter someone... well, she still didn't know what the noise was. She crept downward and turned toward the space she judged to be directly below her bedchamber.

The door was ajar, but there was no light from inside. When she pushed the door and lifted her candle higher, it seemed to be merely a jumble of old furniture. Dust and cobwebs lay thick over many surfaces. She could see nothing that might conceivably be responsible for the noise, which she could not hear now in any case. In fact, it was clearly not in use for anything.

Disappointed, she turned away. As she came to the large, empty room opposite the landing, she thought it would have made a fine banqueting hall two hundred years ago. Or a pleasant, modern drawing room, correctly decorated and furnished. She moved past it to the other side, where the dining room was located. It, too, was in darkness, so she crept past it into unexplored territory. Another door stood ajar, and through the crack, she saw what she had hoped to discover—bookshelves. Full bookshelves.

Smiling, she pushed the door further open—it didn't creak—and walked in. Immediately, she was surrounded by the sight and smell of books. Shelves of them running almost to the ceiling and all the way round the walls, even under the windows and on either side of the huge fireplace…where, she suddenly realized, stood two lamps. Which explained why she could see the room so clearly.

And from the winged armchair beside the mantelpiece, a man rose to his feet and strolled toward her. Above dark trousers, he wore only a white shirt, open at the throat, with no tie, no coat. His black hair was tousled, falling forward over his forehead, his jaw dark with stubble.

And yet, she had never seen a man move with such grace or with such silent, predatory confidence. Her instinct for self-preservation warned her to run, but some other emotion—pride, she hoped—held her rooted to the spot, refusing to as much as step back from his compelling glittering gaze.

He halted a foot away from her, though she didn't breathe any more easily.

"No," he murmured. "I *definitely* don't know you."

But she knew him. Even without the formal attire of Evelina's miniature portrait, this was undoubtedly Sir Nicholas Swan. Only, he wasn't scowling. His eyes were mocking, amused, speculative. A whiff of brandy on his breath explained the hectic glitter in his black eyes. Something dangerous oozed from his every pore, a sense that he was not quite in control, that he didn't want to be. Worse, when his eyes dipped, they seemed to strip her naked while his lips curved in a smile of anticipation.

"I am the governess," she stated baldly, to halt his clear train of thought. "Alexandra Battle."

For an instant, his eyes held hers without blinking as the smile faded. Yet still, he didn't step back. "And how did you know that that would be the one claim to halt me in my dishonorable tracks?"

"You attribute too much calculation to a statement of fact."

The smile was back, though it touched only those amazing, compelling eyes. "I'm not sure I do. But do you know who *I* am, Alexandra Battle?"

"My employer," she said. "My charge's father."

"You don't need to rub it in. And what drives you to seek out your employer in the middle of the night?"

"I didn't seek you out!"

"And yet here you are," he said softly. "Beautifully tousled and tempting in your night attire. What is a man to make of that?"

"Nothing," she retorted. "A gentleman would know that there are no circumstances in which I would seek out a drunk."

As soon as the words were out, she regretted them. Calling her employer a drunk was a step too far. She would be packing her bags in the morning.

But he didn't look angry, only surprised. "Really? Most women find me more acceptable in my cups."

"Why?" she asked, distracted from the main point.

He shrugged. "I don't know. Gets rid of the harsh edges, I suppose." A new challenge gleamed in his eyes. "Well, since you're here, will you drink with me, Alexandra Battle?"

"No, thank you." With that politeness, it was definitely time to flee, but she had not moved more than a muscle before his hand shot out, capturing her chin between finger and thumb, while he stepped closer and gazed fixedly down at her.

She could not breathe. Her heart seemed to drum against her ribs, but instinct told her to remain still, not to begin a fight she could not win. Not that he held her fast. He didn't, and he only touched her at that one point. Nevertheless, there was but a couple of inches between his mouth and hers. She could feel his body heat, smell the brandy he had imbibed, and the lingering, expensive scent of soap on his skin. And if she melted, she didn't know if it was with desire or fear. Either way, she knew better than to move and encourage the wild, male animal to pounce on its prey.

Only when his eyes lightened, did she recognize the challenge that had been there, that vanished as he released her.

With shock, she realized that if she had made any move toward him, kissed him as her wayward mind had tried to imagine, she would have failed his test. But then, just by being here, she could already have failed it. He wanted a respectable lady bringing up his daughter, not an opportunistic girl of loose morals.

There was no point even in indignation. His position and his sex enabled him to make such tests and such judgments. Hers did not.

And she needed the position.

"Good night, Alexandra Battle."

Her candle trembled as she stumbled away from him. Yet, she couldn't resist glancing back into the room. He was back at the armchair, pouring himself another glass of brandy. She fled.

Sir Nicholas Swan smiled as he poured more brandy and threw himself back into his comfortable armchair.

He liked the governess.

In the morning, he supposed, he might be ashamed of his seduction test. Right now, he felt justified by the mere fact that she was wandering his house in her nightclothes. He was a wealthy enough man that women of a certain kind—and this had nothing to do with class—tended to throw themselves at his head, with various motives. He was glad the governess was not one of them.

At least, he thought he was. But he was just drunk enough, and lonely enough, to wish she was not so damned virtuous. For in her thin nightclothes, her shock of auburn hair tumbling about her shoulders, she had been a tempting armful. From her beautiful defiant eyes and sculpted, kissable mouth, down to the outline of her long legs, she was a lovely woman.

Alexandra Battle.

Not even afraid of him. Well, he reconsidered, sipping his brandy, actually she *had* been afraid of him, and rightly so, for he was her employer, and he had not behaved well. But he liked that she had hidden her fear and stood up to him.

Oh well, he thought regretfully, the governess was off-limits if she stayed. If he hadn't scared her off. He raised his glass to the door in a formal farewell to her. He wouldn't touch her, but he found he was looking forward to meeting her again.

Impatiently, he tossed his half-finished brandy on the table and rose to his feet. Time to see if the night's work was done.

"Is there a pianoforte in the house?" Alexandra asked Evelina as they breakfasted together in the schoolroom the next morning. She had been served with no notice to quit, so she had to assume that she was still employed.

Evelina considered. "No," she said in some surprise. "I have never seen one here. In Venice, we had one. Mama used to sing and play. Sometimes people played for her, and she just sang."

"Was she a good singer?"

Evelina nodded seriously.

"I'm sure you take after her. Do you like to sing?"

"Sometimes."

"Did you play the piano also? Or some other musical instrument?"

"Oh, no."

Well, she was only six years old. Still, it was never too young to begin, and not for the first time, Alexandra regretted her sold guitar and harp and the many pianofortes of her youth.

"Perhaps I should speak to your father about an instrument of some kind," she murmured, although her insides twisted up about approaching him on any subject whatsoever. Besides, it would take time to choose and purchase. Until then...there were friends who might lend her a guitar. "Hmm, I'll tell you what, Evelina, if you work hard this morning, perhaps we could take a little picnic lunch and go for a walk this afternoon."

Evelina jumped up with such excitement that Alexandra gathered outings were not common in her life since coming to England.

"Anna doesn't know the way," Evelina explained when asked about previous walks.

"Don't you go out with your Papa, sometimes? To the park, perhaps?"

"Once," she said. "But it was very early, and he couldn't stay long because he had to go to work."

"What does he do?" Alexandra asked, aware she was betraying unseemly curiosity, though children seldom noticed such things. In this case, it earned her nothing, for Evelina merely shrugged.

After breakfast, they pinned the dried paintings from yesterday onto the wall.

"Beautiful!" Alexandra pronounced. "Just what we need to brighten the room. And I hope you'll add to them as we go on."

"I could paint more today," Evelina offered hopefully.

"Not today. This morning, I want you to practice some writing and some counting. And then, if the weather stays fine, we shall go out."

While she spoke, Evelina watched her speculatively, not best pleased. It crossed Alexandra's mind that she was in for the first tantrum, but whether or not the child was distracted by the later outing, she merely shrugged and agreed.

Accordingly, since the sun stayed out, they left the house together at midday, with a small picnic basket, and walked away from the river toward St. James' Park. Evelina bounced along at her side, happy and excited, and took such simple pleasure in their picnic on the edges of the park that Alexandra was quite touched. The girl chattered away, sometimes in English, sometimes in Italian, asking questions, remarking on trees and dogs and people who passed by, recalling snippets of her life in Venice.

"Are we going home now?" she asked in disappointed tones as they began to pack up the meager remains of lunch.

"No, I thought we would walk a bit farther and see if a friend of mine is at home. She might be able to lend us a guitar or know someone who could."

So they walked on from St, James' Park to Green Park. At Piccadilly, Alexandra took Evelina's hand firmly and managed to dodge traffic and cross to the other side, where they walked down the relative quiet of Half-Moon Street.

Although Mayfair was a far better address than Hungerford, Evelina was certainly not overwhelmed by her new surroundings. The girl brought up in a Venetian palace was hardly likely to be impressed by lesser Mayfair mansions.

About halfway down the street, Alexandra turned into a quiet lane that did not lead to the usual mews but to a gate and a garden path up to a smaller, more charming house than those nearby.

The same maid Alexandra remembered from the only other time she had been here opened the door.

"Is Lady Grizelda at home?" Alexandra inquired.

"Please step in while I inquire," the maid replied, smiling at Evelina, who seemed surprised.

Lady Grizelda—whom Alexandra had always called Griz—already had company but was pleased to receive more.

Griz was a musical friend. When they had met and practiced music together, Alexandra had no idea the fun and talented young lady was a duke's daughter. Neither did anyone else. The truth had emerged so gradually that, in the end, no one had been overawed, and she had remained simply Griz.

Lady Grizelda's family, however, was another matter. Her other guests proved to be her sister, Viscountess Trench, and Lady Trench's two children, who were, respectively, slightly older and slightly younger than Evelina.

"And is this your daughter?" Lady Trench inquired in a friendly manner. She was a rather dazzlingly beautiful woman dressed in the finest fashion.

"No, this is Miss Evelina Swan. I am merely her governess."

Not by the flicker of an eyebrow did Lady Trench betray surprise or contempt.

"Alexandra plays music with us," Griz explained, pouring tea. "Sit down, Alex, and the children will take care of themselves."

"Actually, it was about music I came. Evelina's family has only recently arrived in London, and there are no instruments in the house as yet. I was wondering if you had a guitar we could borrow for a few weeks?"

"To teach Evelina? Why yes, I still have the small one I used as a child. It would be perfect for her."

"Thank you," Alexandra said gratefully, accepting the tea and watching uneasily as Evelina stood awkwardly facing the overtures of the other two children.

"Swan," Lady Trench said thoughtfully. "Would that be Mr. and Mrs. Ralph Swan in Brook Street?"

"No, my lady, Sir Nicholas Swan."

"Ah, the older brother! Do you know," she added, lowering her voice slightly, "we thought he was probably dead before my husband ran into him in the city only last week!"

"Dead?" Alexandra repeated, startled. "Because he was abroad?"

To her relief, the little girl was tugging a willing Evelina into the corner, where the boy was holding his aunt's little dog. It sprang free, though instead of running for cover, it jumped into Evelina's lap and licked her face. It didn't seem to care for adults, but it clearly loved children. Evelina laughed, and the boy began to show her the dog's party tricks.

"Well," Lady Trench said, considering, "I think more because his brother moved into the Brook Street house almost as soon as their father died. He didn't assume the title, of course, which should have stopped the silly gossip at once. I suppose no one could recall seeing Sir Nicholas, as he is now, since he was eighteen years old. He was at school with my husband, you know."

"Then you are friends," Alexandra said, covering her unease. Last night's encounter lurked too close to the surface of her mind, and she wasn't sure she would still be employed by the time she got home, which made her angry. She shouldn't have been there, of course, but it was he who had leered. She had done nothing wrong.

"Friends?" Lady Trench said with a shrug. "I would not go so far. Sir Nicholas does not seem to go out in society a great deal."

He wasn't at home a great deal either, according to the household, so where did he spend his time?

Lady Trench stood. "I must go, Griz." Unexpectedly, she held out her hand to Alexandra. "A pleasure to meet you. We're going down to the country tomorrow, but I wish you all success in your new post with the Swans."

"Thank you," Alexandra said, shaking the friendly, aristocratic hand.

"Come, children," Lady Trench commanded. "Say goodbye to your new friend!"

They were laughing with Evelina while the dog ran rings around them at fantastic speed. With reluctance, the Trench children extracted themselves, grinned at Evelina, and accompanied their mother from the room.

"I'll be back in a moment," Griz said, leaving with her sister. The dog ran after them all, then was sent back into the room, and the door closed, much to Evelina's delight. And the dog, easily distracted, bounded back up to her and rolled on its back.

Evelina laughed but looked at Alexandra for guidance.

"I think she wants her tummy tickled," Alexandra said gravely.

Griz came back in then with a guitar in either hand. The dog, without moving from its comfortable position, wagged its tail while Evelina scratched its belly.

"Emmie's gone to dig out the cases," Griz said.

"Yes, but I can't take two from you!"

"It's more fun when you both have one. You can bring it back when we next meet for some music. Do you have a day off?"

"No one has mentioned it," Alexandra said in surprise. "I shall inquire."

"Well, send me a note, and we can work around it. I heard Matthew played excellently at the Braithwaites' soiree the other week."

For the rest of the short visit, they talked about music and their musical friends while Evelina played with the dog. The maid brought in two cases for the guitars, which were then packed away, and

Evelina was summoned for departure.

"Do you think you could carry this one home?" Alexandra asked her, holding out the smaller case.

"Is it far?" Griz asked.

"It's a good walk, almost to Hungerford Bridge."

Griz blinked but made no comment on the odd location. "You need a hackney," she said. "I'll send the lad to fetch one."

"Griz, I can't," Alexandra said awkwardly.

Griz nudged her. "Of course you can. Dragan has been earning pots recently."

Only Griz would have said anything so outrageous, and Alexandra would have laughed, except the drawing room door opened again and, as though conjured up by his wife's words, her husband, Dragan Tizsa, strolled in, his gazed fixed on some pamphlet.

Although jaw-droppingly handsome, he seemed endearingly unaware of the fact, and, having met him before, Alexandra no longer felt the urge to stare.

"Griz, you should read this," he began enthusiastically before he realized he had visitors and broke off to smile distractedly and bow.

"I was about to send for a hackney," Griz remarked.

"I'll send the boy," Mr. Tizsa said, dropping the pamphlet on the table and striding out again.

Idly, Griz picked up the pamphlet and glanced through it. "Goodness," she remarked. "Revolutionary stuff!"

"Then Mr. Tizsa adheres to his old views?" Alexandra said lightly. He was a refugee from the late revolution in Hungary, which had been so brutally put down after holding out against Imperial forces for so long.

"Well, yes," Griz said, frowning, "but he has just come from a meeting with my brother."

Alexandra could not quite grasp the connection, and seeing it, Griz cast her a quick smile. "My brother Horace is a civil servant in a department that keeps track of sedition and anti-government opinions. Dragan told him at the outset of their arrangement that he would not pursue people for their opinions."

A frown had formed on her brow as though the possibility bothered her. Then it cleared. "My brother is an arch-manipulator, but I would still wager on Dragan!"

CHAPTER THREE

D ULY CONVEYED HOME by hackney, they carried their borrowed guitars up the path and into the house, which appeared to be busier than Alexandra had seen it.

Mrs. Dart was saying, "Goodbye, Doctor, and thank you!" to a middle-aged man with a spectacular moustache and beard. Behind them, a maid scurried toward the kitchen, and a manservant strode up the main staircase, where two maids and the footman were dementedly cleaning.

"Oh dear," Alexandra murmured to Mrs. Dart. "Is someone ill?"

"Lady Nora had one of her turns," Mrs. Dart said distractedly. "Evelina, your father is home and eager to talk to you. He's in his library."

With a shriek of joy, Evelina dropped her guitar case and flew across the hall to the stairs. Since it was a summons from her father, Alexandra could hardly stop her. She didn't even want to, except for the unease churning through her, and that was more about the parent than the child.

Was he about to ask Evelina if she would mind losing her new governess? In all honesty, since she had only arrived yesterday, Alexandra could not imagine that she would mind in the least.

And who the devil was Lady Nora?

Mrs. Dart had bustled off again, so there was no one to ask. Alexandra bent and picked up the smaller guitar case, then made her way up to the schoolroom. On the first-floor landing, she heard gales of laughter coming from the half-open library door. She couldn't see either of the occupants, but she heard his voice, light, low, and teasing, and quite different from the voice he had used to her last night.

She was glad that Evelina did not sound in awe of her father, let alone frightened of him. But still, the very joy with which she'd hurled herself upstairs to get at him spoke of a loneliness that was all the more heartbreaking for being easily remedied.

Alexandra went on upstairs and along the passage to the schoolroom, where she left the guitars in their cases, propped up against the wall. There was no note dismissing her on her desk or anywhere else.

As she took off her hat and wrap, Anna came through from the bedchamber.

"Sir Nicholas is home," she said in her careful English. She sounded a trifle smug.

"I know. Evelina is with him."

There was no doubting the triumph in Anna's smile as she swept from the room, though Alexandra could not account for it.

She went to her own room to wash her hands, although this was largely an excuse to be sure no letter of dismissal awaited her there. She would not put it past Sir Nicholas to be so contemptuous of her. But no message awaited her there, and the maid who brought her a cup of tea to the schoolroom, along with a scone and a slice of cake, conveyed none either.

Alexandra would have breathed more freely had it not occurred to her that Sir Nicholas would join them in the dining room that evening. Especially when she glanced out of the window and saw Evelina playing ball in the overgrown garden with her father. Evelina caught sight of her and waved, causing Alexandra to wave back and move hastily out of the way as Sir Nicholas began to look up.

Forcing herself, she sat down at her desk and planned out some lessons for the rest of the week. When she heard Evelina and Anna's voices from the bedchamber beyond the schoolroom, she realized it was time to change for the early dinner prescribed for her and her charge.

Accordingly, she changed from her grey work gown into her dark green evening gown. There was little difference in terms of age or fashion, but at least he could have no possible cause to accuse her of trying to seduce him.

Her face burned. Was that truly what he had thought last night? Why would she—why would anyone?—seduce a stranger? To gain material favor with her employer.

I will not think of that. If he harbors such mean suspicions, they are his problems, not mine.

Unless he dismissed her.

She straightened her shoulders and left her chamber, walking briskly to collect Evelina from the schoolroom.

The child was all smiles as she skipped beside her along the passage and downstairs to the dining room, chattering of her game with Papa mixed in with odd references to Lady Trench's children and Lady Grizelda's dog. By the time they reached the dining room, Alexandra's heart was drumming painfully.

But the table was set for two, and there was no sign of Sir Nicholas.

Alexandra did not know whether to be relieved or indignant. No wonder the child was lonely. But then, had she not been told at the outset that Sir Nicholas dined elsewhere? That she and Evelina would dine alone?

And where on earth did Lady Nora dine? In fact…

"Who is Lady Nora?" she asked Evelina when Clara had cleared the table of their main course.

"She's sick. She wants to die in England, so Papa brought her home with us."

Was this yet another of Sir Nicholas's mistresses? Was it not appallingly bad taste to have her living in the same house as his daughter?

Perhaps not, since he hadn't been married to Evelina's mother either. Such niceties were beyond Alexandra, and none of her business in any case. But she was not sure she cared to be part of quite so unrespectable a household.

"Is she some relation, perhaps?" Alexandra suggested hopefully.

"No, I don't think so. Just an old friend. She's kind to me when she's awake."

"I should hope she is."

Dessert was brought in then, and Alexandra reminded herself that gossiping with her charge about other members of the household was beneath her dignity.

As before, Anna came to collect Eveline from the dining room. When they had gone, Alexandra was conscious of the urge to flee to the safety of her bedchamber, but she forced herself to sit for a few minutes in case he came to dismiss her face to face.

She was not even surprised when Clara came back to clear the last of the plates and presented her with a note. "From Sir Nicholas," she said cheerfully.

"Thank you," Alexandra managed and unfolded it.

N. Swan presents his compliments to Miss Alexandra Battle. It has come to his attention that Miss Battle removed her charge from the premises without permission, taking her into the houses of friends who are not known to her father. Miss Battle should know that this is unacceptable and must not be repeated.

Speechless, Alexandra forced herself to refold the note rather than crumple it and hurl it across the room.

"Thank you," she murmured to the maid and stalked from the room. She did not so much as glance in the direction of the library. The man had probably gone out again in any case, but Alexandra's reply to his ridiculous message would not wait.

Damn the man, how dare he write such an impersonal missive

when she was under his wretched roof?

Hurling herself onto the chair at the desk beneath her window, she turned up the lamp and seized up her pen and paper.

Alexandra Battle returns Sir Nicholas's compliments and begs him to understand that had she been aware of his aversion to fresh air or company for his daughter, she would, of course, have immured them both in the schoolroom for as long as instructed. If Sir Nicholas requires the name of the lady called upon and those others encountered at this address, Miss Battle is happy to supply them.

Since she was still furious, she pulled the bell, then folded the letter and inscribed Sir Nicholas's name on the surface. "Please see that this is given to Sir Nicholas upon his return," she told Clara, who appeared breathlessly at the door.

The girl snatched it and ran off again.

Alexandra collapsed onto the bed, breathing deeply. As she calmed, a suspicion of her own unwisdom began to twist through her and cling.

"Oh, the devil," she whispered ruefully. She rose again and went in search of Clara, whom she found polishing the dining table. "Clara, would you give me back that message I asked you to deliver? I think I might have made a mistake."

"Oh, sorry, I can't. I already gave it to him, and he read it and asked me to give you this. I was going to bring it up when I had finished in here."

Alexandra wanted to close her eyes and slide down the wall. Why could she never control her wretched temper? She seemed to have survived last night's encounter only to be dismissed, deservedly, for blatant rudeness—however stupid and pompous her employer's instructions.

She took the note and trudged back to her room, stepping lightly as she glanced warily toward the closed library door.

In her room, she shook out the note.

That would be acceptable. Feel free to leave the information in the library.

Her face flamed. Was that a reference to last night's encounter there? And did he have to be so wretchedly concise?

She sat down at her desk once more, and so as not to waste her own precious paper, she wrote on the back of his.

Lady Grizelda Tizsa, Half-Moon Street Lane.

Viscountess Trench and her two children, Michael and Elizabeth.

Lady Grizelda's dog, and, briefly, her husband.

She thought of explaining about the guitars and the hackney but then decided his conciseness required the same of her. So, she merely folded the note, and then, reluctant to disturb Clara yet again, she drew in her breath and crept down to the library.

A light shone beneath the door, but she heard nothing from inside. She crouched, slid the note under the door, then rose and walked away, determined not to run.

She had reached the upstairs landing before she heard the library door opening, but she kept on walking to her room. He didn't call her back.

>>>≪≪≪

ON WAKING THE following morning, Alexandra still felt uneasy and again expected the fall of the axe on her position here. But after pacing in her room for an hour last night and realizing Sir Nicholas had no intention of replying further, she had gone to bed and slept peacefully all night. So, at least she was well-rested and ready for anything.

Accordingly, she washed, dressed, brushed and pinned her hair, and sallied forth to the schoolroom where she ate breakfast with

Evelina and drank a welcome cup of coffee, which was brought by Clara without an accompanying note of any kind.

It was after Evelina had impressed her with her reading skills and while the child was copying from a book to practice her handwriting that Sir Nicholas dropped into the schoolroom.

Alexandra was raking through her books at the time, looking for passages that would challenge Evelina without overwhelming her, when Evelina emitted a squeak of joy and rushed from her desk to greet the man strolling into the room from the passage. Unlike their only other encounter, he was fully dressed in dark trousers and coat, his tie neatly in place, and his hair brushed off his face. He appeared to be freshly shaven.

Despite the lack of space, he seized his rushing daughter by the waist and spun her high into the air before depositing her on her feet once more and taking her by the hand to lead her back to her desk.

Alexandra had jumped up in surprise and was now annoyed by her reaction. A slower rise would have fitted more with the dignity she had intended to maintain. But he barely glanced at her.

"Look, Papa, this is my writing," Evelina said proudly as her father pushed her gently into her chair.

"Very fair, in my opinion," he said. "What does Miss Battle think?"

"She hasn't seen it yet, but she liked it yesterday. Mostly. She likes my reading, too."

"I'm very glad to hear it," Sir Nicholas said lazily and at last looked up at Alexandra. "Miss Battle."

"Sir Nicholas."

"Carry on with your work, Evelina," he said without releasing Alexandra's gaze, "while Miss Battle and I talk."

Nerves shot through her as he walked toward her, but she lifted her chin and forced herself to wait calmly for whatever was to come.

"Please, sit," he invited, coming to a halt beside her desk. She sat, which annoyingly meant she had to crane her neck to look at him.

There were other chairs he could have brought up, but he chose instead to perch on her desk.

"I felt we should understand each other," he remarked, watching her.

"I thought we did. Now."

His lips quirked. "I doubt it. First of all, I have no objection to fresh air or exercise. In fact, for Evelina, I fully endorse it." He pronounced his daughter's name with an Italian inflection that was both unexpected and endearing. "But I would like to know in advance where you take her."

"You were not, to my knowledge, at home at the time," Alexandra said. "You may think I should have planned it better to secure your permission, but the day-to-day teaching of a child does not conform to such plans. If she is restless, there is no point in confining her to the schoolroom beyond a certain point. It may be she is lethargic or tired at the time I proposed to take her out and must change my plans accordingly."

"I understand, Miss Battle," he drawled with apparent amusement. "Which is why I propose we agree to a list of places you may take her at your discretion. Providing you tell at least one of the servants when you leave."

"I told Anna," Alexandra said.

His eyes flickered. "I see."

So did Alexandra. Anna had told him only that the governess had taken his daughter out.

"I have heard lots about luncheon on a blanket in the park and about a house with a highly entertaining dog and two children."

"Lady Grizelda's house. She is the Duke of Kelburn's daughter."

"I know who she is," Sir Nicholas said tartly. "I was unaware you are connected to the family."

"I'm not. Lady Griz—Grizelda—is a friend I made when I returned from Europe. We and some amateur musicians play music together when we can."

"Is that why you went there yesterday?" he asked steadily.

"No, I went to see if we could borrow a guitar for Evelina's musical instruction. I understand there is no pianoforte—which situation I would like to ask you to remedy at some point, if at all possible. In the meantime, I shall begin teaching her on the guitar."

For an instant, he frowned as though to forbid it, but his brow cleared almost immediately, and he only nodded. "I will see to it. You are also acquainted with Lady Trench."

"I met her for the first time yesterday. Unfortunately, she is taking her children to the country today, for it would be good for Evelina to have friends to play with."

An arrested look crossed his face. Again, he merely nodded curtly. "What of Lady Grizelda's brothers? Do you know them?"

"No. But as I told you, we met Lady Grizelda's husband."

"Dragan Tizsa," he murmured thoughtfully. "Interesting man."

"You know him?" she asked, surprised.

"Not yet. Lord Trench and I have some common business interests. I have no quarrel with the places you have already taken Evelina. Where else do you imagine taking her?"

"To Hyde Park and the Exhibition. Perhaps to the museum. A walk along the river, perhaps to the market if Mrs. Dart requires anything. I shall keep her with me at all times," she added, sensing his sudden concern.

His lips twisted into a deprecating smile.

She continued hastily. "I would also like to meet up with other governesses and their charges to let Evelina play with other children. I am acquainted with a governess in Mayfair, one in Belgravia, and one in Kensington. Again, their play would be supervised."

He regarded her, unblinking, for so long that she thought she might have missed a patch of jam on her face from breakfast or be growing a pair of horns. "You really are eminently sensible, are you not, Alexandra Battle?"

"Most eminently," she replied, trying not to blush at his mode of address which recalled, as he clearly meant it to, their meeting in the library.

A breath of laughter issued from his lips. Her awareness of him increased tenfold. But fortunately, before breathing became a problem, he eased his hip off the desk.

He said coolly, "Leave me the names of those governesses and their employers, and we are agreed." He began to stroll away, then glanced back over his shoulder. "And Miss Battle? You may browse the library whenever you wish. No permission is necessary for books."

"Thank you," she managed to his back. Fortunately, he did not turn again, for her face was flaming. He ruffled his daughter's hair carelessly on his way out.

⸎

THE FIRST TANTRUM in Alexandra's presence occurred that afternoon and grew out of a simple request to put books and paints away before they went for a walk.

"But I want to go now," Evelina said, staring at Alexandra as if she didn't understand.

"And we shall, as soon as we have cleared up."

"*You* clear up," Evelina said, with her first sign of arrogance. "I'll wait for you in the garden."

"No. We shall each clear up our own desks, and then we'll go together."

"It's boring!" Evelina declared, swiping her books onto the floor with her arm. The little bowl of water tipped up and spilled over her bright, charming painting, and she let out a cry of rage.

Although it was clear what was coming, Alexandra tried her best to divert it. "Oh dear," she said calmly. "I'll fetch the cloth while you—"

"I'm going *out!*" the child claimed and slammed toward the school-room door.

Alexandra was there before her, blocking her way. Evelina stamped her foot and screamed, and in no time, was in the midst of a fully-fledged tantrum. Before she could hurl herself at the wall, Alexandra seized her hand and hurried her toward the inner door.

Surprised, Evelina was in the playroom before she realized it and tried to break free. Alexandra held on grimly and threw open the door of the empty room she had already earmarked for such emergencies. Annoyingly, Anna appeared at the door of Evelina's bedchamber, which made the child scream more loudly and try to throw herself free. Alexandra spun her into the room.

"Sir Nicholas will not have her locked in," Anna remarked with a hint of gloating.

"Later," Alexandra snapped, for she was already inside the room with Evelina and now closed the door on Anna's stunned face.

A cushion landed on Alexandra's head. She ignored it, placed the chair she had put there yesterday in front of the door, and took the book from her pocket as she sat down.

Stunned, Evelina stopped screaming to stare at her, then drew in her breath and yelled with fury. Two more cushions were flung at Alexandra. Another missed its mark. Alexandra ignored all of them, merely continued reading her book. Or at least pretending to.

Evelina hurled herself on the cushions, drumming her feet and crying. Alexandra waited calmly until the storm abated and silenced. Slowly, Evelina sat up, her face red and tearstained, and gazed at Alexandra.

Alexandra gave her a few more moments, then glanced up from her book. "Better? Shall we go and clear up now?"

"I don't want to clear up," Evelina whispered. "I want to go out."

"My dear," Alexandra said gently, "we could *be* out by now if you had cleared up when I asked you."

She had no way of knowing if that point went home just yet, but the tantrum had clearly exhausted her.

Alexandra closed her book, stood, and moved the chair to one side. She held out her hand and, still baffled, Evelina came and took it. They left the room together and returned to the schoolroom.

Five minutes later, with everything cleared, cleaned, and dried, Alexandra took her to the bedchamber to wash her face and hands, while Anna looked on, puzzled.

Alexandra beckoned to the maid and took her into the schoolroom while the child dried her face and put on her hat and coat.

"I would like you to treat any tantrums that way. Take her into the room, block the door, and stay with her, but ignore her. Do something else, mending, knitting, whatever you wish, and don't speak to her until she is calm."

Anna stared at her. "You must have the authority of Sir Nicholas."

"And while I get it, you must do as I ask," Alexandra said steadily. "Trust me, it will make your job easier in the end."

CHAPTER FOUR

WHILE THEY WERE having tea in the schoolroom that afternoon, a maid Alexandra had not seen before came in and said Lady Nora had been asking for Evelina.

"Could she be spared for ten minutes?" the maid asked.

Evelina looked expectantly at Alexandra, without any sign of the earlier, violent tantrum. "May I, Miss Battle?"

"Of course, providing you wash your hands and face first, or Lady Nora won't know who you are."

Evelina giggled, and the maid smiled as she curtseyed and bustled off.

"Come with me?" Evelina invited when she returned from her ablutions. She even held out her hand. "I want to show Lady Nora my new governess."

"Very well," Alexandra said, "if Lady Nora does not mind." In fact, it struck her that Evelina was, if not exactly frightened, then unsure; that she wanted Alexandra there for support rather than display purposes. And yet, she had clearly known Lady Nora longer than she had Alexandra.

But Lady Nora was unwell. Her bedchamber was bright and cheerful and yet smelled somehow of medicine and death. The lady herself was drawn and almost unworldly, propped against a mass of pillows that dwarfed her. Her face was lined with long-endured pain. But she smiled at the sight of the child, and Evelina happily took her hand and sat on the edge of the bed.

"Good day, Lady Nora! This is Miss Battle, my governess. I thought you would like to meet her."

"Lady Nora," Alexandra said, curtseying, while the clouded eyes seemed suddenly sharp.

"Miss Battle," she said and gave a wheezy laugh. "Well, you'll have one. Don't let them defeat you, for there's good in them. Good in him... So, what have you done today, my little angel?"

I had a major tantrum and threw things at my governess, Alexandra thought sardonically, while Evelina recited, "I read and wrote and saw Papa and counted and painted and walked by the river, then up the steps to the market, and I played the guitar. And had tea. And luncheon."

"Busy girl. So, someone is teaching you music at last. I thought they were afraid to."

"Why afraid?" Alexandra asked.

"Oh, her mother, you know. She cast a dazzling light and a long shadow... And where else have you been since I last saw you, Evelina? Anywhere interesting?"

"We had a picnic in the park," Evelina said enthusiastically, "and went to visit a lady with a dog, who runs really fast and likes her tummy tickled!"

"The lady likes her tummy tickled?" Lady Nora asked, apparently astonished.

Evelina laughed. "No, the dog does! And there were other children there, a boy and a girl who seemed to like me."

"Of course they liked you." Lady Nora said, lifting one papery hand to touch Evelina's hair. "*I like you, though I never meant to.*" Her hand fell, and her eyelids fluttered and closed. Then they flew open again. "Come and see me again, little angel. You too, Miss..."

The maid bustled forward. "She'll just sleep for a while now, Miss."

Alexandra took Evelina's hand and drew her away. "Come, we'll have a game in the garden before we get ready for dinner."

Evelina was silent as they went downstairs. Then she asked suddenly, "Do all sick people die?"

"No, they usually get better," Alexandra assured her. "But some are unfortunate."

"Like Mama."

"Yes, like Mama," Alexandra said gently.

"And Lady Nora." She glanced up with haunted eyes. "What if Papa gets sick, too?"

"He seems very healthy to me. And if he falls sick at all, I am sure he would get better again in no time."

"I don't think I have ever been sick."

"Then you are lucky and as healthy as your father."

"Have you?"

"Nothing serious."

"I wouldn't like you to get sick either."

"Thank you," Alexandra said, peculiarly touched, and decided it was time to change the subject. "Do you have the ball?"

ALEXANDRA DIDN'T KNOW whether she was glad or sorry not to see Sir Nicholas for the rest of the day. As requested, she wrote down the names of her governess acquaintances and the names and addresses of their employers and asked one of the servants to give it to him. There was no reply by the time she retired, but during breakfast the next day, Anna came into the schoolroom and deposited a note on the table.

It said only, *Unexceptionable. Proceed according to your good sense.*

She wondered if he meant to compliment or mock her.

Since the early morning mist had lifted by eleven o'clock, revealing a fine summer's day, Alexandra decided on a short walk to blow away the cobwebs before they continued with lessons, and Evelina put away her books quickly and without fuss.

While the child ran to fetch her coat and bonnet, Alexandra unhooked her own from the back of the door and was just tying the ribbons of her bonnet when the door abruptly opened, forcing her to jump back out of the way.

"My apologies," Sir Nicholas said, looking more amused than sorry. "I did not expect to find you lurking behind the door."

"I did not expect anyone to open it, either, so it seems we were both wrong. We were about to take a short walk along the river."

"Then I caught you just in time." He produced what appeared to be a coin purse from his pocket and stepped forward to give it to her. "For incidentals, such as hackneys, since you are not close to genteel company, or any of the places of interest you wished to take Evelina."

"Thank you," Alexandra said, stunned by such thoughtfulness. "I will keep an accounting, of course."

"Of course," he said gravely, though his eyes still seemed to be laughing at her. This had a curious effect on her, causing both indignation and acknowledgment of the man's undoubted attractions. He really didn't need to say or do anything for women to fall into his lap. Women who were not straightlaced governesses, obviously.

She stepped back. "I'll put it in the drawer for safety, for we won't need it just now." It was an excuse to walk away from him, and the quirk of his lips told her he knew that. Worse, he did not immediately vanish, so she was both relieved and disappointed when Evelina rushed in with her coat and bonnet on and flew to her father with delight.

"Papa!"

"Good morning, minx," he said, crouching to hug her. "Are you working hard and being obedient?"

"Oh yes," Evelina said, clinging around his neck. "I have been very good. Since yesterday afternoon," she added with an unexpected streak of honesty. "Are you coming on our walk with us?"

Sir Nicholas extracted himself and straightened. "Not today, my squib. I have business in the city."

She took his hand, tugging and smiling up at him. "But you can make them wait. It's just a short walk, and you'll make it so much fun. Won't he, Miss Battle?"

"I hardly feel qualified to say. But you must not importune your father, Evelina. Perhaps he would prefer to walk with you another time."

"Diplomatically put, Miss Battle," he said wryly.

"But I want you to come this time," Evelina insisted, and there was something in the tone of her voice, in the sudden rigidity of her posture that warned Alexandra another tantrum was looming.

"Come along," she said briskly, hoping to head it off by walking briskly and holding out her hand for Evelina's.

But Evelina hid behind her father's leg. "No! Not without Papa!"

"Evelina, I've told you, I can't today," her father said with gentle firmness.

"You can, you can!"

"I can't, I can't," he said humorously, grasping the door handle and turning away. "Now be good for Miss Battle."

But it was too late for that. The foot stamped, and the angelic little face surged red with fury. "You must come, you must!" she shrieked, throwing herself upon him, beating his thighs with her fist. "You must, you must!"

Alexandra glimpsed the helpless pity in his eyes as he dropped to a crouch once more, clearly meaning to hold her. Quicker than thought, Alexandra grasped one tiny fist in mid-flight and hauled the child away. Again, surprise was her friend, and Evelina was halfway across the schoolroom before she realized what had happened.

"I won't go in there again, I won't!" she yelled, struggling.

"Miss Battle." Sir Nicholas's cold fury broke through the child's screams.

"One moment, if you please," Alexandra said, whipping them out of the schoolroom and into the playroom.

His hasty footsteps followed, but she already had the "tantrum room" door open. Whisking Evelina inside, she closed the door, set the chair in front of it, and sat.

She knew Sir Nicholas stood, stunned, on the other side of it. *Don't try to come in, don't speak. Please don't...*

He didn't. Though it was true, she didn't hear much over Evelina's furious screaming.

The tantrum ended rather quicker than the last one.

She looked up at Alexandra from her tear-stained face, surrounded by a tangle of hair. "He won't come now, will he?" she said in a small voice.

"He wasn't going to come before," Alexandra said honestly. "All you have achieved is that we couldn't go either."

The child nodded miserably. "You didn't lock me in by myself."

"No, and I won't."

"Why?"

"Because I like you when you are well behaved. How old are you now, Evelina?"

"Six."

Alexandra nodded. "Then I think you are old enough to understand that it is really only babies who try to get their own way by temper tantrums. Now that you are six, you must show your father—and me, and Anna and Mrs. Dart—that you are more grown-up than that."

Evelina stared. "Don't you want to h-hug me?" she asked brokenly.

Alexandra, who suddenly felt like crying, opened her arms, and Evelina flew into them. "Everyone loves you, Evelina," she murmured into the girl's hair. "But I think you will get more hugs when you behave well."

She sniffed and nodded into Alexandra's shoulder.

"Perhaps," Alexandra said, "you should apologize to me? And to your father when you next see him. I think it will make you feel better, and we will all see how grown-up you are."

"Sorry," the child whispered, grasping the fabric of her gown.

Alexandra drew her back a little and smiled. "Well done. You are allowed to be angry, you know. Everyone is, sometimes. But anger doesn't change what you might want to change."

She thought about that, and Alexandra decided she had said enough.

"Then go and wash your face and brush your hair again, and we'll have a shorter walk."

Evelina nodded, and Alexandra stood, moving the chair so that they could open the door. Leaving Evelina to wash her face, Alexandra walked into the schoolroom. And found Sir Nicholas scowling at her.

Hastily she closed the door. "Please go," she hissed. "It is vital she achieves nothing by her tantrums. She must not know you stayed because of it!"

"I stayed to be sure you were not being cruel to my daughter," he said coldly.

"But you know I was not, or you would have broken in to stop me."

"I would. You do not have all the facts, Miss Battle."

"Then you must give me them, but not now." She made a hasty shooing motion with her hands, and he blinked.

"I really don't know whether to admire you or dismiss you."

"Decide later."

A moment longer, he stared at her. "Come to the library after dinner," he commanded and turned on his heels.

THEY ENJOYED A curtailed walk to make the point that Evelina had wasted the time, and then completed a little more work before luncheon. Afterward, Alexandra played the guitar and taught Evelina a simple new song. She had a lovely voice, and she clearly enjoyed the music, so they got out the smaller guitar, and Evelina learned how to hold it and strum it.

She then sent the child into the garden with Anna for a short while. Alexandra used the time to write short notes to each of her three London governess acquaintances, proposing dates the following week when they could meet in Hyde Park. As she set them in a neat pile on her desk, it struck her that it was past time for Evelina to be back in the schoolroom.

She crossed to the window, which looked down onto the garden, but there was no one there. Assuming they were on their way upstairs, Alexandra sat down again and opened the nearest book at the story she wished to read with Evelina. After five minutes, she went through to the playroom and bedrooms, but they were empty, too. Sighing, Alexandra set off in search of her errant pupil.

Anna was hurrying along the corridor with an armful of clean linen. For the first time, unease nipped at Alexandra's stomach.

"Where is Evelina?"

"She came in before me," Anna said. "I thought she was with you."

"Look up here, will you? And ask Lady Nora's maid."

It was probably mischief, she assured herself, hurrying downstairs. Children liked to hide. However, Evelina had shown no sign of it before. She seemed to prefer being visible.

With conscious bravery, she knocked loudly on the library door. Receiving no answer, she went in to find the room unoccupied by anyone.

Kitchen, she thought suddenly. Hungry children often gravitated to the source of food and treats. Running down to the ground floor, she pushed open the baize door to the servants' quarters.

Mrs. Dart emerged from a room on the left and paused in astonishment. "Miss Battle? Can I help you?"

"Yes, is Evelina here? In the kitchen?"

"No. No, she—"

"Then I think everyone needs to search the house and gardens until we find her," Alexandra said with a calmness she was far from feeling. Mrs. Dart, thankfully, did not argue but hurried off to order the servants.

Alexandra ran back upstairs in search of Anna, who met her breathlessly on the landing.

"She is not with Lady Nora nor in her father's rooms," she gasped, not bothering to hide her anxiety.

"Exactly when did you see her last?" Alexandra demanded. "In the garden?"

"Yes, we played ball, and then Mary, the laundry maid, called to me that the linen for Evelina's room was ready. I told Evelina it was time to come in. She went to fetch the ball from where it had landed in the bushes, and I went ahead of her to collect the laundry."

"Then you did not *see* her come in?" Alexandra insisted.

"No, I assumed. She was not unhappy to come in."

In other words, she was not throwing a tantrum. "Could she have got out of the garden into the street?" As one, they hurried back downstairs and out the front door, but Clara was already there, outside the gate, looking up and down the street.

Five minutes later, with the house and garden and surrounding lanes thoroughly searched, James, the burly chief manservant, who was not quite a butler or a valet but something of both, was sent to break the news to Sir Nicholas.

CHAPTER FIVE

Nicholas had never known fear like this. Abandoning his carriage to the jammed traffic in the Strand, he strode home, anxiety and hope clawing with equal cruelty at his head and his stomach.

And then hope plummeted like a stone when he saw two of his maids hurrying from the opposite end of the lane, worry etched on their faces.

"Is she found?" he barked, although he already knew the answer.

They shook their heads in terror, and he strode through the open gate toward the house.

"Well?" he snarled at Mrs. Dart, who was rushing down the staircase.

"Oh, sir, we can find no trace of her…"

"Bring me, Miss Battle," he commanded, striding into the bare reception room. "And Anna."

He was aware that anger was growing from fear and helplessness, but until he knew what had already been done to find his daughter, he could not plan. Instead, he paced the room, trying not to think of all the terrible things that could befall a child alone in this city.

Blame, at this point, would waste time, but that didn't mean he did not feel it. He blamed those he had left in charge of her, and he blamed himself for putting them there.

"Stay," he ordered Mrs. Dart as she led the other two women into the reception room. "What has been done to find her?"

"We've searched the house and the gardens and walked around the streets nearby." Inevitably it was Miss Battle who answered. Pretty, intriguing Miss Battle who turned out to be as useless all the rest, damn her. "We spoke to neighbors and people in the street, but no one saw her. And we informed a policeman who is spreading the word amongst his colleagues to look for her."

"Then we must widen the search. Send Ingram to me as soon as he—"

At that moment, Ingram, his trusted lieutenant, who specialized in finding the right people and information, walked into the room.

"You have men at your disposal?" Nicholas flung at him.

Ingram nodded. "Waiting outside."

"They need to spread out from the river in an increasingly wide arc—over the bridge, too. And speak to the boatmen."

"We checked the riverside, sir," Anna all but whispered. "No one had seen her."

He ignored that while Ingram strode off. "Search the house again," he told the women. "She could be hiding somewhere."

Mrs. Dart and Anna scurried off. The governess lingered. "Sir, I want you to know I have also asked friends to join—"

"Have you not done enough?" he burst out.

Despite the force with which he had turned on her, she did not flee. Rather, she took a step closer, her expression anxious and damnably compassionate. "Sir, I must help in any way—"

"By driving my daughter from her home?" he demanded, letting the fury loose.

"Driving...?" she began, bewildered.

"You would not follow my instructions, so convinced you knew better, and this is the result."

She definitely understood that, for her face whitened. "You think...you believe she ran away? From me?" He almost saw the wheels of her mind turn, considering her guilt. "You mean I should have embraced her, held her as you do? Can you not see that hugging her rewards her bad behavior? No, no, she understood me, was quite happy when she went into the garden with Anna."

"Keep telling yourself that," he said savagely. "But it won't be in my character reference." Brushing past her, he strode for the door, desperate to do something, anything to find his lost child.

Abruptly a tall young man and a diminutive young woman in spectacles appeared in the doorway, causing him to halt.

"Who the devil are you?" he demanded rudely.

"My name is Tizsa," said the young man with a bow that was more of a nod.

And then the damned governess was beside him once more. "These are my friends, Mr. and Mrs. Tizsa—Lady Grizelda. I was trying to tell you I have asked them..."

He stared at her. "You are planning on a tea party with friends when you have just lost my daughter?"

"No, sir, I have asked for their help. This is Sir Nicholas Swan, if you haven't guessed." She seemed to throw the introduction to her friends before turning on him once more. "Mr. and Mrs. Tizsa have experience at solving puzzles."

"Puzzles?" He stared at her, unable to believe his ears. "You call my daughter's disappearance a *puzzle?*"

"Well, yes. What would you call it? A child left alone in an enclosed garden for a mere minute has vanished without an obvious trace. Her only exit was into the house, where no one can find her."

He stared at her, unwilling to admit the truth of her words when his every instinct was to panic.

"Perhaps," the tall young man said, "you should show me the garden."

"With your permission," his wife added—a sop, presumably, to Nicholas's dignity.

Without a word, he strode past them, out of the room, and across the hall to the back door. They were right, of course. The headless chicken approach would not help Evelina. He had people scouring the streets. It was time to look more closely at how she could have got out and in which direction.

Tizsa…? "Dragan Tizsa," he said abruptly.

"Have we met?" Tizsa asked in surprise.

"No, but I've heard of you." As a revolutionary thinker and soldier. "What is this experience you have in finding lost children?"

"None," Tizsa said frankly. "But my wife and I have solved a few puzzles."

"The maid who was killed in Covent Garden," Miss Battle said. "And the housing scandal in St. Giles."

That, he did remember, was associated with Tizsa's name. "It's not how I would have chosen to meet you," Nicholas said grimly, pushing open the back door. "But if you can find my daughter before she is killed or becomes another statistic, I will be in your debt."

Tizsa didn't answer that but walked past him into the garden, where he began striding around, checking the walls and gates. Nicholas swallowed his impatience with difficulty. Surely, his own people had done this already?

"Where exactly was Evelina when you last saw her?" asked Mrs. Tizsa, once Lady Grizelda Niven.

Miss Battle went forward toward the overgrown bushes on the left of the lawn. "About here. Anna, the nursemaid, was going inside via the kitchen door and glanced back, she said, and Evelina was looking for her ball among the plants."

Mrs. Tizsa hurried forward with the governess. Since Tizsa was trying the cellar doors, which Nicholas could have told him were shut and locked at all times, Nicholas strode after the women, racking his brains for something more useful to do. Had he set everything in motion that was likely to find her? Ingram would use the neighbors to help scour the streets. The police, the river boatmen, were all looking for her. The servants were tearing the house apart—again—and he was left watching two young women poke among the undergrowth of his shabby garden.

"Is this her ball?" Mrs. Tizsa straightened, holding up the colorful ball that Evelina liked so much.

Nicholas's stomach clenched. It was Miss Battle who whispered, "Yes, it's hers."

"Then either she didn't find it, or she dropped it again. Dragan!" Mrs. Tizsa's unexpected shout jerked Nicholas out of his paralyzing fear once more.

"She would not have come in without the ball," Nicholas blurted, "or at least without raising such a hue and cry for it that she had all the servants searching." Dear God, had she fallen among the bushes, was she lying among them unconscious and unseen?

As one, the four of them began systematically searching the area, but of course, the servants would have found something as large as a child. The ball, they either didn't see or ignored as unimportant.

"It doesn't help," Nicholas burst out at last. "She didn't fall here, and the wall is too high for her to have climbed."

"Someone else could have climbed it," Tizsa said bluntly.

"And taken her?" Nicholas said hoarsely. It had always been a possibility, lurking monstrously at the back of his mind, and yet it was bizarrely shocking to hear it spoken aloud.

Tizsa hesitated. "Someone in another part of the city recently asked me to find a missing child. From what I've learned, he was not the only child of wealthy parents to vanish recently."

"What happened to them?" Miss Battle asked in little more than a whisper.

"That's the mystery." Tizsa kicked at a few plants at his feet. One, clearly rootless, flew to the side, landing on his wife's shoe. "Those rumored to have vanished apparently did not."

"You make no sense," Nicholas snapped.

"I know." Tizsa's foot was swiping loose branches and leaves out of the way, and suddenly his wife was there, helping him, and a small, square clearing near the wall began to take shape.

With a jolt, Nicholas remembered a conversation of months ago and wished he'd paid more attention.

"You have cellars here," Tizsa said.

"I do. They are locked from outside, and only the small wine cellar is accessible from inside."

Tizsa crouched and moved something with his hand. An iron ring attached to the ground. He glanced up at Nicholas in silent question.

"I have no idea," Nicholas answered slowly. Or did he?

It was awkward, with four people surrounded by thick, overgrown bushes and a tall, mossy stone wall, but they all pushed back among the rough branches, and Tizsa pulled the iron ring.

Dirt poured off it as a square door in the ground lifted. The four of them stared down into darkness.

"A sewer?" Mrs. Tizsa asked doubtfully.

"Not this time," her husband answered, which made little sense to Nicholas. "I can't smell it. I think it's another cellar or tunnel of some kind. There's at least one rung and a shaft."

"But she can't have gone down there," Miss Battle exclaimed. "How could she have hidden the door under those twigs and branches if she did?"

"It's possible the servants kicked stuff over it by accident when they were searching," Dragan said. "But on the whole, I think it's unlikely."

"She's afraid of the dark," Nicholas said in anguish. "She would *never* have gone down there willingly." *Oh, dear God, please, no...*

"And no one heard her shouting," Miss Battle said quickly. "I can't imagine her going anywhere without a fuss. And we saw no one in the bushes or climbing the wall, so if she was taken from here, it must have been quick."

"Very quick," Tizsa agreed. He straightened and jumped at the wall, hauling himself up until he sat astride it and gazed down the other side.

"Give me a hand up, Alex," urged the unexpected Mrs. Tizsa.

Without a word, Miss Battle joined her hands as though boosting someone into a saddle. Lady Grizelda stepped onto them, her husband stretched down one hand, and in a moment, she sat on the wall beside him.

"I suggest you investigate down there," Tizsa said, nodding to the hole in the garden. "We'll see what we can learn from this side." With that, he dropped down with a thud, and an instant later, his wife cast herself after him.

On any other day, Nicholas would have thoroughly enjoyed such eccentric behavior. On this day, he was in no condition to enjoy anything. He crouched by the hole, felt with his foot for the first rung.

"I'll fetch a lantern," Miss Battle said, ever practical, and forced her way out of the bushes.

By the time she returned with a lit lantern, he had climbed down several rungs and called his daughter's name several times into the darkness. Miss Battle knelt and handed the lantern down to him. Wordlessly he took it, shining it down the shaft. In fact, he was only one rung from the floor. He shone the lantern around.

He stood at the edge of what seemed a storage cellar, stretching back toward the house and narrowing. Crates and boxes of various sizes were piled as far as the light would stretch.

"Are these your things?" an amazed voice asked beside him. The intrepid Miss Battle, clearly, had followed him down, despite her impeding skirts.

"No. I didn't know this existed, though perhaps I should. I suppose she could have fallen down here." He shone the light on the ground and strode forward, his heart in his mouth. The chamber narrowed into a passage that must have led under the garden. And there was the wall, the blockage he normally looked at from the other side. "My father must have blocked this off," he murmured. "For security. But he never told me, and it doesn't show on any of the house plans."

"Do you suppose it was used by smugglers? Bringing things in via the Thames and avoiding duty?"

"Yes. It seems it still is." He handed her the lantern, then extracted a penknife from his pocket to pry off the nearest lid. "Brandy."

"At least Evelina did not fall down here or get trapped," Miss Battle said.

Another evil possibility struck him. "But she could have been brought here." He couldn't breathe, yet somehow, he fell on the next box, prying off its lid, too. "And hidden to..." The words died in his throat, but she clearly understood, for without a sound, she took something from her pocket and began levering open another box.

A governess who carried a penknife in her pocket. He must have said it aloud, for she murmured prosaically, "I spend a great deal of time sharpening pens and pencils."

And these were the only words between them, as they worked, urgently, grimly, heaving and ripping open every crate, every time terrified of finding a small, lifeless body, or at least a gagged and terrified little girl in the darkness. They did not stop until the last crate was opened and revealed to hold nothing more than spices.

Abruptly, he sat down on the filthy floor and buried his head in his aching, blistered hands. He didn't even know if he was glad or sorry. Or if it was all just soul-gutting guilt. *If only she is unhurt, if only she is alive...*

A great, heaving sob racked his body, and suddenly, soft arms were around him, hugging him, a gentle voice assured him desperately that it would be fine, that Evelina would be fine, and they would find her soon. He felt her cheek, damp with her own tears, pressed to his. And this was the woman he had blamed, in his anger with himself, in his pointless petulance. Yet his was the blame. *His.*

Abruptly, he clutched her to him, the only rock in his crumbling life. There could not be comfort, but at least there was steadiness.

"I'm sorry for what I said," he ground out. "I didn't mean it."

"It doesn't matter," she assured him.

Was she actually stroking his hair? It was a distracting thought, enabling him to pull himself together. He could wallow in guilt and stupidity later when Evelina was found. With a deep breath, he drew back from the governess's arms, which fell immediately to her side.

"I wonder what Griz has discovered?" she said, jumping to her feet and swinging up the lantern.

CHAPTER SIX

GRIZ AND DRAGAN had discovered tracks and footprints on the other side of the garden wall. The lane itself seemed to have no purpose, except as a footpath or a lane for a pony and small cart. Mostly, it seemed merely to separate the Swan house and garden from the tenement building next to it.

Griz gazed up at a windowless gable end. The narrow lane led from the front of the buildings down to the wider alley where the Swans kept their carriage house and stable. A few other storage places for goods and animals lined this alley, and it led directly onto Craven Street.

"So, this narrow lane would hardly ever be used," Griz mused. "There isn't really any need of it. The Swans' servants would take horses and carriages the other direction to the front of the house and back again."

"And yet," Dragan said, rising to his feet, "there are hoof prints here and cart tracks. From where we came over the wall, leading down to the mews."

As one, they followed the tracks into the mews alley, where it was impossible to distinguish them from those of other traffic. Everything was scuffed and manured. And quiet apart from clucking chickens, and, somewhere, a snorting pig.

The mews alley ran to Craven Street at one end, and the other curved into the distance.

"You looking for the little girl?" a woman's voice asked.

Griz swung to face her. A middle-aged woman in a shawl and cap, carrying a bucket, had come out of a small pen where a pig snouted at scraps on the ground.

"Yes," Griz said eagerly, "did you see her?"

"No, I told the maidservant and the other chap that asked. I was here, cleaning out his sty around the time, but I saw no little girl. Not on her own, and not with nobody else neither."

Dragan came up to join them. "Perhaps you saw a vehicle of some kind? A small cart, perhaps drawn by a single pony or a donkey? Coming out of that path?"

The woman began to shake her head, from habit, Griz suspected. Then she paused and frowned. "Actually, yes, I did see a donkey come out of there, pulling a wagon with one man driving it. No little girl with him. Though I suppose she might have been inside."

"Inside?" Griz said quickly.

"Inside the tarpaulin. It was a little covered wagon. Seen it around here before, though I don't know where the blokes work. Came out the path and turned *that* way." The woman pointed away from Craven Street.

"Thank you!" Griz called over her shoulder, already trotting after Dragan, who was striding up the mews alley.

The wagon could have stopped and been hidden at any of the small buildings they passed. It could have cut down Villiers Street, or any of the other crossings leading to the Strand. The alley seemed to run more or less parallel with the Strand, just a couple of narrow streets behind it.

"She could be anywhere between Swan's house and here," Griz said unhappily.

"Would you kidnap a child and hide her somewhere so close that the police would be beating down your door?" Dragan demanded.

"No," she admitted.

"Besides, this does not feel planned. They can't have known she would be in her garden, and why would they have been there in any case?"

"To use the secret door beneath the garden?"

"Probably. It seems likeliest they came upon her by accident and probably snatched her to stop her screaming. They must have had the wagon waiting to receive something. And with the girl as well, I think they would have aimed to get away as fast as possible without being seen."

"But they could more easily be invisible among all the traffic in the Strand than on a quiet muse," Griz protested.

"Except the woman with the pig says they are familiar figures here. She didn't even think of them until I pointed to the path. But you're right, they might have risked being seen by more people in the hope of being lost in the throng. In any case," he added, nodding ahead, "it looks like the alley ends at the Strand."

And from there, Griz thought bleakly, gazing up and down the busy, noisy road, they could have gone anywhere.

Almost directly opposite where they had come out of the alley, on the other side of the Strand, was another narrow street. If their donkey and wagon had actually come this far, there was a maze of streets they could have vanished into.

"Crossing the road, Missus? Sweep it for you!" an urchin offered Griz with an engaging grin.

"Tell me the truth first, and I'll pay you double," Griz offered. "Did you see a donkey pulling a covered wagon here, about an hour ago? Maybe two now."

"Saw two," the boy said happily. "Does that mean you'll pay me twice?"

"Depends if you saw where they went," Dragan said severely.

The boy hastily tugged his forelock, though he didn't actually seem much intimidated. "One went straight up the Strand. I'd been saving half a carrot for him—he's a friend."

"Who does he belong to?" Griz asked quickly.

"Mr. Jarvis, got a fruit and veg shop near Covent Garden."

"And the other donkey?"

"Don't know him, but he was making a racket and playing up. Gave me the chance to sweep for two smart gents while he held up the traffic. Right to-do there was."

"And where did this donkey go?" Griz asked.

"Up there," the boy said, pointing to the lane opposite.

Griz looked at Dragan. "Try along there first, and then move on to Mr. Jarvis's fruit and vegetable shop?"

Dragan nodded and flipped the boy a coin. Immediately, the boy stepped into the street with a practiced hand signal and began sweeping from one side to the other. Griz and Dragan followed his track between the filth to the far side, where Dragan gave him another coin.

"You're an observant lad," Dragan told him. "I'm always happy to pay for useful observation."

The boy grinned, and as they left him, Griz acknowledged that they had added another link in their growing chain of watchers.

As they set off up the next, nameless lane, Griz said, "What do you think of Sir Nicholas Swan?"

"I think he is genuinely frightened for his daughter's safety and not ignorant of the dangers that could befall her. Beyond that... I would say he is a man of secrets and layers. Does your Alexandra like him?"

"I don't know. I don't think she does."

Dragan glanced down at her. "You trust her?"

"Yes," Griz said in surprise. "Oh, Dragan, you don't think she had anything to do with this, do you?"

"I don't know. She was in charge of Evelina when the girl vanished. And Evelina is not the only well-born child to have vanished. Governesses know each other, don't they?"

"Some do, some don't, but I can't imagine Alexandra hurting a *child!*"

"Hmm," Dragan said noncommittally. "I think this lane winds all the way to Covent Garden."

"I don't think I would care to come this way at night." She glanced from darkened doorways to blank windows that seemed to close in on them, and strange, ill-dressed men loitering without purpose. "Or alone at any time."

"Listen out for the braying of donkeys," Dragan advised. He didn't appear tense, but she knew that peculiar, alert poise. He was prepared for anything.

When one of those loiterers moved casually toward them, Griz threw caution to the wind and bestowed upon him a smile that she hoped was dazzling. Certainly, he looked taken aback, which allowed her the moment she needed.

"Good day!" she said brightly. "I'm looking for a donkey, and a boy in the Strand told us someone up this way wished to sell one."

"It ain't me," the man said, staring.

"No, but perhaps you know someone who wants to sell a donkey?"

The man looked stunned. "No. What does the likes of you want with a donkey?"

"When I can afford a carriage and four horses, I'll buy them for her," Dragan said drily. "Until then, a donkey and cart must do."

For a moment, Griz thought it hung in the balance whether he would try and rob them or help them. In the end, he shouted at the nearest window. "Daisy!"

A woman with a child in her arms leaned precariously over the sill and peered down at them. "What?"

"We know anyone with a donkey?"

"Nah." She was about to shut the window again when she said. "One went that way about an hour ago, though." Holding the baby in one hand, she pointed up the lane in the direction Griz and Dragan were already traveling.

"Thank you!" Griz said with genuine gratitude and to the man melting back into his doorway. "And to you. Wish us luck!"

The man made a sound that might have been a laugh. As if he didn't quite know why he'd helped them rather than rob them.

"We're still on the right track, then," Dragan murmured.

"If Evelina is in the wagon. If she isn't, we're wasting a lot of time."

"I know," Dragan said grimly.

It haunted her that the child was afraid of the dark, for she knew there were monsters in the city that a sheltered little girl could not dream of in her worst nightmare.

⫸⫷

HUGGING SIR NICHOLAS had been a purely instinctive gesture of comfort, such as she would have given a distressed child. But with her arms around his broad, muscular shoulders and her cheek pressed to his hair, he felt nothing like a child. He was every inch a big, strong male, smelling of soap and sandalwood and just a trace of recent sweat, an attractive, desirable man. And when his arms came up and held her close, her body answered.

Shocked that such things could even cross her mind in the present circumstances, she was relieved when he released her, even if part of her screamed with disappointment.

"We should go back to the house," he said abruptly. "Someone might have news by now."

She went first up the ladder while he held the lantern. Once above the ground, she took the lantern from him and lit his way out. The sun had moved. Although nowhere near dark on a summer's day, it reminded her that time marched inexorably on.

In silence, they hurried toward the house. Of course, Evelina was not home. Someone would have shouted the good news to them.

"I'll send tea up to the library," Mrs. Dart said.

Sir Nicholas looked as if he were about to refuse, so Alexandra said quickly, "Thank you."

"I should be out looking for my daughter," he uttered, climbing the stairs with impatience, "not swilling tea."

"Swilling tea will give you energy to look longer," Alexandra said calmly. "And while you are swilling, you can be thinking where best to look that is not already covered by everyone else who is out searching."

He cast her a furious look that softened suddenly into rueful amusement. "You are always so sane and sensible, Alexandra Battle. How did my household get by without you all these years?"

"Very well, by all I have witnessed and heard."

He made a sound like a snort as he strode into the library and threw himself into his usual wingback chair. From there, he regarded Alexandra under lowering brows. "Sit, for God's sake. Help me to think straight. Where should I be looking that is not a systematic quartering of the surrounding streets?"

Alexandra chose a hard chair, some distance from him. "Does she know anyone in London that she might have suddenly decided to visit on her own? Your brother, perhaps? I understand he lives in London."

"Ralph? She doesn't know him, has never been to the Brook Street house."

Even as she took that in, it seemed odd. Of course, Evelina might not be considered respectable, being illegitimate. Sir Nicholas, no doubt, was not considered respectable for the same reason and many others.

"And as you have already noted, she has not played with other children here." He sat up suddenly. "Do you suppose she followed some children? To play with them?"

"It is possible," Alexandra said cautiously. "Though I still can't think how she got out of the garden to do so. The mews gate was locked, and she did not go through the kitchen or the main house."

Mrs. Dart wheeled in a tea trolley, briefly distracting them. "I've put a cup for you there, too, Miss Battle. And sir, there is a policeman called to speak to you about Evelina."

Pitiable fear crossed Sir Nicholas's face. "Has he…?"

"He hasn't found her, no, sir, but he wants to talk to you."

"Send him up," Sir Nicholas commanded.

While Alexandra set about pouring tea, a brisk man walked into the room and bowed.

"Sir Nicholas. Ma'am. I'm Inspector Harris, based at Scotland Yard. Word came to me about your daughter's disappearance. I gather she is still not found."

"No," Sir Nicholas said curtly, waving him to a chair.

Since Mrs. Dart had supplied a third cup, Alexandra poured him tea.

He seemed surprised to receive it, though he helped himself to sugar and milk while he talked. "I want you to be aware, sir, that you may receive a ransom demand."

"Ransom?" Sir Nicholas repeated, startled.

"I am investigating one such case, a gentleman's son, and suspect two more who reported missing children and then miraculously found them. It's my belief they paid the ransom. The case I know of, the ransom demand also instructed the parents not to inform anyone, least of all the police. I gather you have not yet received such a note?"

Sir Nicholas shook his head. His face was white.

"You probably wouldn't until tomorrow, if this case follows the same pattern."

"Tomorrow?" Sir Nicholas said hoarsely. "But she cannot be away all night. She will be terrified…"

"It's cruel, sir, I know. On the other hand, it is good to remember that the other children came home unharmed. And, of course, we do not yet know if that is what has befallen your daughter. Children wander, alone and in company, good as well as bad. But I ask you, if you receive a note, to send me word. My men and I wear plain clothes and would not alert people that we are police."

An unhappy smile curved Sir Nicholas's lips. "You may not be in uniform, sir, but I suspect most practiced villains could spot you for what you are a hundred yards away."

"It depends on the villain," Inspector Harris said with dignity. "And the policeman concerned." He hesitated, then added, "I would not normally recommend it, but if you feel you cannot take the risk of the police, then you might contact a man called Tizsa. I can give you his address, and he is *not* a policeman."

"He already has mine, Inspector," Sir Nicholas said dryly. "He is out looking for my daughter as we speak."

"Is he, by God?"

"Miss Battle here is a friend of Mrs. Tizsa."

"I see." Inspector Harris drank his tea, set down his cup, and rose. "Then I have no more to say at the moment, except to assure you of any help you need. I hope she is found before nightfall."

Alexandra rose to see him out since Sir Nicholas seemed to be lost in his own private hell from which he could not move.

However, when she returned to the library, he was at his desk, feverishly jotting things down on a piece of paper.

"I am thinking of places she was interested in. The children who live around the corner will have been asked already. But she also showed interest in her cousins—my brother's children—in Brook Street. And I know she wanted to see where the Queen lives in Buckingham Palace. Then, there is the park where you took her."

"If she walked that way, she will be found quickly," Alexandra assured him, although she still could not see how the child could have got out of the garden so quickly without help. She did not like to think of that help.

"There is also the possibility," he said more heavily, "that some-one, some enemy of mine, might have taken her to get back at me or to force my hand."

"Do you have many such enemies?" she asked, startled.

"I would not have thought so." He straightened, raking his hand through his hair. "I'm clutching at straws. But at least if I look there, I am *doing* something. Miss Battle, I want you to remain here, in case she returns one way or another before I do. She trusts you."

Alexandra did not quite know what to say to that. Nor was she good at simply waiting. But before she could come up with an alternative task for herself, he said abruptly, "I heard what you said to her after her tantrum this morning. And I heard her response. You may only have been here a few days, but you are good for her."

Alexandra swallowed. "I shall remind you of that the next time we disagree, and you threaten to dismiss me."

A brief smile flickered in his eyes, but he was already turning away. "We shall see who dismisses whom in the end."

For lack of anything better to do, Alexandra trailed after Sir Nicholas downstairs, where he grabbed his hat and coat from the stand and strode toward the front door.

"Sir Nicholas!" came Mrs. Dart's voice from the back of the house. "Wait!"

As Alexandra sped up, the housekeeper came into view, hauling a grubby street urchin with her.

"Sir, the boy says they found her!"

Alive or dead?

CHAPTER SEVEN

ALEXANDRA HAD TO grasp the banister in sudden, paralyzing fear. She couldn't begin to imagine Sir Nicholas's feelings.

"She's alive, sir," Mrs. Dart said urgently. "She's fine. The boy has an address and will take you to her."

Nicholas stumbled toward the boy, who held out a grubby, folded piece of paper as though to ward the man off.

Nicholas all but snatched it, while Alexandra ran down the rest of the stairs.

"Not a ransom demand," he threw out. "It's signed *G. Tizsa*. She's at an address in Covent Garden with Evelina. Mrs. Dart, order the carriage brought round."

"I already have. It will be but a moment."

He nodded and swung on Alexandra. "Miss Battle, I am instructed to bring Alex, which I presume means you. Child," he said to the boy, "you shall ride with my coachman to wherever you came from."

In a flurry of breathless activity, Alexandra found herself in a luxurious town coach opposite Sir Nicholas, whose black brows were lowered into a heavy frown. His fingers drummed on his thigh.

"Why did Mrs. Tizsa not bring her home?" he demanded abruptly. "Why send for us, unless she is hurt?"

"The note said she was fine. There will be complications, which Griz attracts like moths to a flame."

He grunted, peering out of the window onto the busy Strand. "We would be quicker walking," he fumed.

With an effort of will, it seemed, he stilled his impatient fingers and focused his attention on Alexandra. She wasn't fooled. She knew she was merely a distraction to an unbearable wait and was happy to oblige.

"Did you work previously for her family?" he asked.

She shook her head. "No. I worked for the Lacey family in Hampshire, and for the Paxtons in London and Essex."

"You can't have worked long for either."

"A year with the Laceys and five with the Paxtons."

"Why did you leave?" he asked curiously.

"I left the Laceys for the Paxtons because they offered a better salary."

"And?" he asked steadily.

She shrugged. "And I did not care for the Lacey family in the end. The Paxtons were a pleasant change."

"And yet you left them, too."

"Only because their children grew up or went away to school. You will find it all in my references. Are you looking for another reason to dismiss me?"

"I am looking for a reason for my luck."

"Was that a compliment?" she asked sardonically.

"Actually, yes. What did you do before? What took you to governessing?"

"I explained it all to Mrs. Dart when she interviewed me for the position."

"You are right, of course. I should have been there, too. You haven't answered my question."

"I lived abroad most of my life. After my father's...demise, I returned to England with the Laceys, who had offered me the position of governess in their family."

"And who was your father? What did he do?"

"Alexander Battle. He was a pianist."

Unexpectedly, Sir Nicholas's eyes widened. "He was indeed! I heard him play in Rome and in Vienna. Alexander Battle was your father?"

"Is that a problem?" she asked, her heart sinking.

"Should it be?"

"I understand the daughter of a public performer is not considered respectable enough to teach English gentlemen's daughters."

"Perhaps, for those more concerned with birth than education," he said with unexpected contempt. "Or for those who want an excuse to pay a qualified person less than their worth."

Which was close enough to the truth to deprive her of words.

"We must be almost there," he said, gazing out of the window once more.

They were skirting the Covent Garden market and soon cut up a nearby lane. Sir Nicholas jumped out almost before the coach had stopped and handed Alexandra down with a hurry that crushed the courtliness of the gesture.

By then, Dragan Tizsa had appeared in the nearest doorway. He led them through a narrow stone close and through a door on the left.

"Papa!" Evelina hurled herself across the bare room and into her father's arms. To Alexandra's anxious eyes, she looked a trifle grubby but unharmed. "Miss Battle!"

Griz stood by the window, looking pleased. At her knees were two small children no older than three. And seated at the table, with a baby, was a gaudily and somewhat scantily dressed female who looked worryingly like a lady of the night.

"I knew you would come!" Evelina exclaimed as her father pushed her a little way from him to scan her face for injury or distress. "I was a bit surprised to see Lady Griz, but Mr. Tizsa sent that boy to find you."

"But how the devil did you get here?" Sir Nicholas asked, clearly too anxious and bewildered to mind his language.

"I ran away from the bad men and hid in here, and then I couldn't leave them, could I? Because they are too young to look after themselves, and they were hungry."

"I think you had better sit down," Griz said. "I've made tea."

Alexandra looked about her. "Are you sure we should be consuming these people's supply of tea?"

"Oh, we bought some," Griz said vaguely. "There's a shop at the corner. I asked you to come too, Alex, because I'm not quite sure what to do with these children."

"George and Jilly," Evelina said, turning to the older children with her father's hand held proudly in both of hers. "This is my Papa. Oh, Lady Griz, we could have the pastries now!"

"We bought those, too," Griz said hastily. "Before we get to explanations, this is Nell." She indicated the gaudily dressed woman, who smiled a challenge to the room. "It's Nell we really owe for Evelina's safety."

Nell got up and fetched some chipped plates from a cupboard, along with a box of pastries. Griz poured tea.

"What happened?" Sir Nicholas demanded of his daughter, who was tugging him to sit down. The tiny children squashed onto the chair beside her, and Alexandra sat next to them.

"I was playing in the garden with Anna," Evelina said, "but it was time to go in. I went to pick up the ball—which Anna, *not* I, threw into the bushes, by the way—and this man appeared on top of the garden wall. I said *Good afternoon*, very politely, and he said something I didn't even understand. Then another man appeared, and before I knew it, the first one leaned down and just hauled me up. I couldn't even scream, though I tried, and then one of them put his hand over my mouth, jumped down with me, and dragged me into a wagon. I bit his hand," Evelina said with satisfaction. "Twice."

"Good for you, my pet," said Nell stoutly.

"I wriggled and kicked as well," Evelina boasted, and her father put his arm around her, hugging her convulsively.

"Did they hit you?" he asked, low. "Hurt you in any way?"

"Well, only in that they wouldn't let me go or make a sound. So I stopped struggling until I could see out the back of the wagon, where the tarpaulin didn't close properly, that we were right by a market. So, while my bad man was talking to the other, I suddenly pulled free and jumped out."

"She did," Nell confirmed. "Exploded out the back of that wagon and ran like a hare. I knew at once she weren't running just from a heavy-handed dad. And I've seen men like that before, too. They knocked over a stall chasing after her. I sent her down this street, and me and some others got in their way. They never saw where she went."

"Did you see where *they* went?" Sir Nicholas asked. Though he sounded calm, there was murder in his eyes.

"They were attracting too much attention," Nell said. "A policeman was running toward them, so they jumped up behind their poor little donkey and headed off in the direction of Long Acre. You won't find them now."

Sir Nicholas held her gaze. "And is this your house, madam?"

She grinned. "Bless you, no, it ain't. *Madam*, though," she added to Griz. "I could get to like him as much as your man."

"What made you come in here?" Alexandra asked Evelina.

"I just tried the doors, and this one opened."

"Dear God," her father whispered.

"It's respectable down here," Nell assured him. "I knew she wouldn't come to no harm."

"And you found these other children on their own?" Alexandra asked Evelina, who nodded. "Have they no parents? No one who looks after them?"

"They have a Papa," Evelina offered.

"Work," uttered the little boy, George.

"Their mum died birthing the youngest," Nell said. "Her next door is meant to look in on them during the day, but she's got her hands full. Expect she forgets sometimes."

Alexandra took in the awfulness of this, of a man who was forced to leave his children in order to work so that he could feed them. Her throat closed up.

Sir Nicholas swung suddenly on Dragan. "When I saw them here with Evelina, it struck me they were the other children taken from their homes for ransom. How do you know they aren't?"

Dragan raised his brows. "Nell."

"He don't trust a witness like me," Nell observed, mocking but apparently unoffended.

"Why not?" Evelina asked her father in surprise. "Nell is kind."

"Oh, I am," Nell agreed, casting a cheeky smile at Sir Nicholas, who seemed more amused than put out.

"I do not doubt it, madam."

"Besides," Griz said, "the children talk to Evelina. She understands them if we do not."

Nicholas glanced from her to Dragan and back. "How did you find them?"

"There were hoof and cart tracks on the other side of your garden wall," Dragan said. "Which meant we had different questions to ask your neighbors. They had not seen Evelina, but they'd seen a donkey and cart emerge from the side path and head toward Covent Garden. We thought we had lost them there, but luck was with us in the shape of Nell, who is an old friend."

"Not so old," Nell objected.

Alexandra gazed at Griz in fascination. She did not appear to mind, or even notice, that her new husband had just claimed old friendship with a woman who was clearly a prostitute.

"If it weren't for Nell and her friends," Dragan said, "we would not have found the murderer of Nancy Barrow, the duchess's maid."

Now Nell did look embarrassed and finished her tea with a hearty slurp. "Yes, well, that was Junie, mostly, but I'm always glad to help *you*, my love," she said cheerfully, "and even your sweet lady. I'd better rush, for their dad won't like to find the likes of me with his kids."

But she was too late. The door opened casually, and a man in working clothes and a cap walked in and stopped dead, his mouth dropping open. His children slid off their chair and waddled toward him.

He scowled, hugging them to his legs. "You ain't taking them to no orphanage," he growled. "They get food and shelter with me."

Sir Nicholas stood. "We wouldn't dream of interfering in such matters. As it is, we must apologize for invading your home. My name is Nicholas Swan, and this is my daughter, who ran in here to escape her kidnappers. This is Mr. and Mrs. Tizsa who found her, and Miss Battle, my daughter's governess."

"And I'm Nell, though you don't want to know."

The man cast her a harassed glance.

"My daughter did not want to leave your children until you came home," Sir Nicholas added.

"We found her cutting bread for them," Griz offered.

The scowl deepened. "Mrs. Brand next door is meant to give them food, make sure they're safe." His gaze flickered to Evelina, who, sensing their imminent departure, had gone to the smaller children. They left their father's legs to hug her.

"I'm afraid they have also had cake," Alexandra offered.

Griz said, "The leftovers are in the cupboard, along with more tea, since we've been drinking it uninvited in your house. But we'll get out of your hair now."

"Can we come back and visit, Miss Battle?" Evelina pleaded.

"Well, that is really up to both fathers," Alexandra said hastily. She fully expected Nicholas to make polite noises and lead Evelina firmly out of the depressing room. But again, he surprised her.

"You cannot be alone in your difficulty," he said to his fellow parent. "If I think up a viable solution, I will be in touch. I'm eternally grateful for your unwitting shelter. Goodbye!"

The other father, who hadn't uttered a word after his initial declaration, gazed after them in bafflement as they left his house. The carriage waited in the street. The coachman appeared to be trading insults with the driver of another vehicle who was having difficulty passing.

Sir Nicholas addressed the Tizsas. "Would you care to squash inside?"

"No, thank you," Griz said cheerfully. "We're going to the market, and then we'll probably take a hackney."

Sir Nicholas offered his free hand to Dragan. Evelina dangled from the other. "I have no words to thank you both for what you've done."

"None are necessary," Dragan assured him, shaking hands.

Alexandra followed Nicholas's gaze toward the market square, where the bright, gaudy figure of Nell was vanishing into the distance.

"Will you thank her, too?"

"We will," Griz said cheerfully, raising a hand in farewell as they turned away.

As Alexandra climbed into the carriage, Dragan suddenly turned back.

"What was in your secret cellar?"

Sir Nicholas said vaguely. "Oh, nothing of interest."

Alexandra glanced at him in surprise, but he was already climbing inside. The coach moved forward toward home.

It seemed a lifetime had passed since Evelina's morning tantrum. And it wasn't even dark yet.

CHAPTER EIGHT

A T EVELINA'S REQUEST—AND indeed, her father seemed to find it difficult to let her out of his sight—Sir Nicholas joined them in the dining room that evening.

Evelina was already in a state of huge excitement. Her welcome home had been overwhelming. Mrs. Dart had hugged her. Anna had wept over her amidst a storm of Italian, and the other servants had been grinning from ear to ear. All the attention on top of her escape and adventure with the Covent Garden children seemed, for the moment, to have blotted out what must have been the terror of her capture. And to crown it all, the unprecedented presence of her father at dinner made her almost delirious.

In fact, Sir Nicholas was waiting for them when they arrived in the dining room, looking very distinguished in his evening clothes—which may have been the reason for Alexandra's sudden shortness of breath.

But he proved to be much more approachable than she had ever seen him: perfectly well mannered, responding indulgently to his daughter's happy chatter, and even telling amusing stories about her babyhood, and about his life abroad. This congenial side of him was curiously beguiling after what she had seen before of the arrogant gentleman and the anguished father.

Nor did he exclude Alexandra, although she was happy enough simply to listen and smile at their talk.

There was wine with this meal, and as he topped up her glass, he said, "You must have been in Rome when I was there in '44."

"Yes, but I doubt we moved in the same circles."

"I met your father," he said unexpectedly. "I don't remember you."

"You wouldn't," she said.

"Why not?" Evelina asked, gazing from one to the other.

"If I was present at all," Alexandra said lightly, "I would have been quite eclipsed by all my father's glittering admirers." Who, generally, he was shamelessly fleecing at the time.

"I would have remembered you," Sir Nicholas said, and something in his tone made her gaze fly to his. Was that warmth in his eyes? Approval? Gratitude for helping in the search for Evelina? Or something more…?

Whatever the emotion, he had no right to look at her like that, to make butterflies flutter in her stomach and sudden, silly hope blossom in her heart.

A swift knock at the door broke their gaze. James came in and spoke quietly in Sir Nicholas's ear. Sir Nicholas nodded, and the man bowed and left the room. Thoughtfully, Sir Nicholas curled his long fingers around the stem of his wine glass and raised it to his lips.

"The large hall off the landing," he observed, "would make a decent drawing room."

"Are you thinking of entertaining, sir?" Alexandra asked.

"It crossed my mind. It is hardly a desirable or attractive address, but I suppose people might come from curiosity."

"Why did you choose to live here?" Alexandra asked.

He gazed into his wine for so long that she thought he wouldn't answer, and Evelina shifted impatiently in her chair. "I had reasons. Reasons I'm not sure were ever valid." He set his glass on the table and pushed it away. "Ladies, it has been a most pleasant evening, and I thank you for your company."

As he made to rise, Evelina looked alarmed for the first time since they had found her in the Covent Garden house. She sprang off her chair and threw herself at his knee. Alexandra didn't have the heart to rebuke her for such table manners. Nor, it appeared, did her father.

After an instant of what might have been surprise, he put his arm around her and bent to kiss the top of her head. "Good night, my brave child."

Releasing her, he rose, and Evelina stepped back. Alexandra prepared for a possible tantrum, but it didn't come. Sir Nicholas ruffled Evelina's head and walked out of the room, while Evelina turned and resumed her seat to finish the last of her dessert.

Not long after, Anna came to take her to bed, and Evelina, who did indeed look exhausted, made no demur. Only at the last minute, as she and Anna reached the dining room doorway, did she turn back, throwing out her hand. "Come, too, Miss Battle."

Alexandra would always have been happy to put the child to bed. In her previous positions, it had been expected of her, but here, it had always seemed like stepping on Anna's toes, and the nurserymaid had already been resentful enough.

"If you wish," Alexandra said, rising.

Evelina clung to both their hands, swinging and chattering between them as they crossed the landing and climbed the stairs. Anna laughed with her, showing no signs of the suspicion usual with her around Alexandra.

While the nursery maid helped Evelina wash and change into her night things, Alexandra browsed the bookshelves for a suitable bedtime story. Drawing out a well-worn edition of Hans Christian Andersen's fairytales, she glanced up at Evelina for approval.

Evelina was sitting in front of the mirror on her dressing table, while Anna brushed her hair. The child gazed at her own face, but it was clear she was not seeing it. Her eyes were frightened, haunted, and Alexandra's heart went out to her.

"I could read you a fairytale," she offered.

Evelina blinked, then nodded, rising from her stool.

"I will fetch a fresh glass of water," Anna said, making for the door.

"No!" Evelina flew after her, seizing her hand. "Don't go."

Anna gazed down at her with pity and murmured in Italian, "You are quite safe, my sweet. Miss Battle will be with you until I come back."

Evelina buried her face in the nursemaid's hand. "Where is Papa?"

"I do not know," Anna said unwisely.

"He did not go out," Alexandra added hastily, hoping it was the truth. "He will be busy in his library, as he always is."

Evelina swallowed and allowed herself to be led into bed, though she still clung onto Anna's hand. Alexandra sat on the chair on the other side of the bed and opened the book. But a tear was squeezing out of Evelina's eye, all the more heartbreaking for being silent and so unlike her usual attention-seeking tantrums.

"Please make him come," she whispered to Alexandra.

Alexandra glanced at the worried maid, who met her gaze. There was really no debate. The child had been through a terrifying ordeal and come out of it with remarkable *sangfroid*. But she was six years old, and rough strangers had seized her from her family home only hours ago.

Alexandra laid aside the book. "I'll speak to him."

As she left the room and made her way to the library, she crossed her fingers among her skirts. *Please don't let him have gone out.* She did not care for lies, but surely in the circumstances, it would be better for Evelina to believe he was in the house, even if he were not?

Hurrying across the landing toward the library, she breathed a sigh of relief, for the door was ajar, and within, she could hear male voices. She advanced with much more confidence that Evelina could now be soothed into sleep, had even raised her hand to knock when Sir Nicholas's distinctive voice reached her, chilling in its icy anger.

"You took my child in broad daylight. Our agreement is at an end."

Alexandra froze. *What?*

"Sir, a genuine mistake..." began a very different male voice, wheedling, yet offhand, very much in the accents of the lower orders of society.

"A final mistake," Sir Nicholas interrupted. "I meant what I said."

The sound of quick footsteps treading across the library floor panicked Alexandra. Though her first instinct was to run, she forced herself to stay put and knock, finally, just as the door flew open.

James stood there, looking larger and considerably more threatening than usual. The man with him was no taller than Alexandra and dressed in the cap and clothing of a working man. His attitude was deprecating to the point of servile, and yet his eyes spat venom.

Alexandra fell back, and this man slid past her, eyes down, with James hard on his heels.

"Miss Battle," Sir Nicholas said from inside the room. "Were you looking for me?"

I was. Before you let your daughter's kidnapper walk out of here, before you implied his only mistake was to do what he did in daylight... Do I really believe that?

"Yes," she managed. "Evelina is asking for you."

He had been walking toward her, but at that, he swung away, dragging his hand through his hair before he spun back to face her. "I am angry, Miss Battle."

"Then perhaps you should not see her," she blurted.

His eyes narrowed as though he suspected hidden meaning to her words. "You don't think much of me, do you, Alexandra Battle?"

"I do not know you," she replied, and that was the truth.

He gazed at her, then without a word, he walked past her and out the door. A moment later, she heard his footsteps running up the stairs two at a time. Alexandra followed more slowly, trying to slow the pounding of her heart.

She could swear his anxiety for Evelina had been genuine, especially those moments in the cellar, and he had seemed to leave no stone unturned in his effort to find her, mobilizing all his employees from all she had seen.

And yet he clearly knew the man responsible, spoke only of broken agreements…

No, that was all you heard, she admonished herself severely. It struck her as she approached the schoolroom area that she was eager to think the worst of him, to counter her own inconvenient attraction to him, which was hardly fair.

She had spoken the truth. She did not know him.

She found him sitting on Evelina's bed, sharing her propped-up pillow, while he read from the fairytale book. Evelina spared her a distracted glance but smiled, and so Alexandra sat next to Anna on the other side of the bed. A fresh glass of water had been brought, perhaps by another maid.

Evelina fell asleep part way through the story, which was probably a good thing, considering the sadness of its ending. Sir Nicholas stopped reading and set aside the book. In fascination, Alexandra watched the tenderness with which he laid her down and drew up the coverlet. As if his conversation in the library had never happened.

Without warning, he glanced up and saw her staring. At once, she looked away and crept from the room while Anna put out all the lamps save the night-light.

"Miss Battle." Sir Nicholas's voice stayed her. "A word, if you please."

He was her employer. She had no choice. Even so, she was conscious of the conflicting powerful pulls of attraction and repulsion. She did not want to go near him at this moment, and yet it was more than the obedience of an employee that caused her to follow him into the library.

He walked across to the table with the decanters and poured brandy into two glasses before holding one out to her.

"No, thank you."

He raised one eyebrow. "You won't drink with me, or you won't drink?"

"I have already had wine this evening."

"Goodness," he remarked. "Any moment now, you will be a fallen woman." He all but dropped her glass on the table between the two chairs. "I wish you'd sit down because I intend to."

She lowered herself, straight-backed, into the second armchair. Was this where Evelina's captor had sat? Sir Nicholas threw himself into the other and frowned at his brandy glass.

"It will make your life difficult," he said abruptly. "But in the immediate future, Evelina must not be left alone outside, anywhere."

"In the immediate future, I do not believe that will be a problem. She does not wish to be left alone anywhere."

"Another issue for you to resolve when this is done."

"When what is done?" she asked uneasily.

"The grounds made safe, and the villains who kidnapped my daughter are behind bars."

She stared at him. *You had him here, sitting where I am now, and you let him go.*

"Miss Battle, I may have no idea how to bring up a child, let alone a daughter," he said impatiently, perhaps misunderstanding her silence, "but I am aware she needs some stability, some security in her life. God knows she had little enough before her mother died, and now I have uprooted her from her home and brought her to a strange country, where Anna and I are her only connection to the past—Anna more so because I did not see her as often as I should." He took a drink, his movements quick and angry. "The point is, this afternoon's adventure can hardly help matters. She has grown fond of you very quickly, and I believe you can help her, but if you are not prepared to take on such a difficult task, I need to know now."

"I believe I already accepted the task."

He sat back in his chair, regarding her over the rim of his glass as he took another sip. "How very stiff you are. How have I offended you?"

"I am your employee. It is not my place to be offended."

"And yet," he mocked, "here you are, rigid with disapproval."

I heard you with him, I saw... "I am tired," she said, taking the coward's way out.

He shook his head. "No."

"By your leave, sir, I should know!"

"Oh, you may well be tired, but that isn't it."

She met his gaze with defiance, saying nothing.

The mockery faded from his eyes, but he did not smile. "Perhaps you overheard some of my conversation with...my visitor."

"I do not eavesdrop."

"Of course, you do not." The mockery was back. "That would be unladylike. On the other hand, catching a few words meant for another and drawing your own conclusions is very different and maintains your honor...or is it self-righteousness?"

She jumped to her feet. "Of what, exactly, are you accusing me, sir?"

His gaze followed her. "Well, here's a heat." He rose deliberately, like a large, predatory cat, all smooth movement and danger. "And yet the question is rather, of what are you accusing me, madam?"

Her heart thundered. It was an effort merely to hold his sardonic gaze as he stood staring down at her, to hide her fear over what he had done and what he was, and why her treacherous body still yearned to be closer.

"Nothing," she managed.

"Oh come," he mocked. "Have the courage of your convictions, and spit it out."

"I would like to retire," she said desperately.

"Would you?" His gaze dipped lower, to her mouth, and back up.

"And if I commanded you stay and keep me company?"

"You won't." With sudden relief, she realized it was true. He was a gentleman, if a somewhat unconventional one, and would not command such a thing. So how could she be suspecting him of something far worse?

Catching a few words meant for another and drawing your own conclusions...

At last, she dragged her gaze free of his, meaning to leave him with a muttered goodnight and whatever dignity she could muster. But his hand shot out, taking her chin in his long fingers, holding her still, forcing her to meet his gaze once more.

He searched her face, no longer mocking but frowning, serious. Almost distractedly, his finger moved beneath her chin like a caress. She could not breathe. "Are you afraid of me, Alexandra Battle?"

"No," she croaked. She swallowed. "Why would I be?"

"I have no idea," he said slowly, "unless it's the same fear I have of you." His lips twisted, and the mockery surged back into his eyes, though whether it was aimed at her or himself, she had no idea. At last, he released her, and relief flooded her.

It is relief, it is...

"Go then, but there will be a reckoning between us one day. Good night, Miss Battle."

"Good night," she managed, trying to gather her dignity. She walked quickly to counteract the foolish, inexplicable urge to return to him.

CHAPTER NINE

EXHAUSTED, ALEXANDRA FELL into a deep, heavy sleep, almost as soon as her head touched the pillow, and she did not open her eyes again until daylight peeked through her bed curtains.

However, as she dragged herself into a sitting position, she did not feel rested. The lingering mists of sleep and disturbing dreams clung to her mind, images of Evelina and Sir Nicholas mixed up with those of Nell and the unpleasant man she had seen in the library. There were noises, too, the strange, rhythmic clanking she had heard on her first night here that turned into much different noises, bumping and rumbling and the low, muffled voices of humans and donkeys. It all felt vaguely ominous.

But as she rose and went through the familiar rituals of washing and dressing and pinning up her hair, her wayward mind kept drifting back to the odd scene with Sir Nicholas in the library. He suspected her of overhearing his conversation with the unpleasant man who had probably, kidnapped Evelina, but he had not asked for her silence or threatened her in any way. Except in his talk of reckoning, and even that had not felt as much a warning as flirtation.

Her whole body heated with embarrassment. Why would he flirt with her except to win her silence? Silence over what? A few words she heard him speak to a shifty character? Words that made no sense besides his care for Evelina, and she could *swear* that was genuine.

She wanted it to be genuine.

As she was about to leave her bedroom for the schoolroom, sounds in the garden drew her to the window. She looked down onto the garden, where a huddle of men stood among the bushes by the righthand garden wall, where they had found the trap door to the cellar yesterday.

One of the men was Sir Nicholas, negligently leaning one shoulder against the wall. Another looked very like Inspector Harris, who had called yesterday about Evelina's disappearance.

Alexandra reached up and opened the window a crack, enough to air the room. And to hear the voices drifting up from the garden.

A policeman's hat appeared through the door, followed by his body. "Nothing down there, sir," he reported. "It's quite empty and seems to have been blocked off decades ago from the cellars beneath the house."

Nothing? It had been *jammed* with brandy and wine, tobacco and spices...

Another policeman followed the first. "Signs of recent movement, though, sir."

"What signs?" Harris asked.

Alexandra made the mistake of glancing at Sir Nicholas, who had not moved, and yet she was sure he gazed straight at her.

She dropped her hand from the window and walked away, thinking furiously. Where had all the contraband—if that is what it was—gone? Had Sir Nicholas got rid of it? Had the man she had seen in the library with him taken it away? Was that the agreement Sir Nicholas had talked about ending? There was, surely, a clear connection between the trap door and the men who had climbed over the wall and kidnapped Evelina. But where on earth did Sir Nicholas fit in? Had he known the contraband was there? Had he turned a blind eye or agreed to its storage?

Alexandra went early to the schoolroom. She wanted to be there when Evelina emerged from her bedchamber. So, she sorted out the lessons for the day while she waited. Clara brought breakfast in, just as Evelina emerged with Anna.

Evelina grinned at Alexandra and ran to the table. "Breakfast!"

"Well, don't fall on it like a little piglet," Alexandra ordered, and Evelina giggled, though she sat calmly down at the table and waited for Alexandra to join her before she reached for the bread and butter. Breakfast here was more in the European manner than the heavier fare of England.

Anna went casually back into the bedchamber, no doubt about her duties, and Evelina did not appear to notice.

They had just finished breakfast when Sir Nicholas strolled into the room.

"Papa!" Evelina greeted him with her usual delight.

"Buttery fingers!" Alexandra warned them both, but Sir Nicholas only laughed and swung his daughter up and around in his usual, boisterous greeting to her.

"I've got something to show you," he said, planting her feet back on the ground. "In the garden."

Something changed in her eyes, an echo of the haunted look Alexandra had seen last night. "In the garden?" she repeated hesitantly.

"Yes. Miss Battle should come, too. And Anna," he added as the nursemaid hovered in the doorway.

Evelina took his hand trustingly, although it was clear she didn't really want to go. Alexandra and Anna exchanged glances and followed.

The sky was overcast, as though it was about to rain. Sir Nicholas led Anna straight toward the spot she had been abducted from. Surprisingly, James lurked there already. Still, Evelina lagged back, looking up at her father in alarm. He smiled reassuringly and said something that made her laugh, and she walked on.

"Look," Sir Nicholas said, pointing to the trap door. "The police came this morning and confirmed there is nothing stored down there, and now nothing will be." He crouched and rubbed his hand over the place the iron ring had been. "We removed the handle, and we're going to cover it up with rocks and earth and plant a tree over it so that no one can get in again. And over there," he pointed to the wall, "we've blocked off either entrance to the passage. I wanted to show you, so you know you'll be quite safe here in your own garden. Now, will Miss Battle permit a quick game of tag before lessons begin?"

"She will," Alexandra said.

She could not deny he was doing the right thing, replacing yesterday's fear with a much more pleasant memory. As she watched him play with his daughter, chasing her and running comically away from her, diving behind trees and leaping over flowerpots, she could not help smiling. Despite what she had overheard yesterday evening, today, her suspicions seemed quite unfounded. Here was no dangerous, arrogant man with criminal connections, merely a doting father with no thought of his dignity.

Despite the rain, which put an end to the tag game, Alexandra made sure that Evelina passed a busy day with lessons, including a little history, painting, and music. They were just having tea when the schoolroom door opened and Griz sauntered in.

"Good afternoon," she said brightly. "I see I am not interrupting important lessons."

"Only tea. Let me send for another cup," Alexandra offered.

"Oh, no, thank you. I am awash with tea."

Evelina laughed at this idea and explained it to Anna in Italian, calling through the schoolroom door to the playroom.

"You may excuse yourself," Alexandra interrupted, "and go and speak to Anna more quietly."

Evelina popped the last of the scone into her mouth and slid off her chair.

"Oh, Evelina," Griz said, "one of the reasons I came was to ask if you had any toys that are too young for you now that you might like to give to George and Jilly."

"They didn't have any toys," Evelina said, frowning.

"Exactly," Griz said.

Evelina, forgetting all about the tea washing around Lady Grizelda's insides, ran through to her playroom with more purpose.

"And your other reason?" Alexandra murmured.

"They fished two bodies out of the Thames this morning," Griz said, low. "We believe they might be Evelina's abductors."

Alexandra blinked. "What makes you think that?"

"One of them owned a donkey. And a covered cart. I know it's hardly conclusive, but the timing makes us suspicious. A botched kidnapping and two men with a donkey are murdered the same night?"

"Murdered?" Evelina repeated, much to Alexandra's horror. She had crept up with her arms full of toys. A small, brightly painted rocking horse fell to the floor, and she bent to pick it up. "Did my father kill them?"

Alexandra's mouth fell open. Her gaze flew wildly to Griz, then back to Evelina, who did not seem remotely upset.

"What makes you think that?" Griz asked lightly, picking the rocking horse up from the table where Evelina had put it.

"He did it before," Evelina said. "I think George would like the horse and the monkey, and Jilly would like this doll and the bear. What do babies like?"

"Perhaps something else cuddly, like the bear," Alexandra said faintly. "Or ask Anna if you have an old teething ring that isn't a family heirloom…"

As Evelina trotted off again, Alexandra and Griz stared at each other.

"Did he?" Griz asked.

"How would I know? I've only just got here."

"But could he have killed our men? For what they did to Evelina?"

Alexandra's breath caught all over again. Was that the reason he had let the man leave last night? So he could *kill* him away from home? "I don't know," she whispered. "I don't know what he's capable of or what he isn't."

There were footsteps in the passage, men's voices.

"You should also know," Griz said hurriedly, "he asked Dragan to find out what he can about you. But I think we need to find out about *him*."

The schoolroom door opened on Alexandra's bemusement, and Sir Nicholas strolled in with Dragan Tizsa.

Predictably, Evelina erupted from her playroom, rushing at her father. A knitted dog with large ears dangled from one hand. "I'm going to give this to George and Jilly's baby because she doesn't have any toys, and neither do they, so I'm giving them a few of mine."

"That is very kind and definitely the right thing to do," Sir Nicholas said.

"If *you* don't mind," Griz murmured.

"Of course not. They are Evelina's toys. Something more basic needs to be done for such families, but this will do to begin with. Have you visited them again, Mrs. Tizsa?"

"No, though Dragan spoke to Nell," Griz replied, apparently unconcerned about her husband consorting with such a woman.

"She'd look in on them if she could," Mr. Tizsa said, "but their father isn't keen on such company for them."

"I don't suppose Nell is very keen on some of the company she keeps either," Sir Nicholas said unexpectedly. "For these people, everything is about survival."

"Is Nell not respectable?" Evelina asked.

"She was kind to you and the other children," Alexandra said hastily, "which is what is important." She felt Sir Nicholas's gaze on her but refused to look round.

"Sit down for a moment," he said to his daughter. "Would you look at a couple of pictures that Mr. Tizsa drew, and tell us if you recognize the people in them?"

She glanced up at him warily, as though she knew what they were going to show her. Then she nodded and sat. Mr. Tizsa took a notebook from his pocket and flipped through it. He showed her first the sketched head and shoulders of a handsome young man. It was extraordinarily detailed and lifelike, from the texture of the hair to facial expression.

Evelina shook her head. "I don't know him."

"What about him?" Dragan turned the page and showed another, very different man. Although he must have drawn it from the dead body rather than the living person, and there was no real expression in the eyes, he did not look like a corpse dragged out of the river. He did not look like the man who had emerged from the library last night either.

Evelina sat back, reaching for her father, and nodded. "That's him," she whispered. "The man who grabbed me. Is he dead?"

"Yes," her father replied, without expression. "What about this one?"

Alexandra pressed a hand to her twisting stomach, but this man was not Sir Nicholas's visitor either. She could think whether that was good or bad.

"It looks like his friend," Evelina said, glancing at the next sketch. "But he was driving the donkey. I didn't see him much."

"Thank you, Evelina," Dragan said, taking the notebook away and shoving it back in his pocket. "You've been very helpful. And you know you'll never run into these characters again."

She nodded.

"Do you have a few minutes, Tizsa?" Sir Nicholas said. "I'd like to talk to you about something else."

Mr. Tizsa exchanged some brief, wordless communication with his wife. "I am at your service," he said civilly and followed Sir Nicholas from the room.

Evelina made no objection, concerned as she was with putting the donated toys in a box. Since it was still raining, Anna took her through the playroom.

"Come to my room," Alexandra murmured and led Griz along the passage to her spacious bedchamber, which Griz duly admired.

"You have found a comfortable position here," she observed.

"Physically, yes. When did he ask Dragan to investigate me?"

"Yesterday."

"But why? What does he suspect me of?"

"I don't believe he truly suspects you of anything. He is merely being careful of the people around his daughter."

Alexandra scowled. "Is that not something he should have done before he engaged me? To have shown any interest at all, rather than palming the trivial task off on his housekeeper?"

"I understand he is new to such matters. Apparently, although he saw Evelina often, he was not involved in her day-to-day upbringing until her mother died. I think what happened yesterday brought a few things home to him. Why are you so upset?"

Alexandra strode to the window, flapping one dismissive hand. "It is the lack of trust when I thought... when I thought we understood each other."

Grizelda's eyes bored into her back. "Is it? Or is there some dark secret in your past that Dragan might find?"

Alexandra flapped one impatient hand. "Of course not. I've never done anything wrong, Griz."

"I know."

Alexandra glanced at her, but she only took off her spectacles, polished them, and put them back on her nose.

"To be honest," Griz said, "I am more concerned with this man Evelina says her father killed. I don't altogether like you being here with such a man."

"We don't know the truth," Alexandra said, her first instinct, stupidly, to defend the man who trusted her so little.

"Well, we can't ask Evelina. The nursemaid came from Italy with them, did she not?"

"Anna? Yes, and James was with him there, too."

"Well, I can talk to Anna under pretense of investigating you and see if I can't learn more about him and this man Evelina said he killed."

"Why don't I talk to Anna?" Alexandra said suddenly. Why shouldn't she question his servants when he was using her friends to investigate her? "She is beginning to trust me now after a rocky beginning. We shared anxiety, I suppose, over Evelina."

"That would probably be simpler," Griz agreed. "Your curiosity would be more natural." She ran her fingers idly over the bed covering. "He is something of a mystery, is he not? Why does he live *here*, of all out-of-the-way places?"

"Apparently, his brother has grown used to the family townhouse in Mayfair."

"Yes, but he could easily rent or buy another in a much better district than this."

"It would be safer," Alexandra agreed, then frowned. "Or would it? There a+re other children vanishing from better addresses than this."

"Which is another odd thing. If there is someone ransoming wealthy children kidnapped in Mayfair, why come all the way to Hungerford for one? Are there not enough of them further west?"

Alexandra walked slowly back to the bed and sank down on the side opposite Griz. Her heart beat fast. The words hovered in her throat, but she didn't know whether or not to speak them, to tell Griz about the man in Sir Nicholas's library last night.

IN HIS LIBRARY, Sir Nicholas took a pamphlet from his desk drawer and threw it down in front of Tizsa, who sat opposite him. "Ever seen this before?"

Tizsa glanced at it but did not pick it up. "Should I have?"

"A man of your political persuasions? It is certainly a possibility."

Tizsa was silent for a moment. For a man with such intense eyes, he was not easy to read. "I have seen it before. Once. When my brother-in-law, Lord Horace Niven, asked me to investigate its origins."

"Did he, by God?" Nicholas murmured.

"I told him what I will tell you," Tizsa said deliberately, "that I will not investigate cases involving free speech and free press." He held Nicholas's gaze. "I had already told him that neither will I indulge in sedition against the country that gives me refuge."

"Is it seditious?"

"I am not a lawyer."

"Nevertheless, I would appreciate your opinion."

"There is little in it I disagree with."

Nicholas smiled. "Then you *have* read it."

"Of course."

"Would you ever consider writing something in the same vein?"

"No," Tizsa replied. "There are too many political points being made. I do not argue that one needs politics to effect necessary change, but I am no politician. I never was."

"And yet you are well acquainted with several figures of radical reform. In Europe and here in England."

"I will discuss poverty, housing, medical care, unemployment, with anyone."

"And if I could find you a platform? An anonymous platform, if you prefer."

Tizsa frowned. "I have never said anything I am not prepared to own publicly. I do not intend to start. But if you know who is responsible for this pamphlet, they should take care. It has disturbed

Lord Horace's department."

"Perhaps I am equally disturbed by it."

"Perhaps you are," Tizsa retorted. "But in a man who has invested so generously in Lord Trench's housing project, I would doubt it."

Nicholas smiled faintly, meeting Tizsa's curious gaze with one of limpid innocence.

"Tell me," Tizsa said. "You are a wealthy man who made his fortune largely abroad. Where, on such a journey, did you develop such reforming tendencies?"

Nicholas shrugged. "I suppose it was gradual. I left home when I was very young, angry and driven, determined to prove myself more successful, a greater provider than my father ever was. I did. Of course, I was lucky from the first ship I bought into, and I have a knack for choosing good people to work for me. Perhaps it was that which made me discontented, restless. To look below the surface of my wealth and that of other people."

"And still, you are angry."

Nicholas blinked. "I?"

"I think so."

"Aren't you?" Nicholas asked, playing for time.

Tizsa shook his head. "Not now. Anger leads to uncontrolled events, to revolution, war, even greater oppression. The evidence is all over Europe."

"But you have not given up," Nicholas said swiftly.

Tizsa's lips twisted. "There are those who will tell you I have. I married an aristocrat and live off her wealth."

"Do you? I thought you held down a government post while running your own business and studying for medical examination."

"Grizelda's dowry and His Grace's gifts are not unwelcome, for all that. Why did you choose this house?"

Again, the sudden question took him by surprise. "It was mine, it was empty, and it was unexpected. Perhaps it was a rude gesture to my origins and the kind of blinkered yet powerful people who live in Mayfair."

"That power keeps the area safer than Hungerford or many other places on the banks of the Thames."

Tizsa was saying nothing Nicholas had not already lashed himself with.

"They seem to have been part of a smuggling gang," Dragan said.

"Who?"

"The men pulled out of the Thames. They moved goods from the river into various parts of the city. They are the first connection I have found between smugglers and the kidnappers of the wealthy children."

"Glad we could help," Nicholas said with a curl of the lip.

"And Miss Battle? Do you still want me to investigate her?"

Nicholas hesitated. There was a reason Alexandra Battle disturbed him. He just wasn't sure what it was. "My instincts tell me she had nothing to do with Evelina's kidnapping. And yet, she is all that has changed in my household in two months. This happened only days after she took up her post. And she is hiding something."

Tizsa raised one brow. "We are all hiding something."

Nicholas said nothing. Tizsa had already revealed—or at least hinted—that he was well aware of at least one of *his* secrets.

"You just told me your instincts are good," Tizsa reminded himself. "So are my wife's, and she and Miss Battle have been friends for almost five years. Have you come across much smuggling since you took this house?"

Nicholas stared at him, then released a breath that was almost laughter. "I imagine you obtain a lot of answers by such sudden questions. I pay my dues, Mr. Tizsa, on everything I import. Nor do I buy smuggled goods. You may leave Miss Battle for now. My request was a moment of panic rather than of thought or even genuine suspicion."

Tizsa inclined his head and rose.

"Tizsa? Who has employed you to investigate the missing children?"

"That," Tizsa said mildly, "is confidential. With your permission, I shall extract my wife and leave you."

"As you wish." Nicholas sat back and watched him depart. He knew Tizsa would not give up on the missing children or on the connection to the dead smugglers. And it was more than possible Miss Battle had already told them about the goods she had seen in the now empty garden cellar.

CHAPTER TEN

ALTHOUGH SIR NICHOLAS did not join them for dinner that evening, he sent a note asking that Miss Battle and Evelina accompany him tomorrow on a morning call. They would travel by carriage.

Fortunately, with this to look forward to, Evelina settled to sleep with a lot less difficulty than the day before. And in the morning, after a quick lesson in arithmetic and a game in the garden, Anna helped dress her in her best frock, ready for the outing.

Alexandra wore her usual work dress and bonnet, which were neat but dull and unflattering, as was only right.

"Who are we going to visit, Papa?" Evelina asked eagerly when they were all in the carriage together, Sir Nicholas with his back to the horses.

"Your uncle Ralph," Sir Nicholas said. "I think it's time we all met."

"You have not seen your brother since you returned to England?" Alexandra asked.

"We did not part on the best of terms," Sir Nicholas said. "And since I came home, we have been avoiding each other. But Evelina should know her cousins."

"It is a family gathering," Alexandra said. "Should I wait in the hall or in the carriage?"

"Oh, you should definitely come in. I don't know that they'll see any of us."

She blinked. "You are turning up unannounced? Do you not think that might be hurtful?" She slewed her gaze to the distracted Evelina to make her point.

His smile was not pleasant. "Since they are living in my house, I shall expect at least some surface courtesy."

The carriage stopped before a large house in Brook Street. Alexandra could not help comparing the gracious surroundings and the elegant building with the smelly, riverside location of the chaotic New Hungerford house, with its many musty, unfurnished rooms.

"How many children does your brother have?" she asked when Sir Nicholas had knocked peremptorily on the door.

"I really have no idea."

The door was opened by a forbidding footman. "Yes, sir?"

"Mr. or Mrs. Swan, if you please," Sir Nicholas said, extending a calling card between two fingers.

The footman had taken it before he noticed the child dangling from Sir Nicholas's other hand and the dowdy governess behind. "I shall inquire if either is at home. Please step inside one moment."

At least he didn't close the door in their faces. Sir Nicholas seemed more amused than offended as he led the way inside. Evelina gazed around her with curiosity but little awe.

"This way." The footman led them to a small, formal reception room on the left-hand side of the entrance hall and departed with the card still held in his gloved hand.

A more superior voice could be heard from the hall, asking whom he had put in "the blue room." An instant later, it said, "*What?* Did you even read this?"

Hasty footsteps heralded an obvious butler of middle years, who stopped dead in the doorway, staring at Sir Nicholas.

"Well met, Stevens," Sir Nicholas said, casually offering his hand. "Glad to see you're not dead yet."

The butler's face dissolved into smiles. "Sir Nicholas! It *is* you! Welcome home, sir, welcome home!" He took Sir Nicholas's hand, at the same time bowing with such fervor that Alexandra thought he might actually kiss Sir Nicholas's fingers.

Sir Nicholas, perhaps fearing the same, withdrew his hand to slap the dignified butler on the shoulder. "How are you, Stevens? I'll swear you haven't aged a day in eighteen years."

"Tell that to my rheumatism, sir."

"You seem pretty spry for a man with rheumatism," Sir Nicholas said. "I look forward to hearing all about your eighteen years, but first, is my brother at home?"

"Of course, sir. Mr. and Mrs. Swan are both in the drawing room with morning callers. Would you care to join them, or would you rather wait for a more private moment?"

"No, no, show us straight in. But you had better announce me to make sure they know who I am."

The butler's smile was slightly pained.

Despite her curiosity, Alexandra had every intention of remaining where she was, but with a hint of mockery, he flung over his shoulder, "Come along, Miss Battle. You are in charge of Evelina."

So, she took Evelina's hand and followed Sir Nicholas and the butler across the hall to the stairs. As they climbed, she was sure she heard the rustling of servants emerging from the kitchen to catch a glimpse of their true master. A maid lurked in the passage upstairs and was swiftly sent about her business by Stevens.

He then opened a set of double doors and walked sedately into a large, gracious room. "Sir Nicholas Swan, ma'am," he announced with a hint of triumph.

Instantly, the talk in the room cut off into shocked silence. Every head in the room snapped around to face Sir Nicholas. Alexandra, gazing at his back, could not see his expression, but she saw that of the lady behind the teapot, presumably their hostess, which betrayed both bewilderment and dismay. The tall man by the mantelpiece looked angry, and yet, somehow, hunted—presumably Mr. Ralph Swan. Their guests displayed only avid curiosity.

Sir Nicholas bowed to the company and strolled into the room. "Well, Ralph," he addressed the man by the mantelpiece. "You've grown."

Ralph's mouth closed with a snap as he wiped all expression from his suddenly pale face. "Nicholas." As though forcing himself, he walked forward, extending his hand. "I heard you were back, though I'd hoped to see you before this."

Nicholas took the outstretched hand. Alexandra could see him in profile now, and he smiled, the faint, sardonic smile he seemed to give to strangers. "Did you?" He dropped his brother's hand after the briefest shake and turned to face his hostess. "Won't you introduce me to your wife?"

"Of course," Ralph said with forced pleasantness, casting a quick, almost agonized glance around his rapt guests. Clearly, he would rather have had this encounter in private. Alexandra suspected Sir Nicholas knew that and had maliciously timed the visit accordingly. "Gertrude, my older brother, Sir Nicholas. Nicholas, my wife, Gertrude."

This time, Nicholas's smile was much more pleasant. Holding his sister-in-law's gaze, he took her hand and bowed over it. "What good fortune my brother has found. Delighted to meet you."

Evelina tugged at Alexandra's hand. "There are no children here," she pointed out in a stage whisper.

Children did not, as a rule, attend drawing rooms when adult callers were present. The many flickering glances at Evelina would have reminded Sir Nicholas of this, had he needed any reminding. But this, too, was part of his little theatre to disconcert his brother. What, Alexandra wondered, was between them to have inspired this? If Nicholas had left at the age of eighteen, then Ralph, surely, couldn't have been more than about sixteen.

"Ah, Evelina," Sir Nicholas said, smiling at her. "Come and be presented to your aunt and uncle."

Since there were several people between Evelina and her father, the child clung to Alexandra's hand as she obeyed, dragging her along.

Mr. and Mrs. Swan had small, rigid smiles affixed to their faces.

"Allow me to introduce my daughter, Evelina. And her governess, Miss Battle."

"She is a pretty child," Mrs. Swan said weakly.

"She takes that from her mother," Sir Nicholas said blandly, and Mrs. Swan colored, presumably at the impropriety. "Perhaps, Miss Battle could take Evelina to your nursery for a few minutes to make the acquaintance of her cousins?"

"I don't think that would be appropriate," Ralph Swan uttered in sudden alarm.

Sir Nicholas smiled, such an unpleasant, dangerous smile that Alexandra was afraid he would actually hit his brother. "You are kind. I'm so glad you will not object to Evelina and Miss Battle playing tag among your guests."

"Nicholas, for God's sake!" Ralph whispered, presumably grasping that it was well within his brother's rights to go wherever he wished in his own house, and do whatever he wished, too. That if Ralph did not like it, it was Ralph and his family who would have to go.

But Alexandra was outraged to have Evelina used as such a tool. She grasped her hand tighter. "Evelina and I shall take a walk and return to the carriage in—"

"No need," Mrs. Swan interrupted. "The footman at the door will escort you to the nursery."

To Alexandra's surprise, Sir Nicholas accompanied them to the door.

"Be good, squib," he adjured his daughter as he held it open, and to Alexandra, he murmured, "We shall talk later."

"Yes," she said grimly, "we will."

"Show my daughter and her governess to the nursery," Sir Nicholas instructed the footman in the passage and, without glancing at them again, shut the door.

⟫⟫⟫⟫⟫⟪⟪⟪⟪⟪

THE OTHER GUESTS only left when they could not, with any civility, linger any longer to observe the Swans' barbed reunion. By dinner time, gossip would be rife all over London and speculation building to a crescendo.

But at the moment, Nicholas sat in the silent drawing room regarding his brother and sister-in-law while he waited to hear what they would say.

Inevitably, Ralph broke the silence first.

"You should have written!" he burst out.

Nicholas raised one eyebrow. "I wrote several times, as I recall. I gave up after about seven years."

Ralph flushed, which told him all he needed to know; that Ralph had indeed received all those letters and never troubled to reply.

"I meant about this visit," he muttered.

Nicholas laughed. "Really?"

"You left this country voluntarily," Ralph snapped. "Mired in so much scandal my mother took to her bed for a month! My father never recovered from it. And this child you now inflict on my children—"

"Children do not care for the niceties of marriage lines," Nicholas interrupted. "What you mean is, I inflicted her on *you*."

"And meant to embarrass me before my guests! Are you trying to drive me from my home, now?"

"Drive you from *my* home," Nicholas corrected gently.

"You will evict us?" Gertrude said, speaking directly to him for the first time.

"Evict you? My dear sister, it was not I but our perverse father who evicted you when he left everything to me. He could have left all the unentailed property, including this house, to Ralph. God knows, he threatened to often enough, even before I left. But he didn't."

"You showed no inclination to come home," Ralph muttered.

"How do you know?" Nicholas retorted. "Did you ask?"

"I asked Figgis."

The solicitor," Nicholas mocked. "He is certainly a great source of information. For example, from him, I know you have already spent more of my money than you could ever repay, even working for your living. What did you think, Ralph? That though I was too awful a person to communicate with, I would be generous enough to neither evict you nor prosecute you?"

Gertrude's teacup rattled in its saucer. She laid it down with trembling hands. Nicholas was more interested in his brother's reaction. Ralph had whitened, his hand flying to his wife's shoulder as though to comfort or perhaps plead forgiveness.

"Think of the family name," Ralph managed. "There would be scandal."

Nicholas laughed with genuine amusement. "Can you think of no better argument for *me*?"

"For God's sake, Nicholas, I have a wife! Children! At least leave this until—"

"For a few days," Gertrude interrupted. "Be assured we will take nothing of yours."

Nicholas glanced at her ironically but said only, "How many children do you have?"

"Three," Ralph replied. "Two sons and a daughter."

"Felicitations. I would be charmed to meet them when Evelina comes back."

"Not today," Gertrude said quickly.

A new suspicion dawned. Perhaps there was more than prejudice or even guilt behind their behavior, which was decidedly odd, even for this awkward situation. "Evelina is rather starved of the company of other children," he said mildly. "Miss Battle is taking steps to change that, but whatever differences exist between you and I, I am eager for Evelina to be friends with her cousins. The child is innocent, you know, of my sins."

"You cannot foist her on society," Ralph said. "Even you must see that."

"I would not be the first," Nicholas said cynically. "I have acknowledged her, and she shares our name."

Ralph's eyes narrowed. "Are you saying that any…generosity on your part is dependent on us acknowledging your illegitimate daughter?"

"Actually, no," Nicholas said, rising to his feet. "I have not yet decided what to do. I won't let your wife and children starve, Ralph, but beyond that…" He shrugged. "Perhaps we would both benefit from a day or so to think of possible solutions. Be so good, if you please, to summon Evelina, and we shall leave you to enjoy the day."

While they waited, Nicholas saw no reason to break the silence with small talk, although he civilly answered remarks flung out to him by Gertrude. Neither of them asked where he was living or about the last eighteen years of his life.

On impulse, he said suddenly, "Did you know Evelina was kidnapped? Only the day before yesterday."

"Dear God," Gertrude whispered.

Ralph's eyes were round, staring at him. "How did you get her back so quickly?"

"I hired a man," Nicholas replied. "Or more accurately, Miss Battle hired a man, who found her within hours. Ah, here they are." He bowed to Gertrude. "Good day, ma'am. Ralph, I shall—er… write. Goodbye."

Evelina, he was glad to see, bounced along happily at Miss Battle's side. The governess, however, barely looked at him as they walked downstairs into the street, even when he handed her into the carriage. He was, he saw, in her black books and was sorry. It was more than time to talk if he wished her good opinion, and for some reason, he did. But the day was not about her.

"Tell me, Miss Battle," he said in the carriage, when Evelina paused for breath, "how many children were in the nursery?"

"Two," she said, and this time, reluctantly met his gaze. "And yet there were three made-up beds."

CHAPTER ELEVEN

SINCE SIR NICHOLAS paused only to leave Evelina and Alexandra at the house before setting off again, there was no opportunity to speak to him until evening.

Evelina, who had played a little shyly with her cousin Eleanor, and been kind and gentle with the baby, remained a little distracted during the afternoon's lessons. However, she did what was required of her in the end, without fuss or tantrum. She was rewarded after tea with a walk along the river in company with both Alexandra and Anna. James plodded watchfully behind, except when Evelina bounced back to talk to him.

Alexandra took advantage of one such occasion to talk to Anna. Since Evelina's return, things had been much easier between them, and she no longer encountered that look of suspicion and resentment in the maid's eyes. But they were hardly friends.

"I wanted to ask you about Evelina's life in Italy," Alexandra said. "To help me understand her better. Have you been with her from her birth?"

"No, I came to her two years ago."

That surprised her. Somehow, she had regarded Anna as an old family retainer. But she pressed on. "I'm concerned because of some of the odd things she says sometimes—for instance, that Sir Nicholas killed someone. Can this be true, or is it some bizarre lie she has made up?"

In quick alarm, Anna cast a glance over her shoulder where the child still chattered away with James.

"No lie," Anna muttered. "She should not know such things—it is her mother's fault. But we do not talk about it." She glared at Alexandra, more pleading than threatening. Her response inspired more questions, but since Evelina skipped ahead to them once more, Alexandra was forced to leave it there. She nodded to the nurserymaid to reassure her she would not speak to their charge on the issue, but inside, she seethed with curiosity. Had Anna meant the killing had been the mother's fault? Or the fact that Evelina knew about it?

When they returned to the house, Alexandra itched to know if Sir Nicholas had come home. No one volunteered the information, and she didn't want to ask in front of Evelina, since she definitely didn't want the child present at the interview. If he showed his face in the dining room, she would ask calmly to speak to him later.

But, of course, whether or not he was at home, he did not join them for dinner. During dessert, Lady Nora's maid, Spencer, appeared and asked if Evelina would be able to join her ladyship for a few minutes before bed. Alexandra agreed, although she made Evelina, who immediately jumped down from the table, jump back up again and finish eating, and then wash her hands and face before they went to call on Lady Nora.

To Alexandra's surprise, they found Sir Nicholas there, sitting on the edge of her bed and holding the invalid's hand while she talked in a low, intense voice. When he heard them approach, he turned quickly but did not change his posture, merely turned back with a word to Lady Nora that made her smile.

Evelina bounced over to him to be hugged and to kiss Lady Nora's papery cheek.

Only then did he stand and make space for them. "Five minutes, squib. Lady Nora is tired." He nodded curtly to Alexandra, smiled at the sick woman, and walked away. At the far end of the room, she could hear him talking with the maid, Spencer, in low, serious voices.

"You are like your Papa," Lady Nora told Evelina, "now that I see you together. I always thought before that you resembled your mother."

"Did you know Mama?" Evelina asked, surprised.

"I saw her," Lady Nora said, "once or twice. I hear you went to see your Uncle Ralph today."

"I met my cousins," Evelina said proudly. "Eleanor and Roger…"

As before, Lady Nora's eyes closed while Evelina was chattering, and after exchanging glances with Spencer, Alexandra took Evelina's hand, and they crept quietly out of the room and along to the child's bedchamber.

After saying goodnight and delivering her to Anna's ministrations, Alexandra took a deep breath and set forth purposefully for the library.

"Enter!" called his familiar voice as soon as she knocked.

She walked in, very conscious of the thumping of her heart and the courage necessary to say what had to be said.

And if I lose my post?

There will be another.

Not like this…

He rose from his desk, where he had been writing in his shirt sleeves, and reached for his coat. "Miss Battle. Thank you for coming."

"Did you send for me?" she asked, surprised.

"No, but you saved me the trouble. Please, sit."

Dash it, why did he have to choose this moment to be so wretchedly polite? Since it seemed unnecessarily pompous to announce that she would rather stand, she sat in the chair on the other side of the desk.

With his coat on, though not fastened, he stood still. She raised her gaze from his chest to his face and found him regarding her with somewhat sardonic amusement.

"Go on then," he said resignedly, casting himself back into his chair. "Rake me over the coals."

Did he think she would not? Did he imagine his invitation would take the wind out of her sails? It did, somewhat, but she refused to back down.

"You cannot use Evelina as a weapon in your fraternal wars," she declared. "It is not—"

"I didn't," he interrupted. "I know what you think, but I took her there to meet her cousins."

"At a time when you knew Mr. and Mrs. Swan were likely to have company? When you could take them and their gossip-hungry guests by surprise? You took her there to discompose them! Did you even consider how it would have affected Evelina if they had denounced her as your illegitimate offspring and sent her away?"

"I know my brother," he said mildly, "and he is not that bad."

"With respect, sir, you do *not* know your brother. You cannot have laid eyes on him since he was a boy. And even if *he* hadn't changed, you certainly did not know his wife, let alone who else you would find there."

His brows lowered in a dark scowl. "You are blaming me for things that did not happen. With what purpose?"

"Can you not see?" Alexandra demanded. "You should not even be *thinking* of her in such a way. Even were there no danger to her whatsoever, she is your *daughter*, not a weapon in your arsenal."

Abruptly, he stood, his expression suddenly frightening. But at least, he turned away from her and strode to the window, where he stood looking out, his back to her. She wondered if it was dismissal, if she was supposed to go now. Pack her bags, no doubt, for departure in the morning. If she had kept her opinions to herself, she could have stayed, provided some kind of stability for Evelina, as she had promised so recently…

"You are right," he snapped and drew in a breath without turning back to her. "I have no idea how to be a parent, how to separate fatherhood from the rest of me. I will protect her, you know. If you protect her from me."

"I?" she said in astonishment, and at last, he turned with an odd, deprecating twist of his lips.

"You have designated yourself my conscience, Miss Battle. There are consequences to that, too."

"I would not presume—"

A bark of laughter interrupted her. "Yes, you would. Let us call a truce." He walked back and threw himself into his chair. It wasn't clear which of them his eyes mocked, until the expression faded, and he said, "I suppose I was killing two birds with one stone. Taking her to meet children who should be friends as well as family, and in disconcerting my brother, giving myself an advantage in our confrontation. It is a hard habit to break."

"Why do you need to confront him?" she asked curiously, then flushed, dragging her eyes free. "Forgive me. That is none of my business."

"Oh, it is, if you are to be my conscience. Since my father died, my brother has lived in my houses and spent my money, without any permission."

"But you know about it. You could, surely, have stopped it at any time."

"I could," he agreed, with a shrug. "I chose not to. I suppose I wanted to see how far he would go, how long it would take before he wrote to me. He never did. Even when I came home, and I *know* word reached him I was here."

"Why did *you* not write to *him?*"

He pushed contemptuously at the papers on the desk. "Pride. I left home in a welter of scandal when I was just nineteen years old. Ralph was not quite sixteen. I spent the next seven years writing to him and to my father. Neither replied. So, I stopped."

"But you did not stop your brother taking your money?"

"He was already married by then. And, frankly, I don't need it."

His eyes dipped. "I suppose I still hoped that one day he would actually contact me and at least ask if I minded. I thought it would be a beginning. It was never about the money."

It was about a family who had rejected him because of the sins of his youth. It wasn't even pride. It was hurt.

"You took Evelina there to be blatant," she guessed. "To show him you apologized for nothing, to throw your sins in his face and prove you thrived without him." And to remind Ralph he had nothing to be self-righteous about.

"All of that," he allowed. "Though I confess also to curiosity and a need to open doors between us. Almost losing Evelina brought many things home to me, including the awareness that this is not, perhaps, the safest environment in which to bring her up."

"And you have a house in Mayfair that might be better."

He inclined his head.

"Did you broach this subject with your brother?"

"In the end, no, I didn't. He was too on edge. They both were."

Her breath caught. "And there were only two children in the house when there should have been three. Do you *really* think theirs is one of the children kidnapped for ransom?"

"It's possible. Of course, the oldest boy could have been anywhere, with family or friends for a few hours or a few days. But when I told them about Evelina, Ralph said, *How did you get her back so quickly?* As though he had to wait for a ransom note, as Inspector Harris warned us, we might have to do."

"Did you offer to help?" she asked carefully.

"We are not in such a relationship of trust that he would tell me anything. If Harris and Tizsa are right, he will have been instructed to tell no one. I sent him Tizsa's card, vouching for his discretion."

During her brief observations, Alexandra had not taken to Mr. or Mrs. Swan, but this possibility changed everything. "They are trying to go on with their lives as normal until they can ransom their son back.

Dear God. And we lost Evelina only for a few hours. I cannot begin to imagine…"

"Don't," Sir Nicholas said, "it will not help him."

"But you could," she blurted. She squeezed her fingers together in her lap, then forced them to relax. If this meeting was to be truthful, she had to speak. "The man in here the night of Evelina's kidnapping. He has something to do with it, has he not? And you must know where to find him."

He did not look angry, nor even like a man found out in sin. He looked more…thoughtful. "Would you be satisfied if I told you he has nothing to do with my nephew's disappearance or any of the ransom kidnappings?"

"No, because you blamed him for Evelina's. I heard you before you let him walk out."

Sir Nicholas sighed. "I thought you probably had. Very well, here it is. That man is a smuggler. He runs a particularly large gang, sneaking goods on which the duty hasn't been paid, up the Thames. I believe they have several safe storage places scattered along both banks, including the cellar we found in the garden, which have been used for the best part of fifty years from all I can gather. It was ideal. The house wasn't lived in, was used only as an office during the day."

He sighed. "My father apparently blocked off access to the house cellars from the garden one, but according to the ruffian you saw, they had an agreement. The smugglers left my father 'presents'—presumably brandy and wine—and he let them use the garden cellar. When I moved in here, he contacted me with the same proposal."

"And you agreed?"

He grimaced. "Smugglers can be a great source of useful information and a useful means of passing it on. I agreed under slightly different terms from my father. I didn't want their goods, but they would keep me informed on certain matters, carry messages when I asked. Most of all, they were only to visit the cellar at night, whether to bring or remove items. I didn't want Evelina running into them, or them into her."

"But that's exactly what happened," Alexandra said hoarsely. Another understanding was fighting for recognition.

He nodded grimly. "They disobeyed their leader's orders for reasons best known to them. And they found Evelina, who was then about to raise the devil of a racket, so they snatched her, probably only to shut her up, and scarpered. I don't know what they meant to do with her, for she could obviously identify them by then."

He swallowed convulsively. "So I ended our agreement."

"And let him go," she whispered, "because you knew he would punish his men."

He stared down at his hands. "They had lost him a hiding place and disobeyed him. They kidnapped the child of a wealthy, well-connected man and nearly brought the law down on him and his operation in massive force. Yes, I knew he would punish them."

"He killed them," Alexandra said hoarsely. "The men in the river." She raised her eyes to his. "You killed them, as surely as if you had shot them yourself."

His lips curved, but his eyes, hard and implacable, chilled her to the bone. "I like to think so."

She closed her eyes, more to blot out his. She could not work out what she actually thought of this, whether she was glad he had not let Evelina's kidnappers go free or was outraged by the cold calculation of what he had done, leaving his own hands clean. There was a frightening ruthlessness about his actions, about *him*.

"I told Griz about the man," she confessed, opening her eyes to meet his gaze.

He looked almost...anxious. Certainly, there was no anger at her admission. "It doesn't matter. Tizsa already suspects. It does not much interest him because the men who took Evelina are not the organized kidnappers he is truly looking for."

She nodded slowly, still trying to think. "Thank you for your honesty. I think."

"Thank you for yours. I hope I haven't appalled you to the extent of leaving us."

She smiled faintly. "I thought you would dismiss me."

"Were you hoping for it?"

She shook her head. "I like Evelina."

"And you can put up with me?"

The half-rueful, half-teasing twinkle in his eyes caused a sudden dive in her stomach. And the realization that whatever he was, whatever he had done, she liked him, too. It was more than the way he looked, all hard, rugged, carelessly attractive male. All the complicated layers beneath his cynicism and sardonic humor, and the conflicting traits of his character that compelled him to care for his daughter and for the sick woman who lived in his house. And yet enabled him to contrive the execution of the errant smugglers who had dared lay a finger on his daughter.

And whatever lay behind the exciting warmth she occasionally read in his eyes when he looked at her, she liked that, too. It was there now, melting, arousing.

She sprang to her feet. "Of course," she said hurriedly. "I should go and write my letters to catch the morning post."

He rose with her, as was only polite. Even though she was only the governess. He even walked to the door at her side and, her heart drumming, she watched his long fingers close around the handle. For a shocking moment, she imagined them touching her skin, caressing, and desperately blinked the fantasy away.

He stood very still, not immediately opening the door. Almost afraid to breathe, she raised her eyes to his face. The oddest fancy struck her that he was all she had ever wanted without even realizing what that was.

But that was foolish, idiotic, plain wrong. Without the light from the window, his face was half-hidden in gloom, reminding her he was little more than a stranger. And yet there was an insidious illusion of closeness in that corner of the room, of an isolated, cozy bubble containing only her and him and whatever this *feeling* was...

"Do you ever have fun, Alexandra Battle?" he asked abruptly. "Apart from making music occasionally with your friends?"

"I am quite capable of enjoying my life," she retorted, and wished she didn't sound quite so defensive.

"Of course you are." At last, he turned the handle. "Would it interfere with your plans to take Evelina to the Exhibition tomorrow afternoon?"

"Not at all. I believe she would enjoy it, and I would like to go."

"Then I shall accompany you."

She could hardly object. God knew she didn't want to.

Somehow, she got past him and out the door to safety, for he did not follow. And she did not go back, though she could not help wondering what would happen if she did.

CHAPTER TWELVE

T HE MORNING SAW an early visit from Griz. Alexandra had not even left her bedchamber for the schoolroom when a knock sounded on the door. For some reason, her mind, which had been dwelling too much on Sir Nicholas, immediately jumped to the conclusion that it was him.

However, when she opened the door, Griz brushed past her into the room, looking rather fetching in a sky-blue gown and matching bonnet, with a paisley shawl picked out in exactly the same shade.

"You look very smart," Alexandra remarked, closing the door.

"Yes, I've been visiting my family."

"Does Sir Nicholas know you are here?"

"Probably. Dragan is with him, so I thought I would step up and see you." Griz sat on the bed while Alexandra finished pinning up her hair. "Did you ask Anna about this murder he is meant to have committed?"

"She seems to think it is true," Alexandra said reluctantly. "Though she would not talk about it. She said something about it being Evelina's mother's fault, but I'm not clear why."

Perhaps it was one of the things she should have asked him last night while they were being honest with each other, but in truth, it had not entered her mind. What was wrong with her that she could forget the possibility of a *murder*? Especially when he had just confessed to that of the dead smugglers. To all intents and purposes.

"I wonder if he killed someone in a quarrel over her," Griz specu-
lated. Her frown cleared. "It's possible. Anyway, I did discover some
other things about his past, mostly from my parents, who remember
the original scandal of him going abroad. And my brother and sister-in-
law, who met him in Venice during their wedding trip."

"He didn't kill the smugglers," Alexandra blurted. "But he had an
agreement with their leader that let them hide things in the garden
cellar. They were only meant to come at night, but when they saw
Evelina, they grabbed her. Sir Nicholas...told the leader what they'd
done. I think he knew they would be killed. Certainly, he is not sorry,
but neither did he do it."

"In the eyes of the law," Griz murmured. She did not seem particularly surprised, and Alexandra suspected she and Dragan had already
worked out as much. "Do you want to know what I've found out
about him?"

"Do I?" Alexandra wondered.

"There's nothing *very* terrible," Griz said cheerfully. "Mostly wild
youth stuff. He caused a huge scandal in 1833 by running away with
one Lady Chivers, wife of Viscount Chivers, daughter of the Earl of
Selpool. Their affair had been pretty much an open secret until then,
to the extent that his parents quarreled with him over it. Anyway,
Nicholas and Lady Chivers eloped to France, where, apparently,
within a week or two, he abandoned her."

"Did she go back to Lord Chivers?" Alexandra wondered.

"No, though Chivers was prepared to accept her. She seems to
have vanished into the demi-monde. Only her old father seems to
remember her now. According to Her Grace, he insists a place is set at
the table for Lady Nora every Christmas. Isn't that sad?"

Alexandra's next question vanished into another. "Lady *Nora*?" she
repeated, spinning around to stare at Griz.

"Why yes. Before her marriage to Chivers, she was Lady Nora
Tranter. Do you *know* her?"

"Well, yes, I think I might. There is a Lady Nora staying here who came with them from Italy. She is very ill, dying, they say. Could it be the same woman?"

"You mean he didn't abandon her at all?" Griz said thoughtfully.

"I don't know. He seems to care for this Lady Nora."

"Well, after he apparently left her in Paris, he set about making his fortune, in shipping and other ventures, eventually with offices all over Europe. He settled in Venice, where my brother met him, living in the lap of luxury. There was talk there of a past duel, too, which might be the root of Evelina's remark about murder, but I don't think they know anything about it. On the other hand, Monkton—my bother— thought Sir Nicholas had some unsavory connections."

"Unsavory?" Alexandra repeated uneasily. "Like our smuggler friend?"

"More like Dragan, to be honest," Griz said with the flicker of a smile. "Revolutionary types. My brother disapproves of such views. He thinks that might have been why Sir Nicholas came home—being persona non grata in Italy when the revolutions there failed."

Alexandra turned back to the mirror to place her last pin. "I do not think," she said carefully, "that Sir Nicholas is a bad man."

Griz was watching her in the mirror, her eyes uncomfortably penetrating.

"I am a governess, Griz," Alexandra said, turning toward the door. "I will never be more or less."

Griz followed her from the room. "See if Sir Nicholas will give you every second Saturday afternoon free. We can have our musical practice then."

Alexandra nodded. "I would like that. Griz?" she added as they parted, and her friend glanced back. "Thank you."

Griz grinned and carried on to the staircase.

Alexandra found it difficult enough to concentrate on teaching Evelina that morning, without all the bumping and frequent, sudden shouts that sounded throughout the house.

"What on earth *is* that?" she demanded around the middle of the morning as another bump echoed from below.

"They are cleaning the big hall to make a drawing room," Evelina offered.

"It sounds like they're knocking down the walls."

Evelina giggled and returned to her work.

A few minutes later came the sound of a musical note, repeated over and over, then silence, then the note again, and again until it was pure. And then another note.

Alexandra's breath caught. "It's a pianoforte being tuned."

"We don't have a pianoforte," Evelina reminded her.

They both began to smile at the same time. For once, Alexandra did not inquire as to the completion of the work she had set. She only stood and made for the door, holding her hand out to Evelina on the way past.

They all but ran along the passage to the stairs and hurried down. The double doors of the new drawing room were thrown wide, and the transformation was all the more astonishing because the doors had been closed the last two days. The room had been cleaned and painted. Beautiful carpets were scattered on the freshly polished floors. Velvet curtains hung from the windows, and in pride of place stood a beautiful walnut piano with its lid wide open. A balding man in an apron stood before it, the tools of his trade clutched in one hand to correct the strings, while with the other, he sounded the notes.

"Morning, ma'am, Miss," he greeted them, then put his finger to his lips and carried on. Alexandra and Evelina crept inside and sat on one of the new sofas. Deciding it was part of her education, Alexandra let the child go up for a closer look until the tuner finished his work, packed up his tools, saluted them, and left.

Evelina sat on the matching stool, gently sounding the notes in random order. "Can you play, Miss Battle?"

"A little," she replied. And suddenly, she was so pleased that Sir Nicholas had done this, that there was such a fine instrument in the house, that she sat down beside Evelina and played some songs Evelina already knew, in both Italian and English. She played with a sense of fun and exuberance, and Evelina joined in, her voice raised with Alexandra's in pure happiness.

"More, more!" Evelina laughed when she stopped.

Alexandra was still smiling as she turned to the child. Something made her glance up. Sir Nicholas stood leaning against the door, large, male, imposing. A faint, enigmatic smile played on his lips as he watched them.

A jumble of anxieties deluged Alexandra. How long had he been there? Was he angry? Why did her heart seem to turn over like this whenever she saw him?

Then the focus of his gaze shifted, their eyes clashed, and her world exploded in intense pain and unimagined joy.

Dear God, I love him. How can this have happened?

⇥⇥⇥⇤⇤⇤

NICHOLAS HAD FELT curiously relieved when Dragan was announced that morning. Having cleared his appointments and told everyone who needed to know that he would be at home that morning, he shut himself in the library after breakfast and gazed unseeingly at the letters before him.

His mind was full of Alexandra Battle, and he did not like that. The body's yearnings one could distract and deal with, but it was so much harder when a web was winding itself around his thoughts, and tugging. The trouble was he liked her. He liked her fearless retorts and her innate compassion. He liked the way she dealt with Evelina. He liked her quick mind and her company. And he liked the way she looked, all prim beauty and neatness tied into a dull gown—beneath which, he was sure, lurked a simmering passion any man would long to taste.

And he did. He wanted her with increasing intensity, no doubt spurred on by the knowledge that he could not have her. One did not seduce the governess, even supposing she would let him. For one thing, it would immediately make her an unsuitable companion for one's daughter. For another, a ruined governess would never get another post. He could not do that to her, or ruin his daughter's burgeoning contentment under the care of her teacher.

And then there was the fact that he liked having her around. He liked the sound of her voice, her rare laughter, her wit, her soothing, comfortable presence. He liked to look at her.

And clearly, he liked to think about her rather than the damned letter he was supposed to be answering. Impatiently, he picked up his pen and dipped it in the ink.

A knock sounded at the door, and he looked up with relief at the distraction.

James walked in. "Mr. and Mrs. Tizsa are here, sir. He asked to see you."

"Send them in," Nicholas said resignedly. He expected some kind of scold from Tizsa about the dead smugglers.

Only Tizsa walked into the room, which meant his wife was running tame about the house, no doubt visiting Miss Battle, whether from friendship or a more practical purpose. Were governesses even supposed to receive visitors? Not on teaching time, he supposed, but then it was not yet nine o'clock.

He rose to shake hands with the Hungarian and invite him to sit. "Did my brother contact you?"

"He did, which is one of the reasons I'm here." Tizsa sat, his dark eyes full of speculation as well as determination. "Mr. Swan has received ransom instructions and is desperate none of this reaches the police to endanger his son."

"And he does not have the money," Nicholas said. "No wonder he was dismayed when I appeared at exactly the wrong moment."

"May he use your money to ransom the boy?"

"Of course," Nicholas said. He twisted his lips. "Though it goes against the grain. He may get Henry back, but it won't stop some other child being taken for the same purpose."

"That is the problem," Tizsa agreed. "I have a plan if you have no objections."

"That is between you and Ralph or any other parents you represent."

"Not if it is your money. I propose to let Ralph hand it over, then follow whoever receives it to discover the culprits. There are no guarantees of success. I may simply lose your money."

"Or die trying to retrieve it," Nicholas said bluntly. "Don't even think of going after them alone."

"Oh, I shan't. Once I know where they are, I shall call on Inspector Harris."

"And if they are gone by the time Harris and his men appear?"

"I hope I will have enough friends scattered about to tell me where they went."

Nicholas stared. "You'll need a lot of friends. This is a large city."

"That is true, but I have narrowed it down to a smaller area."

"How?" Nicholas asked, fascinated.

"Your smugglers. I think, having taken Evelina to shut her up, they decided to get rid of her by taking her to someone they knew who dealt in children. Perhaps they thought they could get a cut of the ransom, or—er... a finder's fee."

An echo of fear clawed at Nicholas's stomach. "There are many in this city who deal in children, and for all sorts of purposes."

"I know. It is a gamble, I admit. But our ransom-seekers are, currently, the talk of the underworld, and our men went via Covent Garden. If I'm wrong, I will find out when I follow your money."

"I have some stout men you might draw upon."

"Thank you," Tizsa said politely. "I might, once I have discovered where our villains are." He delved into his pocket and took out a handful of papers, which he unfolded, smoothed, and passed across the desk.

Nicholas picked them up. "What is this?"

"It is my observations on poverty and sickness in various parts of the city, and my recommendations. It says little that is new, except that it is observed by a foreigner brought up in tyranny. If you know someone who will publish it as it stands, without political comment, you are welcome to arrange it. If you don't, just give it back when you wish."

Nicholas smiled. "Thank you. I shall read it with interest and let you know."

Tizsa nodded and stood.

"Wait," Nicholas said, looking up from the essay, "you haven't told me when the ransom for Henry is to be collected."

"That is true," Tizsa agreed. "I have not. Good day, Sir Nicholas."

Nicholas resisted the urge to throw something after him, then shook his head and read Tizsa's essay with increasing interest. Before he had finished, he was interrupted by the sounds of furniture being lugged upstairs and into the drawing room.

He was glad when it stopped. Until the piano tuner began his work. After that torture stopped, there was a short, blissful silence. And then someone began to play the blasted piano.

Nicholas sprang up and strode purposefully across the room with every intention of closing the drawing room doors to give himself some peace to work. Only, before he even left the library, he heard his daughter's childish voice raised in merry song. He paused, smiling involuntarily, until another, more mature voice lifted to join Evelina's.

Somehow, his purpose had changed, and a moment later, he found himself in the drawing room doorway, watching his daughter and her governess play and sing with such innocent pleasure and laughter that it made his heart ache. Watching them together made his heart ache.

It had been a moment of kind concern that had caused him to ask her last night if she ever had fun. But how superior, how condescending that seemed now. She found fun as it was offered, in a few moments of musical nonsense with her pupil. She did not need to spend huge amounts of money and plan and plot. She lived in the moment and grasped whatever pleasure that offered.

It was beguiling and oddly familiar. He remembered, vaguely, a boy with his name who had once lived by the same instinct. *Carpe diem.* He ached suddenly for that boy, too. But mostly, it seemed, he ached for Alexandra Battle. Especially when her gaze lifted suddenly and caught him watching her.

Something changed in her eyes. The smile begun for his daughter did not quite die, but something else gleamed there, too. It might have been excitement or fear or an acknowledgment of inconvenient desire. Or all three.

Or perhaps she was just embarrassed to have been caught out during lesson time. Whatever, it stirred his already turbulent blood.

Until Evelina cried, "Papa!" And threw herself off the piano stool and across the space between them. "You *did* buy a piano! Thank you, thank you! Isn't it lovely? We *may* practice on it, may we not?"

"Of course," he replied, ruffling her hair. "I can't play the wretched thing, so it is up to you and Miss Battle."

Evelina began to drag him toward the piano. "Come and see Miss Battle play! And you can join in the song, Papa!"

Nicholas laughed, though he allowed himself to be hauled to the instrument, where Miss Battle now stood, smiling faintly at Evelina, not him. "How would that work when I cannot hold a note?"

"Miss Battle will teach you," Evelina said confidently.

Her eyes lifted involuntarily to his and flamed, depriving him of breath. Alexandra Battle could teach him anything she liked. And he would be glad to return the compliment.

"Good grief," said a lazy, amused, female voice from the doorway. "You really do live here."

Nicholas swung around, more annoyed than anything by the interruption. A lady stood framed in the doorway with another, older woman hovering behind. And behind both, James, unable to get past without rudeness, looking at once irritated and guilty.

With an effort, Nicholas recalled his visitors. The beautiful young widow, Mrs. Caroline Jenner, who had visited Venice last year and danced with him. Flirting widows, unlike governesses, were fair game in his book, but she had resisted seduction, probably to intrigue him further. It had worked, too. But it took more than physical desire and the presence of a respectable mother to win an offer of marriage from Nicholas Swan, and he had barely thought of her from that moment to this.

"Mrs. Jenner," he said. "What a pleasant surprise."

"Yes, we have tracked you down," she said gaily, sweeping into the room. "You remember my mother, Mrs. Talley?"

Nicholas bowed to each. "My daughter, Evelina, and Miss Battle, her governess."

Mrs. Talley's nostrils flared.

Caroline Jenner smiled kindly upon Evelina. "What a pretty little girl."

Both of them ignored Miss Battle. Perversely, Nicholas chose to introduce his visitors.

"Mrs. Talley and her daughter, Mrs. Jenner, old acquaintances from Venice," he said.

"Hmm, I'm not sure the Thames has the attraction of the Grand Canal," Caroline Jenner said with amusement. "What on earth possessed you to live here?"

"I like the house. And I had no intention of going into society."

"Well, I hope you will make an exception for us," Caroline said archly. "As soon as we heard you were in London, I thought, we must have Sir Nicholas for our soiree. What a triumph that would be."

"A crusty old hermit will add no cachet to your party, ma'am," Nicholas said dryly.

"Come anyway," Caroline said, presenting him with a card whisked from the reticule on her arm.

"Are we not going to play, Papa?" Evelina asked determinedly.

Miss Battle already had hold of her hand, urging her from the room. "Later, Evelina," she murmured. "We have to have luncheon before we go out in the afternoon."

It was a masterstroke to divert her with the afternoon's treat, and it almost worked. But after an instant's consideration, her brow lowered "There is easily time for both, and Papa said—"

"Papa has visitors," Miss Battle said firmly, tugging her toward the door. Evelina's face had taken on that flushed, furious look. Her body had gone rigid. A tantrum clearly threatened, so in solidarity, he walked with them to the door, hoping Miss Battle wouldn't have too much trouble dragging her upstairs.

"Papa..." Evelina uttered warningly.

"Evelina, remember what we agreed," Miss Battle said calmly, without pausing, "now that you are so grown up and ready to go on outings and meet visitors..." Her voice faded as she hurried the child forward toward the staircase, talking quietly. Evelina's voice sounded once, sulky and petulant, but there was no tantrum. At least not yet.

"Send up some tea, James," Nicholas said wearily, and returned to his guests.

CHAPTER THIRTEEN

I T CROSSED ALEXANDRA'S mind that these intruders from Sir Nicholas's own world would keep him, and that she and Evelina would end up going to the Exhibition without him. She tried not to care, and when she still did, convinced herself it was only for Evelina's sake, and because she doubted she could deflect another tantrum.

However, when they emerged from the schoolroom after luncheon, she could hear his voice in the hall downstairs, asking when the carriage would be ready, and a load seemed to lift from her mind and heart.

It was the beginning of a delightful afternoon. In the carriage, Evelina chattered excitedly and pointed out to her father the patch of park where she and Alexandra had had their picnic. The Exhibition building, the so-called Crystal Palace, all glass and steel, was unique enough to awe her, and once they were inside, she wanted to see everything at once.

Of course, there was far too much to see in one afternoon, though Evelina seemed happy enough to try. In the end, her father enticed her away with the need to buy souvenirs for Lady Nora and the promise of tea in a nearby tearoom.

The tearoom he chose was large, luxurious, and busy, but at a word from Sir Nicholas, they were led immediately to a vacant table by a window. Evelina gazed about her with frank curiosity, which seemed to be returned. Several people gazed at their table, no doubt wondering what the great Sir Nicholas Swan was doing with such a dowdy female.

Who am I trying to fool? Everyone will know by looking at me, I am just the governess.

It was her only moment of self-mockery that afternoon, for she had resolved to enjoy whatever advantages she could in being Evelina's governess. Such as this fine tea and finer company, and the knowledge and the wit that Sir Nicholas had brought to understanding the exhibits. In truth, it also felt good to be treated as a lady, to have doors held for her, and to be handed in and out of the carriage. Just as if she were not merely the governess.

After tea, they walked back through the park for a little before meeting the carriage.

"Will you dine with us too, Papa?" asked Evelina.

"Not tonight, my squib. I have work to do, sadly, to make up for bunking off this afternoon."

Evelina giggled at this turn of phrase. And then, rather cleverly mimicking the visitor this morning, she struck a pose and asked, "When is your soiree? Or will you bunk off that, too?"

Sir Nicholas grinned. He had quite a charming, boyish smile when he chose. "I haven't decided yet," he admitted. "It may be that avoiding society causes more talk than actually going to the occasional party."

"Talk about you?" asked Evelina.

"Yes."

"What do they say?" she asked curiously.

"That I was a wild young man, and they hope I have mended my ways to make me fit for their hallowed homes."

"And have you?" she asked with mock severity.

"I am a perfect model of respectability. Most days."

"A bit like me?" Evelina suggested. "Mostly, I am good, but sometimes I am bad."

Alexandra shifted on her luxurious carriage seat. "The important thing is to keep trying, so that you are bad less often."

"Are you ever bad, Miss Battle?" Evelina asked, gazing up at her with sudden interest.

More disconcertingly, Sir Nicholas seemed to be regarding her in much the same way, and for once, she could think of nothing to say.

"Governesses have to be good," Sir Nicholas said gravely. "Otherwise, they could not put up with naughty minxes like you."

"I am a mostly good minx," Evelina said with dignity and smiled when both her father and Alexandra laughed and agreed that she was.

⇶⫷

ALEXANDRA DID NOT linger in the dining room after Anna took Evelina away. Instead, she retreated to her room, drawn toward music that might soothe her troubled soul, and restore her calm. Grizelda's guitar had become her refuge most evenings, and only today had she begun to understand why.

It was Sir Nicholas who upset her balance. A fascination with her employer, a physical attraction that had been there from the first, those needed some kind of emotional outlet, and music had always been hers. But the realization by the piano this morning... That would take more work.

Piano. She halted outside the open doors of the pleasant new drawing room, gazing at the instrument. If she closed the doors, and played very softly, surely, she would disturb no one? Evelina's bedchamber was on the other side of the house, and she rather thought Sir Nicholas had gone out, for, during dinner, she had heard his voice downstairs in the entrance hall.

Her fingers itched. Before she could change her mind, she walked through the open doors and closed them quietly behind her. She hurried over to the piano and sat, adjusted the position of the stool, then spread her fingers over the keys.

At first, she just played, letting her fingers travel where they willed, until the music soothed and took control of her mind. She played a Chopin Nocturne, moved seamlessly to one of her father's pieces, and on to Beethoven's Moonlight Sonata. The emotion of the music soared with that of her new-found impossible love—tragedy, beauty, and happiness all rolled into one.

With this, inevitably, came past regrets, moments of fun with her father, playing with him, losing him to greed and women and wine... But the memories faded quickly into the image of that other, enigmatic man who, for some reason, held her heart. She would take it back, though; she would. In time.

It was as she finished the sonata and returned to the intensely personal Chopin that she began to imagine him there with her, like a ghostly companion to her loneliness. And she smiled through the pain because she liked the thought. But then, some faint movement penetrated her world, and she glanced around and up to be sure he was not really there.

Her heart plunged. Her fingers stumbled, for he stood only feet away from her in the semi-gloom of dusk that had entered the room while she played.

"Don't stop," he murmured, but she was already on her feet, pushing back the stool.

"I can't," she gasped incoherently.

She felt rather than saw him stride toward her. He seized her in his arms, staring down at her, a frown of bewilderment, of distress, tugging at his brows.

"You are beautiful," he whispered. "Even when you weep."

And then, stunningly, he captured her mouth in his, and God help her, the music was nothing compared to the emotions battering at her now. His kiss was fierce and yet tender, invasive, achingly possessive.

She could do nothing but kiss him back. She had flung out her arms, perhaps in startlement, but now they were around his neck in wonder. His fingers caressed her nape, holding her steady, while his other palm splayed across her back, pressing her to him. Desire, hot and sweet, swept through her.

He seemed to tear his mouth free and held her face between his hands, his thumbs caressing the remaining dampness on her cheeks.

"Why do you weep?" he demanded. "What is wrong?"

You. You are wrong. You... She shook her head and closed her eyes, blotting out the stormy, beloved face. She had never imagined his eyes blazing with such emotion, such passion, not for her.

His mouth came down on hers again, more gently this time, more persuasive than demanding, but no less overwhelming. Only, she could not let herself be overwhelmed. Her survival depended on it.

With a gasp, she pulled back, stumbling away from him. "You mustn't," she said brokenly, raising a hand to ward him off when he followed her. "I mustn't..." She turned and fled, wrenching open the door and not even pausing to close it as she ran across the landing and upstairs to the safety of her chamber.

Trembling, she sank down on the bed, trying to calm her racing heart, wondering what on earth had just happened to her, to *him*.

It was the music... For her, perhaps. And possibly it had some effect on him, too. She knew she played with emotion. On the other hand, he was clearly a man used to women. Lady Nora. Evelina's mother. Whomever he had fought a duel over. The beautiful widow, Mrs. Jenner, who had been here only this morning, courting him, Alexandra was sure.

Oh, yes, he was a womanizer. And she, Alexandra, was a woman. There at the right time, tugging his emotions with her music.

Having explained things to her intellectual satisfaction, she drew in a deep breath. It didn't stop the pain.

Footsteps in the passage jolted her back to reality. Her heartbeat quickening once more, she listened to their approach, quick and firm…and they stopped at her door.

She knew instinctively this was no servant. It was a male tread, and she was sure it was Sir Nicholas's. Afraid to breathe, she sat perfectly still on the bed, staring at the door.

She hadn't locked it. What if he came in?

Heat flamed through her like wildfire, and temptation surged in its wake. *Where would be the harm? Who would know?*

She imagined his fingers grasping the handle. She even imagined it turning, and was afraid to breathe.

And then the footsteps moved on in the direction of the school-room.

She exhaled in a rush. She did not want to think she was more disappointed than relieved, so she jumped up, hurrying to the door, where she turned the key deliberately in the lock.

That done, she moved to her desk and sat down determinedly to finish her letter to one of her old pupils. Not long after, she heard the footsteps returning, but they did not pause at her door, merely went evenly on toward the stairs.

FOR THE FIRST time since the night of her arrival, Alexandra woke to the sound of that muffled, rhythmic clanking. It seemed to have been part of her woolly dream, so she had no idea how long it had been going on. As on the first night, curiosity blossomed. But she remembered all over again what had occurred when she had wandered the house in her nightgown looking for the source of the noise. She spent some time recalling every word, every look of that warning encounter. And then his every expression, every touch this evening.

It was some time before she noticed the noise had stopped. She closed her eyes to go back to sleep, no easy task when her every sense, every nerve was awash with memory. At some point, the clanking started up again, but she was already half asleep and had no intention of pursuing it.

NICHOLAS LEFT THE house early the following morning and walked to the city to keep several appointments. He liked to walk, and often did when time permitted, but on this particular morning, he was very aware his prime motive was to clear his head of Alexandra Battle.

What in God's name was I doing? Touching her, kissing her had been unforgivably wrong, and yet when he had done it, while he was doing it, it had felt very right. He had been correct about how she would feel in his arms, all softness and curves and feminine strength. And he had been right about the passion smoldering beneath the calm exterior. Only he hadn't guessed quite how sweet her lips would feel beneath his, how moved he would be by her blind, almost desperate response.

Of course, he had been moved before he entered the room when her music had drawn him there against his better judgment. She hadn't even noticed as he'd opened and closed the door, walked across the room to her like the proverbial moth on its way to burn itself.

Fascinated, awed, he had been unable to look away from her rapt face. He had loved watching the expressions play across her face, mirroring that inspired by the music. She had never looked so beautiful, so unguarded. The tear he had first seen sparkling at the corner of her eye, then trickling down her cheek, had touched him to the core, even though she didn't seem to notice it.

And when she'd noticed *him*... Dear God, emotion had *crashed* through him, longing to comfort as well as possess and defend...and make wild, passionate love to. All the emotion of the music had been alive in her unguarded face, her lovely, passionate eyes. And so, he'd taken her in his arms and kissed her while he wiped her tears, and rejoiced in every response of her lips and her clinging, caressing hands.

Carpe diem, the only principle of his untamed youth, had possessed him once more. Unforgivably. One did not kiss the governess. One did not make a mistress of the governess. She was a young lady whose survival depended on her reputation, which he had so nearly stolen. He had, in effect, insulted her. She would be well within her rights to leave her post, to leave Evelina and him far behind. Part of him knew she should, since he seemed to have relapsed into the boy who could not keep his hands to himself in the face of physical attraction.

But he did not want her to go.

He strode through the familiar streets, as far as St. Paul's Cathedral, trying to clear his head and compose a humble, respectful apology. And a promise, which he could not then break, never to touch her again.

He didn't like that idea either, but it was the least of all the evils he could see opening like a chasm in front of them both. With that decided, he turned his mind determinedly to the appointments ahead of him.

More than two hours later, as he walked home, he decided to take a slight detour to Whitehall and call in at the office where Dragan Tizsa was often to be found in his capacity as an employee of the government. He was lucky enough to find him picking up his hat and coat to leave.

"Is it time for luncheon already?" Nicholas inquired.

"No. I only called in to collect some papers. I prefer to work away from the office. I spent some time with your brother earlier. Is that why you are looking for me?"

"Yes," Nicholas admitted.

Tizsa held the door for him, and he passed back into the street.

"I went to my bank," Nicholas said. "They were worried by a large withdrawal requested by Ralph. I told them to allow it. I presume it is the ransom for Henry."

"I presume so, too." He cast a quick glance at Nicholas. "He will deliver the ransom tonight in return for his son."

"Someone should be there," Nicholas said abruptly. "Not just to be with you in pursuit of the villains, but to look after Ralph and Henry. What if they cheat him at the last moment and keep the boy to extort even more money? What if something goes wrong and they try to hurt or even kill one of them?"

"I will be there," Tizsa said. "Hidden. You are not an inconspicuous man."

Nicholas blinked. "And you are?"

"Yes," Tizsa said in apparent surprise. "And I know how to remain unseen. I tracked Romanian guerrilla fighters through Transylvania for months."

"Catch any?"

"Yes, actually. Much good as it did us in the end."

"Tell me where the exchange is to take place," Nicholas said. "Let's make a plan that will keep everyone safe."

"You don't trust me," Tizsa observed.

"If there were four or five of you," Nicholas retorted, "in this particular situation, I would certainly trust you more."

Tizsa was quiet for so long that Nicholas began to get irritated. Then the Hungarian said, "We'll speak to Griz."

Nicholas blinked. "Lady Grizelda?"

Tizsa nodded. He cast Nicholas a glance, and his lips twitched. "She is wise in many things. Lots of women are. Haven't you found that?"

Nicholas thought about it. "No. Though that may be because of the women I have pursued. Or who pursued me." Unbidden, Alexandra Battle swam back to the front of his mind. He suspected she was wise. After all, it was she who had broken from him last night. All he had done was manage not to pursue her, though he had been sorely tempted by the sight of her bedroom door as he had gone to look in on Evelina. "By all means, let us consult your wife."

The Tizsas, it transpired, lived in a sprawling, half-hidden little house reached from a lane off Half Moon Street. It somehow suited the eccentric couple, as did the lively little greyhound with the blue-grey coat who leapt on Tizsa as soon as they entered the front door. Taking shelter behind Tizsa's legs, it regarded Nicholas with an amusing mixture of smugness and suspicion.

"This is Vicky," Tizsa explained, bending to stroke the dog and tickle it behind the ears. "After Her Majesty, of course, because on better days, she can look quite regal. Or so Griz says."

While the greyhound condescended to sniff Nicholas's feet, Tizsa turned to the maid emerging from the back of the house.

"Is Lady Griz in?"

"In the drawing room, sir. Will the gentleman be staying for luncheon?"

"Let's say, yes," Tizsa replied without consulting his guest. "And if he tires of us before that, there will be all the more for me. This way."

Tizsa led him up a staircase and into a rather fine room with paintings and framed pencil portraits on the wall. It was more of lived-in sitting room than a drawing room, not least because Lady Grizelda sat at a table surrounded by books and papers.

Her face lit up as her husband walked into the room. "Dragan!" She jumped up to meet him, and quite unself-consciously, he threw an arm around her and kissed her on the lips. Only then did she seem to see Nicholas and leave her husband to greet him with surprise. "Sir Nicholas. An unexpected pleasure."

"I hope I am not inconvenient. Your husband believes we should consult you, and I am interested in your view."

"I'm very glad to see you. Would you like tea? A glass of wine?"

They settled on a pre-luncheon sherry, which Lady Griz poured while her husband spread out a map of London on the table. The three of them gathered around it.

"Your brother," Tizsa said, pointing on the map, "has been instructed to come *here*, to a corner coffee house just off King Street. At half-past nine this evening."

"Near Covent Garden again," Nicholas said thoughtfully. "You think Henry and perhaps other children are being kept near there?"

Tizsa shrugged. "I doubt it would be *too* close to where they want to meet. Just in case witnesses see where they come from."

"Is a coffee house not a rather public place to conduct such business?" Nicholas said.

"There is no guarantee the coffee house will be the final place. My guess is the coffee house was chosen to make your brother feel safe, but once he brings the money, he will be enticed from the coffee house into one of the quieter alleys."

Nicholas nodded thoughtfully. "Have you been there? Could we pack the house with Inspector Harris's plainclothes policemen?"

"I thought of Harris himself, but he is not an unknown figure around the area. Besides, the house is frequented largely by actors and people associated with the opera house. Harris would stand out a mile even he wasn't a known Peeler."

Nicholas regarded him. "You look like an actor, I suppose, or a struggling writer, perhaps. I could be your financier."

Tizsa grinned, but his wife said seriously, "That isn't such a bad idea. I would be happier if you had company inside. And I was thinking, I could watch from the outside. With Nell."

Even Tizsa blinked at that.

"In disguise," Griz clarified.

"I know," Dragan said grimly. "And I cannot protect you outside when I am inside."

"I won't need protection when I'm with Nell," Griz assured him.

Nicholas turned to Tizsa with amused interest. "Wisdom, eh?" he murmured.

Tizsa ignored him. "And if Nell goes off to work?"

"I'll pay her to say she's waiting for someone."

"And if the police move you on?"

"Dragan," Griz reproved. "You know the police will have been well paid to stay away. It makes sense. We'll see who else is waiting or watching and what direction anyone takes who bolts out of the coffee house ahead of you. And then, while you and Sir Nicholas follow the villain, I can go and help Mr. Swan and his son."

Nicholas laughed aloud. "I can just see Ralph's face when you appear to help, dressed as a—"

"Actually, it would be a good idea to have a carriage waiting," Tizsa interrupted, glaring at him. "Perhaps with Miss Battle."

Nicholas drew himself up, scowling. "I will not have Miss Battle—"

"That *is* a good idea," Lady Griz interrupted. "And Alex will like to help. A hired carriage, perhaps, rather than one emblazoned with the Swan's arms."

Tizsa, frowning, appeared to be reconsidering. "A carriage would make a useful means of escape, too, should anything go wrong. Or a means of pursuit if the villains have their own vehicle."

"Good," Lady Griz pronounced. She smiled dazzlingly at Nicholas. "Will you speak to Alex? Or shall I?"

CHAPTER FOURTEEN

THAT AFTERNOON, ALEXANDRA took Evelina to the first of their arranged meetings with other children. It was an informal affair, the governesses sitting on benches, while their charges circled each other warily and eventually began to play. Since Miss Farnsworth had two pupils, Alexandra had worried that Evelina might be overwhelmed, and indeed she was, just at first, but she soon joined in the games, while the governesses chatted together and dispensed snacks as required.

As they returned home, Alexandra felt pleased with the outing, for Evelina had clearly enjoyed it. And for Alexandra, it had been a blessed relief from the oppression of her own feelings.

Back in the house, as they climbed the stairs, Alexandra laughing at one of Evelina's stories about her new friends, she saw at once that the drawing room doors were open. And when Sir Nicholas strolled through them, her heart plunged. She felt like a trapped deer.

Fortunately, before she was forced to meet his gaze, Evelina flew at him with her usual joy, diverting all attention as she poured out to her father where she had been and whom she had met.

He listened patiently, even asking questions that made her laugh, while Alexandra stood awkwardly to one side, trying to make herself invisible. And then a female figure appeared from the drawing room.

"Griz?" Alexandra said faintly.

"Off you go to Anna," Sir Nicholas said, "and I will hear the rest at dinner."

So, he was going dine with them? The butterflies in her stomach began to panic.

"Miss Battle," Sir Nicholas said amiably, "join us for a few minutes if you please. Lady Griz has a proposition you may happily reject."

Alexandra glanced warily from one to the other, then at Sir Nicholas's ironic bow, she followed Griz into the drawing room in front of him. Since Griz sat on the new sofa near the impressive but empty fireplace, Alexandra sat beside her, removing her bonnet, while Sir Nicholas chose to stand leaning negligently against the fireplace. She wished she wasn't so aware of his presence, his tall, muscular body, which had been pressed so close to hers last night.

Griz spoke quietly and matter-of-factly. "Tonight, Sir Nicholas's brother is paying the ransom for his son. The exchange is meant to take place in or near a coffee shop by Covent Garden. Dragan means to follow the kidnappers once young Henry is safe. I will watch from close by, but we thought it would be good to have someone else close by in a carriage, hopefully merely to look after Mr. Swan and Henry, but possibly to rescue anyone else in need of it, or even to follow the kidnappers if they have a vehicle of their own."

Alexandra followed all this with unusual difficulty, finally working out who she had in mind. She blinked. *"Me?"*

"It is not part of your duties and not required," Sir Nicholas said sternly.

Alexandra thought of Evelina's abduction and Sir Nicholas's terrible anxiety. His brother's had been going on for several days, and the boy was still in danger. "I would like to help if I can."

"I told you she would," Griz said to Sir Nicholas, whose enigmatic gaze was focused on Alexandra.

"I believed you," he said. "Which is why I have already arranged for my man Ingram to accompany you. He is quick, observant, and useful in a fight."

"A fight?" Alexandra repeated, startled.

"Let us hope not. The alternative, of course," he added, including Griz in his sweeping gaze, "is that we send Ingram without you."

"Though he is likely to be less use in comforting Henry," Griz pointed out.

Alexandra gazed at her. "And you will be no use in such a role because you will be with Dragan."

Griz smiled.

"Does he know?" Alexandra asked cynically.

"Probably."

With fresh courage, Alexandra met Sir Nicholas's gaze. "And you, sir?"

"With Tizsa, if all goes as planned."

"Good," Griz said, rising to her feet. "Then I will go and prepare. I'll let Sir Nicholas tell you the finer details. Until tonight!"

Any panic she might have felt at being left alone with Sir Nicholas vanished as he unfolded a map and spread it out on the table. Wordlessly, she went over to join him, and he pointed out the location of the coffee house, where Griz would be standing, and where they wanted the carriage to be waiting.

It struck her that her role was largely superfluous. That Henry would have the comfort of his father and, very soon after, his mother. If there was any trouble, Mr. Ingram would be far more use than she. However, there was a certain pleasure in being part of the plan, in bending her head so close to Sir Nicholas's as they studied the map.

And, she acknowledged to herself, part of her hoped there would be cause to chase the villains, for the sake of pure excitement as well as satisfaction from bringing them down. It was a long time since she had done anything riskier than prevent a child from falling in a shallow pond. Such reprehensible longings were, she supposed, part of the attraction of Griz, about whom had always hung an air of chaos that seemed to have blossomed into constant, thrilling adventure since the advent of Dragan Tizsa in her life.

Sir Nicholas glanced at her. "You are taking this very much in your stride."

"I lived with my father for twenty years," she said wryly, and hastily straightened, because he was too close, and because the flash of interest in his eyes warned her to be careful. "Is the ransom being paid with your money?"

"Why else would I involve myself?"

She couldn't help searching his eyes or the faint smile that curved his lips. "Because he is your brother, and the boy, your nephew."

"That's part of the same thing."

She shook her head. "No, it isn't. Please excuse me while I change for dinner."

⟫⟫⟩✦⟨⟨⟨

NICHOLAS ALWAYS LIKED to see Alexandra in her evening gown. Not that it was much more elaborate than her dull, grey day gown, but the color became her, and he could admire the elegant, creamy slope of her shoulders.

Funnily enough, despite the increasingly intense desire she engendered, he also liked to see her in company with Evelina. He hadn't realized it before, but she behaved more as a mother to the child than Eva ever had. She seemed genuinely interested in Evelina's chatter, asked questions, and laughed at her jokes. She gently corrected the child when she grew too loud or broke table manner rules. As a result, Nicholas, who would always have died for his daughter, began to appreciate her more as a person than a possession to be taken care of.

It was, he thought ruefully that evening, as if they had become a little family. And it had taken the outsider, Alexandra Battle, to make them so.

When Evelina had gone upstairs with Anna, and Ingram arrived, he realized with irritation that he was not the only man to recognize Alexandra's charms. Ingram, of course, was perfectly polite and would remain so, but Nicholas did not like the admiring look in the other man's eyes.

It was with some reluctance that he left them alone together while he changed his clothes for the outing. Returning ten minutes later in a lacy shirt and loud waistcoat with a red kerchief knotted at his throat, he saw Ingram grin openly.

"You find something to amuse you in my appearance?" Nicholas drawled, slurring his words just a little, as though well on his way to inebriation. "You will laugh on the other side of your face when my play is the toast of Europe!"

"I certainly will," Ingram agreed.

"I'm reverting to my youth," Nicholas told Alexandra. "The role comes worryingly easily."

"I look forward to seeing you on stage," she said lightly.

He wondered if he imagined her face tinged with color, as though she found his new character not unattractive.

"Mr. Tizsa is at the door with a hackney," James announced.

Nicholas nodded and turned briefly back to the others. But they both had their instructions. There was no more to say.

"Thank you both for this," he said abruptly and strode from the room. In the hall, he snatched up his hat, which he wore at a rakish angle, and an ornate walking stick, and went out to meet Tizsa.

Lady Griz was in the carriage with him, enveloped in a large cloak. God knew what she was wearing beneath.

"What does the duke, your father, think of your mad starts?" he asked suddenly.

"I imagine if he ever heard of them, he would be displeased," Griz said without much interest. "You do look the part, Sir Nicholas. Well done. Dragan just looks as he always looks."

"My wife is disappointed I won't play dressing-up." Dragan observed.

"It doesn't seem to matter," Nicholas replied. Somehow, the man could pass in any company. "As long as you can play the unthreatening drunk."

"I was a soldier for nearly two years. I can be any drunk you like."

At Covent Garden, the carriage drove around the back streets until, at the corner of the square, Dragan said, "There's Nell," and knocked on the carriage roof for the driver to halt.

"And Junie," Griz said, throwing off her cloak to reveal an astonishingly gaudy gown of sparkling pink and some clashing dyed and drooping feathers in her hair.

As she was about to jump out, Dragan leaned forward suddenly and caught her wrist. "Griz. Be careful."

Griz cast him one of her unexpectedly dazzling smiles and dragged his hand up to kiss it. "And you."

The last Nicholas saw of her as she sidled up to the screeching women, she had her hand on her hip and was tossing her head until she was drawn in among them.

"Is she really safe there?" Nicholas asked.

"As safe as they can make her," Tizsa said grimly. "But I'll be glad when we can get this over with."

The carriage dropped them on King Street, and they sauntered up the road, weaving slightly, before turning the corner into a narrower, quieter street that led to the coffee house. No obvious watchers hung around the area. A hackney was driving past. Two respectable looking women hurried home from whatever work they did.

A man was just leaving the coffee house. Tizsa performed an amusing "excuse me" dance in the doorway with him before simply falling back and raising his hat with the exaggerated civility of the amiable drunk. The man muttered rudely and stalked off toward King Street.

Nicholas laughed, and pushed Tizsa in before him. They were, it seemed, the only customers at that point. But since the shop could have been watched surreptitiously from outside, or the staff themselves could be complicit, they did not allow their roles to falter. While they drank copious amounts of coffee, and the street outside darkened, they got into discussions about Shakespeare, quarreled about the qualities of various playwrights and actors, and moved onto an invented play featuring lots of classical allusions. Throughout it all, they kept taking nips from their flasks to reassure watchers that the coffee was doing little to sober them up.

Ralph came in during one such tipple. Nicholas snorted out a laugh to have been caught, but Ralph, well instructed, ignored them both, merely took a table at the window, and ordered coffee.

On the empty chair beside him, he placed a small carpetbag, presumably containing the ransom money. He looked nervous, his eyes darting, his fingers drumming, his shoulders rigid. Nicholas, reminded brutally of his own emotions when Evelina had vanished, knew a surge of pity for his brother.

It would change nothing, of course. But it was interesting he could still sympathize with him.

No sooner had Ralph's coffee arrived than a face suddenly darkened the window beside him. A boy's face was pressed to the glass from outside.

"The thing you are missing," Tizsa said insistently, stabbing his finger on the table in front of Nicholas, to drag back his attention, "is the completely unfeasible…"

With an audible gasp, Ralph jumped to his feet, so it was definitely Henry at the window. From the corner of his eye, Nicholas saw the boy beckon. So the exchange would *not* happen in the glare of the coffee house lights.

Ralph stumbled forward toward the door in his desperation to get to his son.

"Your bag, sir," Tizsa called politely after Ralph, who dashed back in some horror at his narrowly averted mistake, seized the bag, and bolted outside. By which time Tizsa was holding forth some other rubbish as though paying no attention to the drama unfolding.

"Oh, take a powder, Tizzy," Nicholas said impatiently as an excuse to stand and throw down some coins to pay for their coffee. "I'm off."

"I'll come with you," Tizsa said generously. "Happy to take powders."

"You're three sheets to the wind," Nicholas said contemptuously.

"It's nearly ten in the evening, old boy. No point in being sober, and if you try to tell me *you* are…"

This exchange got them as far as the door. In the shadows further down the road, a gaudy gaggle of women lurked. Griz, looking as outrageous as any of them, swigging something from a flask, jerked her feathers to the lane beside them. As one, Tizsa and Nicholas started toward them, remembering to keep up their slightly weaving gait.

Some yards beyond the women, Nicholas made out a carriage and two horses. Its lamps were lit, and the coachman remained aloft, as though his master was visiting someone in one of the houses nearby. Inside, Alexandra and Ingram should be waiting.

"Ladies!" Tizsa beamed at the very unladylike group of females. "May we buy you a drink?"

Of course, his gaze was not really on the women, and neither was Nicholas's. A group of men lurked in the lane. Ralph was easily recognizable, rigid and several feet from the others whom he faced. He dropped the bag and kicked it some feet to a space roughly halfway between him and the others.

A man detached himself from his companion and came forward, holding the arm of a boy perhaps eight years old. In his other hand, he carried a dim lantern. They stopped, and the man crouched down, opened the bag, and peered into it.

He said something and rose, giving the boy a little push.

"Ladies, if you will," Dragan murmured, and the "ladies" stomped off down the lane, hurling abuse at their drunken admirers, who followed, wheedling.

At any other time, Nicholas would have been vastly entertained by the insults flung at his head. But his attention was on his brother, now clutching the boy to him. The man with the bag and the lantern was vanishing into the darkness with his companion.

"I'm so glad to see you, Papa!" the boy's muffled voice exclaimed, not quite steadily. "I have had such an adventure!"

Nicholas glanced over his shoulder. Alexandra's carriage had edged nearer the coffee house and stopped. Its door opened, and Ingram's face peered out, lit up clearly by the carriage lamp.

"The coach at the end of the lane," Dragan said to Ralph, low and insistent. "Get in it, and my friends will take you straight home."

Ralph, looking like a terrified, hunted rabbit, nodded as though he *needed* to be told what to do and began to hurry his son along the lane. At one point, his eyes met Nicholas's, and he actually nodded. An acknowledgment of his help? Or a mechanical politeness to someone he did not recognize?

It didn't matter. Henry was safe. And he and Dragan—and possibly Dragan's wife and three prostitutes—were in pursuit of the villains.

CHAPTER FIFTEEN

"**H**AVE YOU WORKED a long time for Sir Nicholas?" Alexandra asked Mr. Ingram as the carriage waited fifty yards or so down the road from the coffee house.

"Almost ten years," Ingram replied.

"What exactly is it you do for him?" She spoke mainly to fill the tedious waiting time, but having asked, she found she really wanted to know the answer.

Ingram smiled faintly. "Whatever he asks me to. For the last six years or so, I have carried out his orders concerning the British parts of his business. I am a good organizer. Since he has come home, my duties have become more…diverse."

"Such as looking for his lost daughter and helping find his brother's abducted child?"

"Among other things. It has been…*interesting* to meet him at last."

Alexandra dragged her gaze away from the fascinating sight of a gaudily dressed Griz walking among several "ladies of the night."

"Interesting in what way?" she asked.

"All ways. Until I met him, I thought he was just another wealthy gentleman getting richer off the backs of the poor souls who worked for him. Though admittedly, he paid better than most."

"I believe he is involved in several charitable projects," Alexandra remarked. A man had fallen out of a nearby public house and was heading straight for Grizelda's group, who had paused at the corner of a lane.

"And some," Ingram said, faintly amused.

Alexandra glanced at him inquiringly.

Ingram shrugged. "I mean, he is doing some good with his pots of money. He isn't as heartless as he would have you believe."

Alexandra had already come to the same conclusion herself, but now that she had heard it confirmed, she wanted to know more. She had to bite her lip to prevent displaying unseemly interest. She was only the governess, after all. What he did with his money was not her concern, as long as he provided what Evelina needed for her education.

In the street, the drunk she had noticed earlier, seemed to have taken a shine to Griz, perhaps sensing her differentness. This was one of those dangerous moments when they must be ready to rescue her.

"I see," Ingram murmured when she glanced at him. "But I don't think he wants to get on the wrong side of her companions."

He was right. The other women were seeing him off with insults and ridicule. One was even waving a bottle at him in a threatening kind of way. The man, after hurling a few vicious insults back, loped off toward King Street.

"You can't imagine they make much money that way," Ingram observed.

"*We* are paying them," Alexandra said wryly. "Otherwise, they would be in trouble with the men who take most of their earnings."

Ingram blinked at her, clearly intrigued. "How do you know so much about the unseemly side of life?"

"I have eyes," she retorted. "And I have lived in many cities across Europe." And her father, while looking after her in his own way, had seen no point in sheltering her from the harsh realities of life—not least to illustrate why he broke the law to keep her safe from such an existence as these poor women led.

Two working men and a boy emerged from the lane near where

Griz and her friends stood. Alexandra's heart began to race, for surely there was no need for one of the men to be holding the boy's arm? The child must have been about eight or nine, his clothes too grubby to reveal their quality. And his hair stuck up as though it hadn't been brushed for days.

As they watched breathlessly, the man with the boy halted at the edge of the coffee house window. The other man walked on to the other side of the door and lounged against the wall.

The first man shoved the boy toward the window, and he flattened his face against the glass. He didn't seem frightened, Alexandra thought, wondering if this was really Henry Swan or some other random child. But then he jumped up and down with excitement at what he saw inside the coffee house—presumably his father—and began gesticulating.

"They're coming out," Ingram breathed.

The boy was hauled back from the window and all but dragged back toward the lane. He didn't protest, but he clearly didn't want to stray again from his father. Ralph Swan bolted from the coffee house, a carpetbag in his hand, and caught sight of his son waving to him as he was hurried round the corner of the lane. Ralph, looking pitiably demented in his anxiety, ran after them.

Ingram stuck his head out of the carriage window. "Wait a moment, then move forward to the edge of the lane, so that we can see…"

While he gave his instruction, Alexandra watched the other man at the coffee house, who slouched off after Ralph. This made her uneasy. Did they mean to trap Ralph, hurt him? The man turned his head, looking across the road, and gave a definite nod before he sped up and strode after Ralph.

Alarmed, Alexandra tried to make out who or what he had nodded to. A shadowed doorway seemed to move. But then she was distracted by the sight of Sir Nicholas and Dragan Tizsa weaving down the road and raising their hats to Griz and her companions. Clearly, a reason to be there while secretly peering down the lane at whatever was going on. Unexpected laughter caught at her breath. Who would have thought the imposing Sir Nicholas would be such an actor?

As the carriage ambled forward, a movement near that same shadowy doorway seized her attention. A shapeless man enveloped in a cloak moved rapidly away from them in the direction of King Street.

"I think there's someone else, Mr. Ingram," Alexandra said urgently. "He's just left that doorway across the road and is hurrying away from us."

By then, the carriage had halted again opposite the lane, where Nicholas and Dragan were in apparent pursuit of the women.

"There's an exchange going on in the lane," Ingram replied. "Watch your man. Mr. Swan and the boy are coming this way…"

This was their task. To receive the no doubt traumatized boy and his father and take them home quickly and safely. And yet, the cloaked man worried Alexandra. Of the men involved, only he had been hidden, while the others risked themselves openly. And he had done nothing but supervise from a safe place. Was this their leader? The man who organized the abduction of children from their wealthy parents for ransom?

Ingram was hanging out of the coach, waving encouragingly to Mr. Swan and the boy. He got down to help them inside, and Ralph blinked in surprise to find her there.

"We have met," Alexandra said comfortingly. "I'm governess to Sir Nicholas's daughter." She smiled at the slightly bewildered boy. As far as she could tell in the carriage's poor light, he seemed unhurt and not particularly afraid, although he sat very close to his father. "You must be Henry. I am Miss Battle, and this gentleman is Mr. Ingram, who works for your uncle. Did these men treat you well?"

"Yes, I suppose so…"

"Did they feed you, Henry? Did they hurt you?" Ralph burst out, clutching the boy's hand convulsively.

"Yes to food, no to hurt," Henry said with surprising cheerfulness. "I was so glad to see you, Papa! It has been quite an adventure, but I've had enough now and want to go home."

Alexandra, along with everyone else, searched his face again. "Home is clearly the best place for you," she said with resolution as the coach moved on its way toward King Street. She peered out of the window, looking for any cloaked figures.

She could be quite wrong about him, of course. The nod of the kidnapper could have been that of mere acquaintance or not aimed at the cloaked figure at all. He could have nothing to do with the kidnappings. But he *could* have been watching everything unseen. He *could* have suspected the inebriated actors were more than they seemed.

Sir Nicholas and Dragan were following two men, and could be trapped by others, under the command of the cloaked man, coming from a different direction.

Anxiety gone mad, she chided herself. *Pure speculation.*

And yet, if the cloaked man was involved and he got away... If Nicholas walked into a trap...

And there he was! Surely that was her cloaked man crossing King Street and vanishing up a lane leading away from Covent Garden.

"That's him," she exclaimed, rapping on the carriage ceiling to tell the coachman to halt his horses. "Mr. Ingram, I believe I might need your protection. Mr. Swan, you will be taken directly home. Good evening!"

"Miss Battle!" Ingram exclaimed as she leapt down from the carriage. "You cannot go—"

"I will, whether you come with me or not," she said calmly and strode across the street without waiting to see if he followed. She had to admit she was glad when he did, especially when the coach continued on its way west toward Mayfair, and she realized he had thought to bring a lantern.

"Miss Battle, this is madness!" Ingram protested, striding along by her side. "Sir Nicholas will string me up if I allow you—"

"You cannot stop me, and Sir Nicholas, I hope, will be glad of your presence with me."

"In pursuit of someone we don't even know is involved?" He glanced suspiciously up the lane as Alexandra strode boldly into it.

A cloak fluttered around the corner at the end.

"He's heading toward Bow Street," Ingram said. "What if he is a policeman?"

"Then why take the back alleys?" Alexandra demanded.

Unseen eyes seemed to bore into her from all sides, making her hair stand on end. The stench of waste she didn't like to think about filled her nostrils, while rubbish she didn't look at crunched under her feet.

Ingram held his walking stick like a weapon, his gaze darting all around as they hurried along. "We're skirting Bow Street. That's Drury Lane. Seems to me we're now heading in the same direction as Sir Nicholas."

"Then perhaps he *is* one of the kidnappers."

They moved quickly, yet never seemed to draw any closer to their quarry. At least they were lucky enough not to be attacked or robbed or even accosted. So lucky, in fact, that Alexandra began to wonder if they were benefiting from whatever protection hung over their quarry.

And then, they lost him.

By this time, they were deep into St. Giles slum territory, surrounded by tiny, almost-hidden passages. He could have hidden down any of them, and they would never have seen him, even with their own lantern. They stood at the end of the alley, looking in either direction, up and down the next. A few people hung around here, gossiping or drinking on doorsteps, though none of them wore a cloak. Opposite was a rare open space scattered with stone rubble, perhaps from a building that had been knocked down or simply collapsed. It was surrounded on three sides by other tall, dreary buildings.

"Now what?" Ingram asked flatly. "We have no clue. We might have come too far. He might have gone into any of these buildings, and we have no business, let alone ability, to search them."

"Let's just cross this clearing—it's open enough that we shouldn't be attacked—and see what we can from the far side. And if nothing, we will have to give up."

With the end in sight—although they would still have to negotiate their way to respectable streets and a hackney stand—Ingram set off across the rubbly ground with renewed vigor, pausing only to help Alexandra over difficult obstacles.

They were almost at the end of this difficult ground, and able to see further alleys leading through the buildings ahead, when she noticed the shadows.

They approached from either side, and when she jerked her head around, she saw they were behind them as well.

"Mr. Ingram," she said warningly.

He raised the flickering lantern—another worry, because if it went out, they would have an even harder time finding their way out of this dangerous warren. As it was, it still supplied enough light to make out the figures of three men to the left, another three to the right, and two more behind.

There was nothing to do but hurry on and hope to prevent themselves being encircled by people who clearly meant them no good. But when they sped up, so did the men, and it was clearly only a matter of time until they were surrounded.

Ingram halted and swung up his stick, trying to ward them off. They crowded closer, sneaking up behind so quickly that Ingram spun around, waving his stick in a wide arc that halted only just short of

Alexandra before he whipped it back again. The men halted, some even stepped back, though most were grinning in amusement.

"Stay close," Ingram hissed between gritted teeth and charged between the nearest two men in the hope of breaking through. But one merely made a grab for his stick, and the two men tussled for it, while the others crowded Alexandra.

She had nothing worth stealing, save the purse Sir Nicholas had given her for expenses. And then she realized the wretched poverty of these people. Her ten-year-old evening gown and bonnet could be sold for a few meals. The purse would not buy them off. They would have everything.

Someone aimed a punch at Ingram, who ducked, wrenching his stick free at last, and lashed out with it at his most immediate attacker, taking him across the ribs. But someone else lashed out with his feet, hacking at Ingram's ankles to trip him. It would have worked, too, had Alexandra not grabbed his elbow to steady him. But a punch from behind sent him staggering, and hands pawed at Alexandra's wrap.

Whose idea was this? Why do I never listen to good sense from anyone else?

And then a shout went up, loud and commanding, and another man all but catapulted out of one of the alleys ahead and strode toward them.

"Stop that!" he ordered. "Stand back, or by God, I'll have your hides!"

The shout was that of a sergeant major, but the accent was cultured, and the voice sounded ridiculously like Sir Nicholas's. Oddly enough, the men did pause and turn uncertainly to face the newcomer, giving Ingram time to stagger to his feet.

The newcomer wore a top hat and was dressed like a gentleman. In the gloom, no one could see the ridiculous waistcoat or the bohemian shirt and necktie. But it was undoubtedly Sir Nicholas.

"Get going," he growled, "before I flay the skin off your miserable backs. Madam, this way."

And astonishingly, a path opened up. Alexandra and Ingram stumbled forward toward Sir Nicholas. She expected a blow, a snatch, at any moment, but none came. Sir Nicholas took her arm, turning his back on the dog-like pack behind.

"Hurry," Sir Nicholas muttered. "We haven't got long."

Somehow, the three of them were off and hurrying down the alley Sir Nicholas had emerged from.

"How on earth did you do that?" Alexandra asked in awe.

"I have no idea," he all but snarled in response, though he was glaring over her head at Ingram. "But you're damned lucky I took it into my head to examine the lay of the land when I did! What the devil do you mean bringing her here? Where is my nephew? My brother?"

"In the carriage going home," Alexandra replied before Ingram could open his mouth. "In fact, I imagine they are safe in Brook Street by now. We saw another man and wanted to be sure he was not part of a trap for you. Besides, if you had lost the others, I thought he might lead us to their den."

In the gloom, his eyes blazed fury at her.

She tilted her chin. "You may thank me later. Or dismiss me. Mr. Ingram, who could not stop me, only came to protect me."

To her surprise, a grunt of laughter escaped him. "You have my pity, Ingram."

"Where are the others?" Alexandra demanded. "Did you see where the kidnappers went?"

"Here," Sir Nicholas said, pointing down a narrow passage to a door, before which, in the glow of a dim lantern, huddled Dragan and Griz. Her gaudy costume was now covered with Dragan's coat, though her feathers still nodded sadly. "Reinforcements," he added to the Tizsas as they turned.

"Did our man come here, too, then?" Alexandra wondered. "Just a few minutes ago? A man in a cloak?"

"No one's gone in since our men with the money," Griz replied in a whisper as she moved back toward them. "We've looked through the keyhole, and they're definitely in there. As are at least three sleeping children and two women who are talking to the men."

"Are they abducted children?" Alexandra asked.

"No way of telling for certain until we get in there," Dragan said. "But I could swear the child who asked for a drink of water doesn't belong here."

Griz said, "We're trying to decide whether to go to the police or barge in now and take the children away. Unless they're the women's children, of course, but at least we could get Mr. Swan's money back."

"If we wait for the police, the men could scarper with the money," Nicholas said impatiently. "And the children."

"Well, now that there are so many of us," Dragan said, "some could wait here while the rest fetch the police."

"There aren't many policemen about here," Ingram said dryly. "How do you even get out of this warren? Alive, I mean."

"That's a good point," Nicholas agreed. "We need to keep together for safety."

"Between those buildings *there*..." Dragan pointed to the right, "...is the way through to Holborn, a policeman, and a hackney stand. Five minutes at the most."

Griz gazed at him thoughtfully.

"If those children are frightened," Alexandra said firmly, "we have to take them out of there tonight. Imagine if one of them was Evelina. Or your sister's child," she added to Griz.

"Three of us and two of them," Sir Nicholas said, with an expressive shrug.

"Provided the neighbors don't rush in to help," Dragan said dryly. "And don't discount the women!"

"Let's get on with it," Nicholas said impatiently.

Dragan shrugged. "Very well. I suggest we take them by surprise. I'll pick the lock, and we'll charge in. Griz and Alex, you try and keep the children calm and safe until we have the adults secure."

Ignoring the fact that lock-picking was hardly a gentlemanly talent, Alexandra focused on the practicalities. "How long would that take? They would probably hear you. Besides, the door is probably bolted."

They all looked at her. "Good point." Nicholas allowed. "I'm sure you have a suggestion."

"Knock on the door. If I'm right, they're expecting the cloaked man. And even if they're not, surely curiosity would make them answer."

"And then we charge in."

CHAPTER SIXTEEN

I N CASE THE villains looked through the keyhole, as Griz and Dragan had done from the other side, they hid on either side of the door while Sir Nicholas scratched at it in a furtive manner. Receiving no response, he knocked loudly, and that inspired sudden commotion within, chairs being pushed back, hasty footsteps, and the sound of bolts being pulled back.

The door opened a mere crack, but Sir Nicholas shoved it hard with his shoulder and barged in, Dragan and Ingram at his heels.

"Hey!" a man's voice shouted. "You ain't—"

Slipping inside behind the men, Alexandra had to step nimbly out of the way as one of the villains shoved Sir Nicholas in the chest. He was a large bruiser of a man, not the one who had carried the lantern and made the exchange earlier. That individual was lunging at Dragan, fists flying.

Sir Nicholas, meanwhile, brought the wrought silver head of his walking stick up smartly under the chin of his attacker. Even through the sudden din in the room, Alexandra heard the snap of the man's teeth before he collapsed to the floor. Sir Nicholas stepped elegantly over him to haul the other man off Dragan.

Alexandra and Griz edged quickly past to the back of the room, where the three children were standing, looking terrified.

"Just stay where you are," Alexandra said calmly. "No one will hurt you. My name's Miss Battle, and I'm a governess."

"Governess?" a boy repeated blankly. "Do we have to have lessons here, too?" His tone implied that that would be the last straw.

"Goodness, no," Alexandra replied. "We've come to rescue you and take you home."

The remaining man would not have been much threat to the combined forces of Sir Nicholas, Dragan, and Ingram, but they had reckoned without the women. With a shriek of rage, one, who looked quite young, had launched herself on Sir Nicholas's back.

"Where's Henry?" another of the boys demanded in panic.

"With his father," Alexandra replied.

"Did you do that?" the third boy asked with clear awe.

"No," Alexandra said, distracted by the fracas in the room. "But I saw them going home together."

The woman, still firmly attached to Sir Nicholas's back, snatched up a pitcher from the table, with the clear aim of bringing it down on his head—she knocked his hat off, presumably with the express purpose. But Dragan, to Alexandra's relief, suddenly leapt up, snatched the pitcher from her hand, and instead brought it down on the head of the second male kidnapper.

He stumbled backward, clutching his head, and tripped over the body of his friend. As he fell, the older woman charged Dragan with a howl of rage. Ingram grabbed her arm to slow her down and received a buffet to the face from her other hand.

In other circumstances, it might have been funny. As it was, a surge of hysterical laughter threatened Alexandra's calm demeanor. It was clear none of the men were used to dealing with violent women, and as gentlemen, they were held back by chivalry as they were not against men.

"I would like to go home," the first boy said firmly. "Now."

"Are you all dressed?"

"We sleep in our clothes here. It's cold otherwise, and there are no nightgowns."

"What are your names?" Alexandra asked desperately, more to distract them than because she cared much at this precise point in proceedings.

Griz, meanwhile, had moved to the wooden chair where the neglected carpetbag full of Swan money resided, watching as Nicholas spun around in an effort to dislodge his shrieking burden, and the older woman snatched up a kitchen knife from the table.

Things had turned suddenly much more dangerous.

Griz snatched up the bag. "Oh, for the love of—" She marched straight up to Nicholas and swung the bag high and accurately. With a yelp, his attacker dropped off, falling to the floor with a clatter.

The older woman with the knife glanced round, distracted, and Dragan managed to grasp the wrist that held the knife. As she brought up her other fist with clear intent, Griz grasped it and twisted it up her back.

She dropped the knife, and Ingram picked it up, keeping warily away from her feet.

"Come along, boys," Alexandra said, herding them together.

"You," Griz uttered, pointing from one woman to the other, "are in so much trouble. What do you mean by keeping other people's children here? The police are on their way, and if you don't want to have assaulting a duke's daughter added to your charges, you had better keep out of my way."

Amazingly enough, for the first time since Alexandra had known her, she looked and sounded exactly like a duke's daughter, even with the wilted pink feathers falling over her face.

Sir Nicholas strode to the door, and Alexandra hurried past them with the boys. Only when they were outside did Dragan and Griz follow.

Nicholas led the way between the buildings Dragan had indicated earlier, and in a swift, silent column, they bolted for Holborn. From where, in two hired cabs, they drove to Scotland Yard.

TWO HOURS LATER, Sir Nicholas handed Alexandra down from another hackney outside New Hungerford House, and they made their weary way up the path to the front door, where Sir Nicholas let them in with his key.

The house was in darkness, save for one lamp by the door, turned down low. Sir Nicholas turned it up and used spills to light two waiting candles from it. One, he handed politely to Alexandra, who took it with a grateful murmur.

The long and exciting evening spent as his equal had made her quite comfortable in his presence, but as their fingers brushed, a jolt of fresh awareness shot through her. Ignoring it, she walked calmly to the staircase and began to climb. He walked beside her, tall and imposing, no longer just her employer but her comrade, which, for some reason, made her inconvenient feelings for him easier to bear.

"I don't know about you," he murmured, "but after an evening like that, I need a large glass of brandy."

"I could hardly blame you."

"That harpy kicked me black and blue. I am only grateful she did not scratch my eyes out."

"She was an enthusiastic but not very efficient harpy," Alexandra agreed.

They reached the landing opposite the dark drawing room. Deliberately, she did not look at it.

"Goodnight," she murmured, at the same time as Sir Nicholas said, "Will you join me?"

She drew in her breath and met his gaze. Candlelight flickered across his lean, saturnine face. "I don't think that would be a good idea," she said firmly, while she longed to go with him to the drawing room, the library, or anywhere at all.

A rueful smile tugged at his lips and her heart. "I promise, I shan't touch you. If you don't play the piano."

She should keep to her original plan and her own good advice and retire immediately to her chamber. Though it seemed somehow cowardly, as well as churlish. After all, he had more or less admitted it was the music that had led him astray.

"I would like your opinion," he said casually, "about our kidnappers."

Her heart beat drummed. She was too tired to care what it meant. "Very well," she said calmly and walked past him in the direction of the library. Making it clear there would be no music and no excuse.

He followed but reached the door in time to open it for her. The room was in darkness save for their own candles, but he moved past her, lighting more lamps before setting down his candle beside hers. He walked to the decanter on the table and poured two glasses of brandy, while she went to the armchairs and sank gratefully into one.

"Thank you." She took the proffered glass from him, making sure this time not to touch his fingers.

He took the other chair. For a moment, he sat back with a sigh of satisfaction, then leaned forward again to clink glasses with her. With his disordered hair and his grazed knuckles, in his unconventional "poetic" garb, he looked peculiarly decadent. And desirable enough to melt her heart all over again.

But she clinked glasses with the devil and drank, hoping the burning liquid would shock her into reality. But it was smooth and warm and served rather to soothe her.

"So, what *do* you think of our kidnappers?" he asked, sitting back once more.

Two police constables had brought them in while they were still at Scotland Yard with the children. The women had fled, but Inspector Harris, who had been roused from his well-earned rest and dragged across town to deal with the situation, seemed confident of finding them again. He seemed to know who they were.

"I think," Alexandra replied, "that none of them are bright enough to have arranged this. They had a clever little game going on, only taking eldest sons, presumably for maximum value, warning the parents to silence on pain of death to their children, and accepting large ransoms, after which the boys were freed unharmed and the parents still too frightened, for the most part, to tell the authorities what had happened."

"So even with the women, we do not have the whole gang," Sir Nicholas said. "Your cloaked man?"

"In the absence of anyone else. But he seemed to vanish altogether, leaving the money with our poor fools."

"Perhaps you and Ingram scared him off. Perhaps he sicked that lot on you in the clearing to be rid of you, and stayed out of the way when that didn't work." He shifted and waved his glass dismissively. "Whatever, I think we've broken up the game. He won't try it again for a long time."

"Do you think the police will still look for him?"

"I think Tizsa and Griz will." He smiled. "They are quite a pair."

An unladylike snort of laughter shook Alexandra. "When she knocked that woman off your back with the carpetbag...!"

Nicholas grinned. "I was very grateful. I have no idea how to fight women, though you'd think I'd have learned by now."

She took another sip of brandy. "Do women attack you very often?"

"No." The smile died on his lips. "Though Eva—Evelina's mother—used to throw things." He stroked his jaw. "And she had quite an effective right hook."

Alexandra gazed at him. "Did you deserve it?"

"Sometimes," he admitted. "But usually not."

"Why did you stay with her?" she blurted.

"Oh, I didn't. But then, there was Evelina." He broke off with a shrug and drank. "I regret nothing because of Evelina."

An ache grew in Alexandra's heart. She wondered how much he had loved Evelina's mother, how much he had been hurt by her behavior, and yet was forced to keep seeing her in order to see his daughter.

He drew in a sharp breath. "Evelina loved her mother, but Eva was not kind to her either. It was Eva who shut her in a dark cupboard for whining and then went out and forgot about her. The maid found her the next morning. Eva thought a little petting and a nice present would make everything right again, but it didn't. That is when I found Anna and insisted she live with them to look after Evelina."

Alexandra swallowed. No wonder he refused to allow the child to be locked alone in a room under any circumstances. There were many forms of cruelty.

"Was your duel over Evelina's mother?" The words tumbled out with her sudden thought, appalling her. It seemed she had become too comfortable with him.

His gaze snapped up from his glass to her face, but he looked more rueful than angry. "You heard about that? No, the duel was fought long before I ever met Eva, when I was still young enough to imagine I had to kill a man to prove my honor. Or at least be prepared to wound or die. It was a waste of life, over a trivial quarrel that should never—" He broke off, his lips twisting. "I still see his face when I close my eyes. I always will."

"I'm sorry," she whispered.

"Don't be. Not for me, at any rate." He drew a quick breath. "You should probably know that, too, was one of Eva's weapons. She knew it hurt me, so she told Evelina I had murdered someone. Evelina didn't know what it meant, but she would repeat it occasionally. I expect she still does."

Alexandra looked away as anger with Evelina's dead mother rose painfully to her chest. She sipped her brandy and was aware of him raising his own glass to his lips.

"Those boys tonight were not frightened or hurt," Nicholas said, abruptly changing the subject. "They were well-cared for."

"Apart from the dirt and the imprisonment."

"Most boys do not notice dirt. And the imprisonment seemed to have been made into a game, like extended hide-and-seek. There were always several children at a time, so they had company. Two of them tonight even knew each other before they were kidnapped. Before they could tire very much of the adventure, they seem to have been returned to their parents for considerable amounts of money, judging by Henry's ransom."

He glanced up and smiled at her, depriving her of breath. "I don't know whether or not I should apologize for dragging you into this mess."

"No, for I went willingly. And it was fun—in a very strange way. Besides, it is less of a mess now. Your nephew is home with his parents, and three more boys are back with theirs without having to pay a ransom."

The smile lingered on his lips and in his eyes. "You took the nasty, seamy side of life in your stride."

"So did you."

"Well, it is hardly new to me. When I first ran away from home, I lived among the poorest and saw the worst—and the best—of life. What is your excuse?"

She hesitated, fighting a sudden desire to tell him everything. The habit of secrecy was well ingrained. So, she compromised. "Living with my father was not all salons and palaces and concert halls. I, too, saw different aspects of the world. An itinerant musician does not earn a steady income. Besides which, my father was given to gambling and to luxury when he could obtain it."

"And when he couldn't?"

She shrugged. "Grubby lodgings." Until he could fleece some unsuspecting music lover or worm his way into the home of a wealthy, tolerant patron. To say nothing of the outright theft. But she would not think of that.

She blinked the images away and found Sir Nicholas's perceptive gaze on her face.

"Someday, we must compare grubby lodgings," he said humorously. "I am glad, at least, to see you out of such a situation now."

She nodded. "I used to remind myself of the worst times when I felt put upon as a governess. Even with the Laceys, I had a safe and decent home and never went hungry." She set down the brandy, afraid she was talking too much. "Thank you for the brandy. I must go to bed now, or I will be quite useless tomorrow."

He rose when she did. "Take an extra hour in the morning. Anna will cope if I cannot be there."

"No," she said at once, "I would rather be there." The necessity of being indispensable to the family who employed her was hard to overlook. Besides which, stability and routine were good for Evelina.

"Very well." He stood too close to her, gazing down at her but making no attempt to touch her.

She wondered what would happen if she touched him. If she reached up and brushed her lips across his, would his mouth fasten to hers again in another of those wild kisses? Would he jerk away, his honor offended by her boldness?

Well, she was not bold enough to find out. Or face the consequences of either.

"Goodnight, Sir Nicholas," she said formally, moving hastily away from him.

"Good night, Alexandra Battle."

It took peculiar effort to leave him, and yet when she closed the door on him and made her way upstairs to bed, she found she was smiling because they were friends.

SHE DID SLEEP later than normal the following morning, which meant she had little time to herself before she had to throw on her clothes, cram her hair into some kind of order, and stagger downstairs to the schoolroom for breakfast with the unreasonably lively Evelina. For the first time, she asked for more coffee.

However, they began lessons on time, which was a matter of pride for Alexandra. While Evelina worked on her arithmetic exercises, Alexandra began planning a game that would use the globe in the corner to teach Evelina about other countries and their location compared to Britain. Keeping busy was the only way she knew to prevent her mind dwelling on Sir Nicholas.

A knock on the schoolroom door made her heart leap with hope, before she remembered that Sir Nicholas never knocked, and scolded herself for foolishness. It was Clara who entered at her bidding.

"Beg your pardon, Miss. Sir Nicholas is asking for a few moments of your time."

Evelina looked up so eagerly that the maid added apologetically, "Just Miss Battle. It's a grown-up meeting."

"Of course," Alexandra said calmly, hoping this would not initiate a tantrum. "Evelina, see if you can finish the exercise before I return, and if it's very neat and all correct, we can put it aside to show your father later on so that he can see how well you are doing."

The stratagem seemed to work, for by the time she had gone into the playroom to ask Anna to keep an eye on the child, there were no sounds of temper.

Sir Nicholas, of course, was in the library. Crossing the first-floor landing, she was surprised, when she glanced downstairs, to see the figures of two uniformed policemen in the hall. The reason became plain, for on entering the library with a drumming heart, she found Inspector Harris with Sir Nicholas.

Both men rose from the large desk when she entered.

"Good morning, ma'am," Inspector Harris said with a short bow. "I have just been telling Sir Nicholas how we've found the two women and talked to them, as well as to the children you freed. And Henry Swan. Mr. Ralph Swan has identified one of the men as the kidnapper who brought Ralph to meet him and took the ransom."

Alexandra sat in the chair which had already been set for her at the side of the desk between the inspector and Sir Nicholas. For some reason, it struck her that he could thus see both of them at the same time.

"How are the children?" she asked.

"Very well, all things considered," Harris replied. "Surprisingly so. None of them were hurt, nor even particularly frightened by their experience. No one hit them or tied them up, or even gagged them. In fact, the women played with them, fed them well, and generally looked after them. Their imprisonment was made into a game, a joke which they'd soon get to appreciate."

Alexandra nodded. "Yes, that's the impression they gave us."

"Neither the men who took them nor the women who looked after them, so much as clipped them round the ear for talking too loudly or squabbling." Harris smiled thinly. "That isn't natural."

"Sir, I never strike my pupils," Alexandra said, faintly amused.

"Forgive me, but you're employed by their parents. Men like Gorey and Burke—the kidnappers—are not known for keeping their hands to themselves. And you may trust me when I tell you the women are not known for the gentle natures."

"Oh, we definitely trust you on that score," Sir Nicholas murmured, rubbing his neck beneath the collar where the older woman had tried to strangle him.

"So why in the four days he was away, did Henry Swan not receive so much as a slap on the wrist? In the two and three days, the other boys were there, not so much as a shove. They're well brought up children, but they *are* children, and you're not telling me they behaved *that* well for *that* length of time."

"Your point being?" Sir Nicholas asked impatiently.

"That someone instructed the adults to treat them well," Alexandra said slowly. She glanced at Sir Nicholas triumphantly. "The cloaked man, just as we said! Have you found him, Inspector?"

"Certainly, someone was giving the orders," Harris said, without answering the question. "Gorey and Burke didn't plan these abductions. They're not capable of it. Neither are the women. Someone was pulling their strings, keeping an eye on them, too. Henry Swan recalls a third man being in that room on two different occasions. One was during the night when he probably came to pick up someone else's ransom. The other was in daylight, but the women kept the boys at the back, near their beds, and they never saw the man's face, only his back."

"Did he wear a cloak?" Alexandra asked eagerly.

"They didn't say," Harris replied. "However, they all claimed that he didn't speak like the others."

Alexandra frowned. "You mean, he had a different accent? From where? Was he foreign?"

"No, he was a gentleman." Harris smiled faintly at Sir Nicholas. "Like you."

Alexandra's stomach seemed to plunge. Although the inspector was not quite accusing, neither was he quite joking.

Nicholas's brows flew up in surprise. "In nothing but accent, I assure you. I have never knowingly hurt a child in my life. At least, not since I stopped being one."

Harris held his haughty gaze. "Have we not just established the wonder of these children not being hurt?"

Sir Nicholas stared, then flung himself back in his chair. "Are you actually accusing me, Inspector?"

"That is nonsense!" Alexandra burst out. "It was he who rescued them!"

"Perhaps because the game was up," Harris said softly. "And he'd done what he'd really intended all along—made his brother suffer."

Alexandra could not quite believe her ears. She could find no words nor breath with which to utter them.

Nicholas's lips curled. "Then what were all the other children? Practice?"

"Perhaps," Harris replied with a shrug. "I never heard that you were averse to making money."

"But did you ever hear I did so by breaking the law of whatever land I was in?"

"No," Harris admitted. "Which is one reason I am sitting here talking to you rather than arresting you."

"The other reason being that you have no evidence against me," Nicholas said dryly.

"Not yet," Harris agreed.

"I have never heard such nonsense in my life!" Alexandra burst out. "If you had seen him strike that man, if you had seen that awful woman clinging to his back, trying to strangle him, you wouldn't dream of uttering such arrant rubbish!"

"A spirited defense," Harris allowed. "Tell me about this incident when a gathering of men threatened you and Mr. Ingram."

Alexandra blinked at the sudden change of subject. "It was on that waste ground close to where we found the children. Men loomed out of the darkness, surrounding us. It was quite frightening, and Mr. Ingram had to use his stick to ward them off. But they would easily have overcome us if Sir Nicholas had not come."

"And did what?" Harris asked curiously. "Set about all of them at once with a club? Threatened them with a pistol?"

"No. He just commanded them to leave us alone, and they were so surprised, and not quite sure, I suppose, what power he held, that they backed off, and we escaped."

"Yes, that is more or less what Mr. Ingram said." Harris fixed her with his very sharp eyes. "Did this not seem odd to you?"

"I was too grateful to be curious. Though it did strike me it might have been his accent—" She broke off, her eyes widening.

Harris smiled faintly. "His accent. And his appearance. Is it not likely the men knew and feared him because he was a commanding presence in their world? A man who made criminal money for all who served him?"

Alexandra blinked several times. "Well, yes," she admitted. "That would be a possibility, were it not for the fact that I saw Sir Nicholas and the cloaked man in different places at exactly the same time. Sir Nicholas could not possibly be the cloaked man."

"But your cloaked man could be anyone. There is no proof he went anywhere near the children. You had no reason to suspect him, except that he was in the wrong place at the wrong time."

"And one of the abductors nodded to him," Alexandra pointed out.

Harris shrugged. "You *think* he did. Mr. Ingram saw none of this. It was you who led the pursuit of the man, and he followed because he was charged by Sir Nicholas with your protection."

"What exactly are you saying now?" Sir Nicholas snapped.

"That it is also possible that Miss Battle is your ally. That she made up the cloaked man to avert suspicion from you."

A frightening surge of anger flamed in Sir Nicholas's eyes, and thinned his lips. And yet, he spoke with perfect calm. "Let me be sure I understand this. You are accusing me of kidnapping a bunch of children, including my own nephew, for ransom, just to be able to wreak some bizarre vengeance on my brother? And you are further accusing Miss Battle, who has been with us for barely a week, of being my accomplice?"

Harris should have shriveled beneath that contempt. He didn't, though, neither did he raise his voice. "No, sir. Not yet. I am merely explaining why I would like your permission to search your house. So that I can eliminate you from my list of suspects and move on."

Sir Nicholas's lips curved into a dangerous smile. "My permission," he repeated. "Because you do not have the evidence to warrant such a search."

"I do not. But an innocent man would be happy to be free of suspicion."

"An innocent man has no need to allow the ransacking of his home, the frightening of his daughter, or the upsetting of his servants. I do not grant permission."

That surprised Alexandra. She had expected him to maintain his contempt while allowing Inspector Harris to do his worst.

"What exactly do you hope to find?" she asked the inspector. "More children? Carpetbags full of money?"

"Something like that," Harris said steadily, "though I assure you, I hope for no such thing. I merely wish to search for them."

"Well, you can't," Sir Nicholas said, standing to indicate the interview was at an end. "Good morning, Inspector."

Harris rose, too, though more slowly. "I would like you to think about it, sir. It is the quickest way to remove suspicion."

"Your suspicions do not interest me." Sir Nicholas uttered. "My money is on Mr. Tizsa to discover the true culprit."

Although he had not rung, James appeared at the door.

Sir Nicholas remained behind his desk. "James will show you out, Inspector. Miss Battle, thank you for your time. Please, do not let us keep you longer from your duties."

He was not rude, but from a friend, such an abrupt dismissal cut her to the heart. She left wordlessly, without looking back at either Sir Nicholas or the inspector, who was descending the stairs without noticeable hurry, James close on his heels.

CHAPTER SEVENTEEN

S OMEHOW, ALEXANDRA KEPT her focus on Evelina and teaching for the rest of the day, even when they played in the garden and went for a walk.

Only in her free time before dinner did she sit down and write a panicked note to Griz, informing her of Inspector Harris's visit and his ridiculous suspicion of Sir Nicholas and herself. But as she wrote down his arguments, she began to see their logic, and how what they had done and what had happened to them appeared to fit the inspector's theory.

She stopped writing and sat back, clutching her hair. She knew she was innocent. And she believed in Sir Nicholas's innocence, too, even if she did not *know* it. But that crowd of men had obeyed him. She had put it down to his force of presence, but she could see the unlikelihood. And the treatment of the kidnapped children was equally improbable. Surely, no normal villain would have taken quite such care of them. And Sir Nicholas *had* insisted on accompanying Dragan that night. To Harris, he had done it to be seen as the rescuer, not the chief perpetrator, to avert suspicion, instead of which it seemed to have heaped accusations on his head.

She did not believe those suspicions. Of course, she did not. And yet, he had not let Harris search the house. The police would hardly have "ransacked" a gentleman's property. And Alexandra could easily have taken Evelina out the way for a couple of hours, so none of his reasons for refusing were truly valid. It was his right, of course, at this stage, at least. But it was odd.

She got up, pacing restlessly to the window. She could see over the garden wall to the mews lane behind. A man loitered, leaning against the fence opposite. And yet he did not look like a groom or a coach-man nor like one of the local tradesmen. He was, she suspected, a policeman. There was probably another at the front, watching to see if Sir Nicholas tried to smuggle anything—or anyone—out of the house.

They believe it. They truly believe it.

She went back to her desk and snatched up the letter to Griz, tear-ing it into tiny pieces, which she swept into a drawer. Her stomach churning, she changed for dinner and re-brushed and pinned her tangled hair. Then, she walked to the schoolroom to find Evelina had already gone downstairs. Did Sir Nicholas mean to join them for dinner?

The library door was open when she reached the landing. And she could hear Evelina's voice piping up, "...to dine with us, Papa?"

"Not tonight, minx," he said, sounding genuinely sorry. "I'm going to this dreadful party."

"Why would you, if it's going to be dreadful?" Evelina asked.

"Good question," he said. "To show my face is the only answer I have. To any of it. I'll look in on you when I come home, though."

"Wake me up!" she begged.

He laughed. "No, I won't do that, but I'll leave something by your bedside. Off you go, squib. I can hear your tummy rumbling from here."

Alexandra hurried toward the dining room, where Evelina joined her a moment or two later.

After dinner, they again paid a visit to Lady Nora, who looked a little brighter than the last time they had seen her.

"Papa has gone out," Evelina told her. "To some dreadful party. Mrs. Jenner invited him. She came here the other day and stopped

Miss Battle and me playing the piano."

"Caroline Jenner?" Lady Nora said, apparently amused. "She is wasting her time. She will never hold him."

"Hold him where?" Evelina asked.

Lady Nora released a breath of laughter. "It's just a saying. Don't regard it or me. Tell me about your day."

Ten minutes later, Anna came looking for Evelina, who was quite ready to go to her own rooms for some quiet play and stories before bed.

"Perhaps you could stay another few minutes?" Lady Nora said unexpectedly when Alexandra stood to leave, too.

"Of course, if you are not too tired. Can I bring you anything?"

"Just your company. I thrive on society and have known so little recently, for obvious reasons."

"I'm glad to see you looking a little better today."

The pain-filled eyes regarded her with unexpected perception. "While you look as if you have the cares of the world on your shoulders. She is a challenging child, I believe, but she seems much more contented since you came."

"I am glad."

"So does he."

"Who?" Alexandra asked, bewildered.

"Nicholas, of course."

Warm blood seeped into Alexandra's face. She hoped the gloom hid it from Lady Nora. "I think he is pleased to have his worry over Evelina eased a little."

Lady Nora nodded. "Of course, there is that. You are good with the child. You are good with him, too."

"Well, despite a few rocky moments, he has not yet dismissed me," Alexandra said lightly.

"He likes you because you stand up to him. But he looks at you for quite other reasons."

Alexandra scrambled for some other topic of conversation. She did want to think of him looking at her in any way at all. And yet she did, all the time.

"I embarrass you," Lady Nora observed.

"I am the governess," Alexandra said, low. "It is not appropriate to speculate on such matters, even in fun."

"Oh, I wasn't joking. I have no time for jokes, Miss Battle. I am dying, and I would die more peacefully if I knew you were there to care for him."

"I will care for Evelina, who will care for him. I am the governess."

"So you said." Again, she sounded faintly amused. "You should know—perhaps you already do—that Nicholas does not care for differences in rank, birth, or social status. If he likes you, he likes you." She must have caught some desperate expression in Alexandra's face, for she smiled and said, "I am not hurt. Why should you suppose I could be hurt by his affection for you?"

She was wrong, of course she was, but if she wished to speak plainly, Alexandra rarely backed off.

"Because I know you and he ran away together when you were very young, and that he deserted you in Paris," she said flatly. "Not his finest hour."

"Then you know nothing. He was very young. I was—as I still am—eight years older. And he didn't desert me. I used him as the means of escaping my vile husband, and then I deserted him in Paris. For a very talented artist, as it happens, who was more suited to me in age and character."

Alexandra blinked to cover her surprise.

"You will think me heartless now. But you already know the narrowness of the paths we women are permitted to walk. I was ruined and could never go home. I never wanted to, but in my defense, I thought Nicholas would. He certainly *could* have, but he never did. He went off and made his fortune, just as he said he would, only he did it without me, without anyone."

Alexandra took it in, readjusting what she knew of Sir Nicholas to Lady Nora's story. "What happened to your artist?" she asked at last.

"He died. And I moved on, through the demimonde. Occasionally, I met Nicholas again. I liked to keep up with his life and his successes."

"Did you regret leaving him?"

Lady Nora shook her head emphatically. "No. It was the making of both of us. But he loved me once, and so he looks after me now when the world has turned its back on me. *That* is your Nicholas."

"He is not mine," she whispered in sudden distress.

"Then make him so. He needs you. And bless you, child, I know you will never admit it, but you love him. I hear it in your voice. Don't tell me again that you are the governess."

Alexandra gave a watery laugh and dashed her hand across her eyes. "I somehow imagined he left you for Evelina's mother."

"Lord, no, there were many years between those relationships. And Evelina's mother was hardly the best decision he ever made, either. The woman was beautiful and sang like an angel, but she was volatile, unpredictable, selfish enough to make me look like a nun. I would not even be sure the child is his, though she always maintained it, and he acknowledges her. He loves her as his own."

Lady Nora lapsed into silence. Her eyes began to close.

"Why do you tell me all this?" Alexandra asked, and the sick woman's eyes flew open again.

"Because he won't. Because you *should* know." She smiled, moving her thin, papery hand. Alexandra put hers into it, and Lady Nora's fingers grasped and released her.

"She'll sleep now," Spencer said, bustling over.

Alexandra left with her mind buzzing. She did not put a great deal of faith in the dying woman's reading of Sir Nicholas's affections for her. But what she had said of his past was more than interesting. This was a man who took care of a child who might not be his, of an old lover who had used him and left him. This was a man with an over-developed sense of responsibility. Not, surely, a man who took other people's children away and only gave them back for money.

IT TOOK A long time for Alexandra to fall asleep that night. Her mind flitted from problem to problem concerning the cloaked man and the police suspicion of Sir Nicholas. A well-spoken man would certainly stand out in the slums of St. Giles, but that didn't make him a gentleman. It certainly didn't make him Nicholas Swan, who, in his own practical, understated fashion, seemed to take care of everyone. As far as she knew, he had made no effort to take control of his inherited property from his brother. And he did not appear to need more money. He just would not endanger other people's children for money or any other reward.

Why could the police not see that?

Did Griz and Dragan? Were they suspicious? Had they put the notion into Inspector Harris's head? Surely they could not be so...so blind, foolish, wrong-headed, so...

Besotted, she finished bitterly. And clearly, *they* were not.

Her thoughts strayed to the soiree Sir Nicholas was attending. She expected Mrs. Jenner was all over him, taking possessive hold of his arm, holding discreet and sophisticated conversation, inveigling him into some private corner to force his hand, perhaps, into marriage. She couldn't imagine Sir Nicholas being caught in such a way...unless he wanted to be.

Restlessly, she turned over, punching the pillow to make it more comfortable. Sir Nicholas would marry one day. She would have to get used to that idea, to be able to accept it without this foolish jealousy eating into her. Caroline Jenner did not deserve him. She did not love him. She wanted to be Lady Swan, married to one of the wealthiest men in the country. And she did not like Evelina. She would work to have her sent away to school, to keep her away while she had children of her own to distract Sir Nicholas.

Nicholas would not be distracted. He would never send Evelina away.

Would the Jenner woman want him if she knew what Inspector Harris had accused him of? Would she defend him?

She would never get the chance. He does not look at her. He could not... And it makes no difference to me. Whatever Lady Nora says, I am only the governess.

With the thoughts swirling and circling like vultures, she, at last, fell into exhausted sleep.

She woke again to darkness and that strange, rhythmic clanking she had heard before. Annoyed, for it seemed she would never get any sleep, she lit her bedside lamp and flounced out of bed. A glance at her watch told her it was after three in the morning. Everyone, even Sir Nicholas, would surely be tucked up in bed. Did no one but her ever hear this noise? Or had they learned to ignore it?

She thrust her arms into her robe, left the lamp, and took a lit candle with her as she left the room. As on her first night here, the sound seemed to fade as she closed the door and walked toward the stairs. But since she was sure it had been coming from below, she descended the staircase, studiously ignoring the library. This was no time for an unplanned encounter with Sir Nicholas.

Although I would not mind, she thought wistfully.

Yes, you would, she berated herself. *And besides, he's asleep.*

She paused for a moment on the first-floor landing. Then, sure she could hear an echo of the clanking, she began to descend further.

A sudden creak and the swish of an opening door below startled her. She fell back against the wall, almost losing her footing, and hastily shaded her candle as it threatened to go out.

From below, the clanking sound was suddenly apparent once more.

"James." Sir Nicholas's voice called from somewhere toward the back of the house. "You can go to bed after that. I'll bring the rest."

"Thank you, sir."

Frozen to the spot, Alexandra saw James walk into view, setting a lamp down on the table that stood by the chairs the policemen had sat in yesterday morning. He carried a sack-like bag over one shoulder as he walked into one of the unused rooms on the ground floor.

A door closed again somewhere, muffling the machinery sounds. Afraid one or both men would find her skulking on the stairs, she fled back up, hoping she was unseen and unheard.

But the incident hardly quenched her curiosity. What were they up to? And *where* were they up to it? She had been down to the kitchen with Evelina to "help" Cook bake some cakes. There had been no sign of any kind of machinery that could make that kind of noise, just the usual oven and stove. And access to the cellars.

Her heart beat fast as she closed her bedchamber door once more and blew out the candle.

Perhaps Harris thought he kept his extorted money and more abducted children in those cellars. Or used child labor to operate whatever that machine was. Except Griz and Dragan knew different-ly—a man of radical, even revolutionary principles would hardly do such a thing.

And yet, he was clearly up to something.

Before she retired, she peered out of her window. She could see no one in the garden, and the policeman who had been skulking in the mews was no longer visible either.

Alexandra dropped the curtain and padded back into bed. Deter-minedly, she closed her eyes to sleep, for she wanted to be up early enough to investigate both the room with the sack and the servants' hall.

ALTHOUGH SHE SLEPT a little later than she meant to, she still rose well before breakfast time in the schoolroom. Hastily washed and dressed, she walked briskly downstairs and, finding the hallway deserted, she went straight across, and into the room James had entered several hours before.

It was empty.

There were shutters across the window, but no curtains, no furniture, no sacks. Layers of dust crunched under her feet. Perplexed, she gazed around her, wondering if there was a trapdoor from here into the cellar or some way into the garden.

The shutters parted easily to her touch. Behind them, the window was grimy and locked and looked as if it hadn't been opened in decades. The floorboards were grubby and a bit uneven but showed no obvious signs of disguising a door of any kind.

Then she paused. By the light from the doorway, she could see scuff marks in the dust and a cleaner patch. As though a sack, or sacks, had lifted the dirt from the floor.

But whatever had been there was gone.

Frustrated, she left the room and walked purposefully to the green baize-covered door. She had not gone far along the passage that divided the servants' hall from the kitchen when Mrs. Dart emerged from her sitting room and stopped, clearly startled to see her.

"Miss Battle! What brings you down here?"

"I was looking for you," Alexandra said promptly. "I hear strange noises at night, sometimes, a bit like machinery of some kind. What on earth could that be?"

Mrs. Dart didn't look remotely furtive. "Probably wind and rain in the chimneys," she replied. "They make funny noises sometimes, especially with the fires not being lit in summer. It's a mad old house!"

Alexandra smiled back. "I wondered if it was coming from the cellar."

Mrs. Dart laughed. "No room in there—look." She lifted a large key from the loop at her waist and walked swiftly to the door at the end of the passage, where she inserted the key and threw the door wide.

Alexandra glanced in and saw all four walls of a small, cavernous room lined with racks of wine and spirits and casks of ale.

"Crammed to the gunnels with wine," Mrs. Dart said cheerfully. "I tell Sir Nicholas he'll never drink it all, but there it is!"

"Are there no other cellars? I'm sure Sir Nicholas mentioned there were. They must stretch under the house and part of the garden, too."

"Oh, they're all blocked off. Even before the incident with Evelina, no one could get into the other house cellars."

You mean you don't have a key to them. But I'll bet Sir Nicholas does. And James.

"Oh, Sir Nicholas left a note for you," Mrs. Dart said suddenly. "About dinner tonight. It's in the schoolroom—the note, I mean, not the dinner!"

Laughing, she locked the cellar door again, and Alexandra, having run out of time, left the servants' quarters for the schoolroom, trying not to speculate on what Sir Nicholas had to say about dinner.

It tended toward the curt, as did most of his communications. It seemed he had encountered his brother at Mrs. Jenner's and invited him to dinner, along with his wife and three children. He suggested the children have their dinner party in the schoolroom for the sake of his civilized guests, supervised by Anna.

He didn't even trouble to sign it, although he had added a postscript at the bottom of the page, to the effect that he meant also to invite Mr. and Mrs....

She turned the page over. *Mr. and Mrs. Tizsa.*

She wondered if she would get the chance to consult with Griz before she read the second postscript.

By the way, you have grasped that you will be in the dining room and not in the schoolroom? You are the nearest thing I have to a hostess.

ALTHOUGH RATHER A noxious fog was coming off the Thames, Alexandra found it something of a relief to escape the schoolroom and take Evelina shopping to see if she could find a pretty new ribbon for her hair. Mrs. Dart had mentioned a little shop off the Strand, where they did indeed find pretty, embroidered pink ribbon. Alexandra bought a length with the money Sir Nicholas had given her and then decided to go home via Hungerford Market.

Evelina was not much interested in fruit and vegetables, and she wrinkled her nose as they descended the steps toward the smelly fish market, but she did gaze curiously at the stallholders and the buyers.

As they pushed through the fish stalls toward the river, Alexandra felt her skin prickle as though she were being watched. But Evelina bounced happily at her hand, and James still hovered watchfully behind. She squeezed past an enormously fat woman, who was clearly extremely particular about which fish she was prepared to buy.

Abruptly, instinct drew Alexandra's gaze from the woman, past the stall-keeper to the other side. And there, bold as brass, stood her father.

CHAPTER EIGHTEEN

"THIS IS THE place?" Griz followed Inspector Harris through the door. It had been locked, but one of Harris's men had put his shoulder to it.

"According to Betty Bryce," Harris replied, looking about him, "the younger of the women we arrested. She claims to have come here on a couple of occasions, that Ricco, the man who ordered and arranged the abductions, was definitely living here."

"He doesn't appear to be here now," Dragan observed.

They were in a suite of three decent rooms, including a separate bedchamber and kitchen, a bit of a luxury for this part of town. It was clean and tidy and decently furnished. And when Griz pulled open the door of a wardrobe, she found two smart suits of clothes hanging there.

"He doesn't seem to have gone far," she said. She felt the fabric of the coat. "Good quality."

"I'm sure," Harris said ironically. "And I doubt he's gone farther than Hungerford. They're about Swan's size, too."

"I do not see Sir Nicholas as the villain," Dragan stated, looking under the bed.

"Nor do I," Griz said. "Alex trusts him. And if you had seen how upset he was about his own daughter's disappearance—"

"I did see," Harris interrupted. "And in my opinion, that tells against him. He didn't want his own child hurt. Nor anyone else's.

Those boys you freed were well fed and entertained. They weren't remotely frightened, and that all came from *this* man's orders."

"Ricco," Dragan said thoughtfully. "An unusual name."

"Made up," Harris said with certainty. "It means *rich* in Italian. He's having a laugh at the ignorant thieves working for him."

"That doesn't sound like Sir Nicholas either," Griz said.

"No, but he's lived most of his adult life in Italy," Harris retorted. "And everyone says this Ricco is English, not foreign." He strode off into the kitchen to search there.

"If he's left everything," Griz said thoughtfully, opening a drawer, "he'll be back."

"Maybe he took the important things, like carpetbags full of money, and fled."

"But not to Hungerford House." Griz rifled the next drawers, which were mostly empty apart from a couple of shirts, collars, and ties. "Surely Harris is wrong about that."

"Yes." Dragan hefted up the mattress and let it fall again with a sigh.

"He could have saved himself—and Alex—a good deal of trouble," Griz said, shutting the last drawer with force, "if he had just let the inspector search the house as he wanted. I don't understand why he didn't."

"I do," Dragan said vaguely, walking slowly across the room and trying the balance of all the floorboards.

Griz joined him, but none of the boards seemed to be loose. "Wretched pride, I suppose. Did you try the wardrobe base?"

"Yes."

Together, they left the bedroom and walked through the rest of the rooms, where Harris and his men were searching the furniture with no more luck.

"There's nothing," Harris said with dissatisfaction as they continued testing the floorboards. "Nothing but Betty's word to connect whoever lives here with the kidnapped boys. No ransom notes, though there are pens, ink, and paper, no rolls of money or children's stolen toys."

"No, he kept the children, all the actual crimes away from himself," Dragan said. "The men took the children at his orders, and the women looked after them. He might have watched the exchanges of boys for money, but it was men who made them."

Harris nodded. "He came later to collect the money and give the others their share. Betty says he wasn't ungenerous. It's just a pity he wasn't there to collect when you barged in. In fact, Betty was surprised he wasn't there by that time."

"He knew Miss Battle and Mr. Ingram were following him," Griz said firmly. "He took care in his approach and probably saw us lurking around Betty's door."

"Or he was with you," Harris said stubbornly.

"Then why did none of the villains recognize him?" Dragan asked mildly. He followed the floorboards out of the sitting room and into the narrow hallway. "Why not give him up when he was clearly responsible for their arrest?"

Harris glared at the floorboards as if daring them not to move. "I don't believe they knew. It wasn't exactly bright in there. They just saw a man barging in and fighting. I'm sure he altered his posture and manner and even his accent. Or perhaps they trust him so implicitly, they go along with everything he does, convinced he'll reward them in the end. I don't know. I *do* know it's odd for a man of his birth and wealth to be living in that house in that location. If he doesn't want to evict his brother from Brook Street—and I would have thought he would enjoy doing so!—why doesn't he just buy another property? Not as if he can't afford it."

"No, but you can't accuse a man of kidnapping just because you don't like his house," Griz said. "*None* of these wretched floorboards are loose."

Dragan paused and looked at her. "Which is itself odd. This place is pretty decent for its location, but you would expect the odd creak." His breath caught. "Move out of the light, if you please, inspector…" He crouched down, inspecting the boards more closely before moving awkwardly forward.

"What are we looking for?" Griz asked, bewildered but game.

Behind them, the constables snickered, until Harris cast them a glower.

"Shiny, new nails," Dragan replied. "I think he suspected the police might trace him here and search. So, he nailed his treasure in with the intention of coming back when the police give up and leave."

"Or took it away and doesn't care," Griz argued.

"Also possible," Dragan admitted. "But a man like that *must* have a hiding place, and we certainly haven't found it. Griz, is there a lantern?"

Wordlessly, Griz lit one and brought it to her husband in the dark corner behind the kitchen door. The police constables looked on with amusement and some doubt, though the inspector wasn't laughing. Especially not when Dragan looked up with one of his rare, dazzling smiles that still made butterflies gambol in her stomach.

He took out his penknife and began prizing out nails. Two minutes later, a floorboard was lifted, and from underneath it, Dragan pulled out an oiled canvas bag. It looked heavy, but he tossed it up to Harris, who pulled it open to reveal rolls of banknotes.

"A few ransoms, I'd say," the inspector remarked, hefting it in one hand.

As SOON AS she saw her father standing there, in the middle of the fish market, the years fell away, and the old deluge of frustration, anger, and hopeless love flooded her. She saw at once that he looked well.

Tired and a little creased, but well. His clothes were decent, too, those of a casual gentleman wasting time.

Wasting *her* time. *Spoiling* her time. Again.

He was not remotely surprised to see her. Had he known she was in the area? Or was he here by some unkind accident and spotted her from afar? Either way, her duty was to Evelina, and she deliberately looked away from him to march on to the steps.

When she next spared him a glance, he had moved to the next stall. He held a walking cane in one hand, which he tapped lightly on the ground twice. He would stay there until they could speak.

Why do you do this to me now? Am I never to be free of you?

And yet, as always, the fury came with pleasure because she had seen him again. Because he was her father.

Although she tried very hard to pay attention, the short journey home passed in something of a blur. She smiled at Evelina's innocent pleasure in her new ribbon, though she barely heard the words, and somehow, she got through tea in the schoolroom. From then, as Evelina returned to Anna's care, Alexandra was more or less free.

Seizing her bonnet and shawl, she walked swiftly along the passage, downstairs, across the hall, and out of the front door once more. It was not far to the market, but her stomach felt as if a stone sat in it, weighing her down.

She found Alexander Battle easily enough, sitting at the side of the steps up to the fish market, his hat off and his face turned up to the sun. He hadn't been worried that she wouldn't come. He had known she would.

"What a fetching sight," she remarked, "for a dead man. What do you want, Papa?"

He smiled without opening his eyes. "Is that any way to greet a parent? I'm disappointed in you, too, my dear. I had hoped to see you established in Mayfair, not *Hungerford*."

"I don't have long," she said impatiently. "Why are you here?"

He opened his eyes and patted the step beside him. Alexandra stayed standing where she was. He sighed. "I need a favor."

"Sell your coat."

"It is not money," he said with dignity. "As it happens, I am currently in funds. However, I do find myself—temporarily—without a roof over my head."

She stared at him. "The city is full of hotels, hostels, common lodging houses, take your pick."

"Even if I were prepared to tolerate a common lodging house, I doubt I could cram myself in. And there are reasons I would rather lie low."

"Of course there are. What do you expect me to do?"

"You have a decent lodging close by, I presume."

"You expect me to take you to dinner with my employer's family? And introduce you as what? The ghost of my father? A long-lost uncle?"

"Very kind of you," her father said sarcastically, "but I shan't embarrass you or your employer. I shall merely pass the time in your rooms, sleeping. And in the morning, I shall be gone about my own arrangements."

"Merely," she repeated. "Papa, I am the governess, not a guest. I don't have a suite of rooms at my disposal. I have one room, and the house is full of servants. My pupil *visits* me in that room."

"Lexie, I wouldn't ask if I wasn't desperate. I have nowhere else to go."

"Yes, you do," she retorted. "You always do."

He rose to his feet and nudged her gently with his elbow. "Is that a *yes?*"

"I suppose it must be," she said bitterly, "but only because I know you'll hang around the house and cause more trouble if I refuse. But you must do exactly as I say."

Without waiting to see if he followed, she turned and walked back down the steps. After a time, as they walked up Craven Street, she said abruptly. "I will take you into the reception room as my guest, a visiting cousin, and when the coast is clear, I'll smuggle you up to my room. But if you are discovered, Papa, I will be turned off without a character reference and be as good as ruined, with no means of earning my living except that from which you always claimed to be saving me."

"I'll be good," he promised. "I hope your employer is good to you. And respectful."

For the first time, it struck her that he had taken the trouble to discover who her employer was. It mollified her a little, even warmed her. "How long have you been in England?" she asked.

"Oh, a few months," he said vaguely.

She didn't ask what he had been doing. She really didn't want to know. But she did remember the times she had imagined someone was watching her and wondered if it had been him. In his own way, he did love her.

James opened the door, looking harassed, and blinked at the sight of the slightly rumpled gentleman beside her.

"Thank you, James," she said cheerfully, stepping inside. "This is my cousin, who is passing through London. I shall take him into the reception room for half an hour."

"Very good, Miss," James replied. "Shall I have them bring tea? A glass of sherry?"

"Sherry would be most welcome," her father said predictably.

"Thank you," Alexandra murmured, leading her father into the uncomfortable room she had waited in when she first arrived.

"I must say, I'd hoped for something a bit better for you," he said, looking about him with displeasure.

"Sir Nicholas has not long moved in," she snapped. "And you may believe it is considerably better than my first post."

"I did try to warn you about the Laceys."

"There are not a lot of choices available to a lady whose father only escaped the gallows by supposedly dying of natural causes." There was more to say, but she swallowed it back. It was not the sort of conversation she wanted to be overheard.

"I did foul things up a little," he admitted, the master of understatement.

Footstep heralded James with a tray on which resided a decanter and two glasses. He placed it on the small, bare table beside her father and poured a glass, which he presented to the guest with a bow. "And for you, Miss?"

"No, thank you," she said hastily. "I won't trouble you further, James. I know you're busy."

James hurried off again.

"Why so busy?" her father asked when he had taken an appreciative sip of the sherry. "What are they flapping about?"

"Nothing, just a family dinner party."

"Family?"

"Sir Nicholas's brother, his wife, and children. Why do you care?"

"I don't," he assured her. "But I promise to stay well out of the way. This sherry is really very good." He poured himself another.

After a few moments, she rose. "Wait there." She walked into the hall, looking and listening. Most of the servants' work would be in the kitchen, and things would be carried up via the separate servants' staircase, but there was always the danger of being seen from the dining room or even the drawing room.

But all seemed quiet for the moment. She beckoned her father, who drained his glass and set it down reluctantly. Together they crept upstairs, Alexandra straining to hear any sounds. Abruptly, just as they reached the half-landing, Clara flew out of the dining room and hurried toward the drawing room.

Quick as lightening, Alexandra wrenched open the door of the walk-in cupboard and shoved her father inside. The maid turned just as she closed the door.

"Miss Battle? Is something wrong?" Clara asked anxiously.

"No, no, I just stupidly lost my footing and knocked into the cupboard," she said cheerfully. "All is well."

Clara carried on into the drawing room, leaving the door open, so she was forced to carry on upstairs without her father. Fortunately, Clara dashed out again, clutching a vase of drooping flowers, and with a quick smile, hurried past her toward the servants' stairs.

Alexandra carried on another few paces, then flew back across the hallway and coughed. When her father emerged warily from the cupboard, she beckoned urgently, and he closed the door and followed, less speedily than she would have liked.

She opened her bedchamber door with relief but remembered to look around first to make sure Evelina wasn't waiting for her there before she pulled her father inside and closed the door. She turned the key in the lock and leaned her back against the wood.

Her father grinned at her. "Confess, you have missed the old days."

"In some ways," she said tightly. "But I value my position here. I *like* these people, and I do not relish sneaking behind their backs."

"Of course not," her father soothed. He walked across to the window, checking the view, then drew the curtains. He sat down on the bed and regarded her. "So, what are your duties for the evening?"

"I suppose I shall take my pupil downstairs to greet the guests and perhaps settle her in the schoolroom afterward, although she will have her nursemaid there and possibly her cousins' nurse, too. Then I am expected to make up the numbers in the dining room."

"Excellent." He beamed and stretched out on the bed, kicking off his shoes. "See if you can't smuggle your old dad up a bit of supper. But I think I'll take a nap now."

Sighing, she kicked his shoes under the bed and drew the curtains around it. At the last moment, she tossed in the hat he'd abandoned on the bedside table, and he grunted as it clearly landed on him.

"Please don't snore," she begged. "And when I leave, I shall lock you in."

"Don't trust me, little one?"

"I don't want you frightening the children if they come looking for me!"

"Good point," he agreed after a moment. "Very well."

She didn't need his permission, but his cooperation was usually helpful.

Trying to pretend he wasn't there, she washed and changed for dinner, then brushed out her hair to pin it. Just for a moment, as she caught her gaze in the glass, she was tempted to brush her hair up into a softer, more becoming style. Nicholas liked her in this dress...

Sir Nicholas was being polite, she scolded herself, and tightened her hand on her hair once more. The usual, severe governess style would suffice.

In order to have somewhere to put the bedroom key, she dusted off an old reticule and dangled it from her wrist. It added a note of greater formality, she decided.

She glanced through the bed curtains at her father, who was clearly sound asleep. He had never used to snore. She hoped he hadn't acquired the habit in the last few years. Pulling her shoulders back, she left the room, locked the door, and dropped the key into her reticule.

She went first to the schoolroom, where a vastly excited Evelina was clearly itching to be free of Anna, tying the last ribbon in her hair.

"Hold still!" Alexandra laughed. "Considering the trouble you went to choosing those ribbons, you might as well wear them!"

Evelina subsided while Alexandra glanced around the schoolroom. The table had been set with three chairs and a baby's highchair.

When they finally proceeded downstairs, at last, Alexandra's heart was bumping uncomfortably. While she reminded Evelina to be on her best behavior and to curtsey to her aunt and uncle, she was also reminding herself that she must not take offense at any slights cast her way by Mr. or Mrs. Swan, or be hurt by any slight change in attitude on Nicholas's part. For she had told her father the truth. Whatever Nicholas had said, she was not his hostess. She was the governess and present only to even the numbers.

She had hoped to get there early and be safely ensconced before either Sir Nicholas or his guests appeared. But she could see Mrs. Swan at once, seated on a sofa with her husband standing at her side holding a glass of sherry. Beside him stood young Henry, holding the hand of his little sister.

The girl's eyes lit up when she caught sight of Evelina, but beyond a smile, she gave no sign, even when Evelina waved to her.

"Miss Battle," Nicholas acknowledged her from the table beside the door, where he had been pouring himself a drink. "Sherry?"

"Thank you," Alexandra replied. In this company, she felt she needed it. She gave Evelina's hand a little squeeze by way of reminder and released her.

Evelina immediately went to her aunt and uncle and curtseyed prettily. "Good evening, Aunt. Good evening, Uncle."

Though their smiles might have remained a little fixed, they made no objection to this mode of address.

"How very nice to see you again, Evelina," Ralph said with a trace of nervousness.

"How are you, child?" his wife managed.

"I am very well, thank you," Evelina replied. "How are you?"

But her question remained unanswered, as both adults were, at that moment, distracted by the announcement of Mr. and Mrs. Tizsa.

Evelina relaxed enough to greet the newcomers cheerfully. "'Evening, Lady Griz! Mr. Tizsa!"

Dragan actually bowed to her, which made her giggle until she remembered to curtsey back, and Griz bade her good evening in a teasing kind of way.

Dragan was obviously acquainted with Ralph, but while Nicholas performed the other introductions, the children gravitated toward each other, and the girls were soon giggling together, while Henry tried to look superior.

Mrs. Swan turned to Alexandra. "Feel free to take them to the nursery whenever you wish, Miss...um. Our nursemaid is already there with the baby."

"Oh, Evelina can take them," Nicholas said carelessly, handing Alexandra a glass with a flicker of one eyelid that looked very like a wink before he turned back to face his brother. "It's good to see Henry looking so well." He glanced after the children's fast-retreating backs. "I hope he is as unhurt by his experience as he seems."

"So far as we can tell," Ralph replied with a quick look at his wife. "There is no physical injury. Certainly, he was more than ready to come home, but he seemed surprised that we hadn't known where he was. Those villains told him—and the other boys—that it was all a game arranged by their parents to see how brave they were away from home."

"I don't think I would ever have believed such a tale," Nicholas remarked.

"No, well," Ralph said ruefully, "our father wasn't really much of a man for games. Not with children, at any rate."

It was a rare, momentary connection between the brothers, who exchanged smiles that were more of a reflected grimace. Then, into the short silence, Ralph said awkwardly, "I have not thanked you, Nicholas, for the part you played in Henry's rescue. And that of the other boys. Mr. Tizsa, of course, knows he has our undying gratitude. But so do you."

Nicholas betrayed neither gratification nor annoyance, merely smiled. "Miss Battle and Lady Grizelda did at least as much."

Ralph blinked in surprise at this shocking revelation. His wife, however, had fixed on the name.

"Lady Grizelda?" she repeated. "Mrs. Tizsa is Lady Grizelda? The Duke of Kelburn's daughter?"

"If he has not yet disowned me," Griz said lightly, sitting on the sofa beside Alexandra.

"I think he is secretly proud of you," Dragan remarked and accepted his glass from Nicholas.

"To the children," Nicholas said, raising his glass.

Everyone repeated the toast, and they all drank.

"You won't know, of course," Mrs. Swan said, "but before all this wretched upheaval, we had actually been planning a ball in Brook Street for the day after tomorrow. And now that Henry is home, we do not need to cancel it. I would be so glad if you could all come. It is all we can do to prove our gratitude."

Though interestingly enough, Alexandra thought cynically, she had not issued the invitation until she had realized Griz was a duke's daughter, and she could not invite Griz and her handsome husband, even at the last minute, without inviting Ralph's brother, too. After all, Nicholas was, presumably, paying for it.

"Thank you," Griz replied, without looking at Dragan. "We would be delighted."

"Lovely! Nicholas, you will be there, will you not?"

"If Miss Battle wishes to go, I shall be happy to escort her."

Alexandra's startled gaze flew up to meet his. "What?"

"Of course, Miss Battle is as welcome as the rest of the heroic warriors," Ralph said jovially. "I think my wife is merely concerned she might feel a little overwhelmed."

"Never underestimate a governess," Nicholas drawled. "Ours has danced in Venetian palaces and waltzed before the Emperor at the Hofburg in Vienna. I don't believe the Brook Street ballroom will frighten her."

Alexandra was appalled. In fact, she *had* done those things, though she had no idea how Nicholas knew of them. Nor did she wish either to be thought above her profession or to inflict herself on an unwilling host. To say nothing of that universal female problem of not having anything to wear.

"Why then, of course, you are invited, my dear," Mrs. Swan said kindly, although her eyes were not warm. "Because, naturally, our gratitude includes you."

"I can be your chaperone," Griz said with a dancing grin. "One of the more unexpected benefits of marriage!"

Dinner was announced then, which came as something of a relief to Alexandra. Fortunately, Nicholas seemed to have decided he had put enough cats among the pigeons for one day and became the perfect, genial host. Since they were a small party, he introduced topics of conversation that included everyone. His remarks were witty, his questions light-hearted, and under his subtle leadership, everyone began to relax into good humor and enjoyment.

Ralph turned out to be not quite so stiff, and his wife not quite so worldly. Only Griz and Dragan seemed exactly as they always were—fun, clever, and knowledgeable. They happily answered questions about how Dragan came to England and how they met but also asked many questions of their own of Ralph and Nicholas.

Alexandra, who talked least, stored up little pieces of information about her employer that she learned that evening. About the pet dog he had loved as a boy, about the job he took on a cargo ship sailing from France to Italy, and a host of funny stories poking fun at himself as he learned new languages and made mistakes in building his business. He seemed so open, so charming. And yet he was hiding something, probably in the cellars, that he didn't want anyone, least of all the police, to know about. Something to do with the kidnapped children? She could not believe so, and yet Inspector Harris, who was by no means a stupid man, had accused him. And one could never tell what Dragan was thinking.

As she ate and thought and listened, she forgot the oddity of her position. The servants, surprisingly well-trained, did not need to be told when to clear a course away and bring in the next.

But when everyone had finished with the pastries and the cheese, she rose quite naturally from the table, saying, "Ladies, shall we withdraw?"

Only when she caught a look of irritation from Mrs. Swan did she realize she was behaving like the hostess Nicholas had asked her to be. A position that probably belonged more rightly to his sister-in-law than his daughter's governess.

Mrs. Swan inquired rather stiffly for a cloakroom to refresh herself. Having directed her, Alexandra walked into the drawing room with Griz.

"The perfect hostess," Griz remarked admiringly.

Alexandra grimaced. "I am in an impossible position. But Sir Nicholas, not Mrs. Swan, pays my salary."

"He likes you," Griz observed, sounding a key on the piano at random. "This is a lovely instrument."

Glad of the change of subject, Alexandra agreed. "It is."

"Tell me," Griz said, pulling something from what must have been a large, hidden pocket in her gown, "have you ever seen anything like this before?"

Alexandra took a slightly crumpled pamphlet from her and smoothed it out. She scanned it quickly. "It's quite like the one your husband had the day I visited you with Evelina. Political, radical. Aimed, I'd say from the language, at the educated classes. Where did you get it? From your brother again?"

Griz shook her head. "No, in the secret hiding place of the man we think is behind the kidnappings. It was in among the banknotes."

"The cloaked man?" Alexandra said eagerly. "I didn't think Inspector Harris believed me about him."

"We didn't find a cloak. But one of the women certainly gave the police the name and address of the man she claims gave the orders and took the bulk of the ransom."

"But that is excellent news! Do they have this man?"

"No, but they are watching his rooms. He left his money hidden there, so he's likely to come back."

"Won't he see them watching and stay away? After all, he managed to avoid all of us before."

"Maybe." Griz sat on the piano stool, with her back to the instrument.

Alexandra handed her back the pamphlet. "Why do you suppose he kept this? Is he some revolutionary type who believes it's acceptable to ransom rich people's children?"

"It's possible, I suppose, but it isn't much of a defense before the law."

"Or anyone else." Alexandra sat on the stool beside her but facing the piano. "Griz, have the police told Ralph Swan their suspicions of Sir Nicholas?"

It was clear at once Griz knew what she meant. "I don't know. But I rather think it was Ralph that put the idea in *their* heads—at the beginning when he was angry and upset at his son being taken. In my judgment, Ralph has dropped such a belief."

"But the police have not." Alexandra frowned. "I wonder why?"

CHAPTER NINETEEN

I N THE DINING room, while Nicholas pushed the port toward him, Tizsa bent to pick up something that had fallen out of his pocket. He tossed it on the table while he poured himself some port and passed the decanter back.

"What have you there?" Ralph asked. As Nicholas was fairly sure he was meant to.

"Just a pamphlet. Your brother is kindly publishing it for me."

"They should be ready for distribution tomorrow," Nicholas said mildly.

"May I see?" Ralph asked, reaching across the table.

Tizsa shoved it toward him and sipped his port.

Ralph flicked through it. "Conditions of the poor again," he observed with a shade of impatience.

"From a medical perspective," Tizsa pointed out.

"Why do you say 'again'?" Nicholas asked.

Ralph gave a crooked smile and reached into his pocket. "I was going to ask you, Nicholas, what you thought of *that*. It seems to be more of the same. Intentionally or not, fomenting unrest and revolution."

Nicholas took it, and Tizsa dragged his chair closer in order to peer at it, too.

"It's not the same thing at all," Tizsa stated, saving Nicholas the trouble. "One is a factual account. Yours is more political. Neither, in my opinion, are in any danger of arousing revolution."

"Seriously?" Ralph demanded. "If you tell the poor they're down-trodden often enough, they will grow to resent it!"

"The poor already know they're downtrodden," Tizsa retorted. "I would say, though, that both these pamphlets are aimed at the rich and the powerful. Who, if they are not already aware, need to be made so."

"Isn't that how you bring about revolution?" Ralph snapped back. "Make the powerful aware of the danger of the supposedly power-less?"

"A directed mob can be frightening," Tizsa allowed—speaking, presumably as one who had done his share of directing. "English mobs only riot. There is no direction. And there is nothing in my pamphlet that tries to do so."

"Perhaps not," Ralph said grudgingly, "but the other sails too close to the wind for my taste. It must be illegal."

"That is probably true," Tizsa allowed. "At least in so far as it has no printer's mark." He shrugged. "Where did you get it?"

"It was pushed under my front door." Ralph was clearly outraged, which made Nicholas smile faintly.

Tizsa glanced from one to the other. "What do you think of it, Sir Nicholas? Will you treat your workers better on the strength of it?"

"My workers are pretty well treated as it is. I am hoping it rubs off on other employers."

"They'll just undercut you," Ralph said.

Nicholas shrugged. "But I have happier and more productive workers."

Ralph adopted a faint sneer. "I don't see you giving away all your wealth to the masses."

"Oh, I give away a fair bit," Nicholas murmured.

Ralph flushed painfully. "I suppose I deserved that. You were not here when Papa died. What was I supposed to do?"

"I haven't accused you of anything," Nicholas pointed out. "You don't need to be so defensive. I shan't demand you pay it all back to the estate. You deserve a share."

Ralph paused in his angry reach for the decanter. "I am glad you see it that way." He poured himself more port before he raised his gaze to Nicholas's. "Will you further agree that I continue to live in the Brook Street house?"

Nicholas shrugged. "It seems to have become your home more than it was ever mine."

Ralph relaxed visibly. "Thank you. That has been preying on our minds."

"Don't thank me too soon. I will make you an allowance from the estate, Ralph, but I'm taking back control."

"Damn it, you don't *need* that money," Ralph said irritably. "The world knows you have *pots* more!"

"Which I earned," Nicholas pointed out.

Ralph's chin came out. "*I* earned my share. *I* remained with Papa. *I* put up with him. *I* looked after the estate when he died."

Nicholas blinked sleepily. "If by looking after it, you mean you spent it…"

"When was the last time you were in Sussex?" he demanded.

"Last month, as you would know if you troubled to read the steward's reports. Look, Ralph, I'm not depriving you of anything except the misplaced notion that you deserve anything. You won't go short. You'll have Brook Street and an allowance, and I'll pay for the education of your children. Beyond that, you're on your own." *As I have been since I was nineteen years old.*

He closed his mouth, refusing to speak the last thought, which was petty as well as self-pitying, and he had no wish to be either. Instead, he raised his glass and smiled. "Cheer up, Ralph. Admit it's more than you hoped for when you saw me arrive on your doorstep."

After an instant's glare, Ralph smiled reluctantly. "Damn you."

"By all means."

Ralph let out a bark of laughter and glanced at the silent Tizsa. "I'm sorry you had to witness our quarrel."

"Don't be. I am frequently deaf and always discreet."

"Perhaps we should join the ladies," Nicholas suggested. "And see if we can persuade them to indulge us in some music."

He had thought of spending more time over the port and trying to discover if Ralph or Tizsa or both were suspicious of him. He tried not to care, but he liked Tizsa, and Ralph, in spite of everything, was his brother. He should have been used to betrayal, but somehow, he never was. However, something insistent was pulling him toward the drawing room and Alexandra Battle, to soak in the comfort of her presence, to hear her play, watch her expressions... Just to be in the same room had become a treat he looked forward to.

Except, it seemed a treat now and again was no longer enough. He had liked seeing her at the opposite end of his table, an unassuming, dignified presence. It had made him wonder what life would be like now without her. Evelina would miss her. *He* would miss her.

And yet he didn't know her. She didn't know him.

Stepping into the drawing room, his hungry gaze found her at once, and at just the right moment. Her face, quietly, austerely beautiful, was turned toward the door, lit in a moment of laughter as she glanced at Lady Griz in a teasing, humorous way that was as rare as it was delightful. He could not help the smile curving his own lips.

Her gaze flickered to him, and their eyes met. She looked away again almost at once, but a delicate, tell-tale flush seeped into her neck and cheeks. A fierce surge of triumph exploded through him because she was not indifferent. That he could affect her melted his bones.

And yet she had brought a man into this house, her supposed cousin, a man important enough to her to be shown out personally, not left to the servants. Nicholas was not proud of his twinge of jealousy, but he waited impatiently to be told about him, who he was, what he was to her.

None of your business, Nicholas Swan, he scolded himself impatiently, then turned to his sister-in-law, who was closest to the piano. "Are you musically inclined, Gertrude? Do you play?"

After a pretty show of reluctance, and the persuasion of her husband, who informed the company how gifted she was, Gertrude submitted gracefully and played and sang a pleasant French song.

Gifted she was not, but she had skill enough to charm most ears.

"Perhaps we could persuade you to another?" Alexandra suggested when the appreciative applause died down.

"Oh, you are *too* kind to ask me again. In truth, I do not wish to be late home with the children, and we have not yet heard Lady Grizelda. Your husband was telling me how musical you are."

Lady Griz cast a quick glance at her husband that spoke of unexpected and oddly endearing doubt. Then, the doubt vanished into something that wasn't quite mischief, but a mixture of relief and calculation.

"I do love music, but I hate to play in public," Griz said frankly. "But if we played a duet, Alexandra?"

Alexandra's eyes widened in clear alarm. "Oh, no, I was about to ring for tea since Mrs. Swan—"

"*I* shall ring for tea," Sir Nicholas said. "You ladies must play."

"The Spanish piece?" Griz suggested, walking to the guitar that was propped up against one of the piano legs.

Alexandra opened her mouth, clearly to object. She even glanced at Nicholas rather wildly, perhaps for moral support, but for motives he did not wish to analyze right now, he wanted her to shine.

"We are all ears, ladies."

Gertrude was no doubt appalled to have to listen to the governess, but she could hardly go against her host's request without insulting Lady Grizelda. That amused Nicholas, too.

He placed a chair beside the piano for Griz and then stood back.

He wanted to watch Alexandra as they played, but, knowing it would draw too much attention to both of them, he opted for discretion and watched the effect of the music on his other guests instead.

He already knew Alexandra to be a highly skilled musician, but Griz with her guitar was the perfect foil. They had clearly played together often, for the music flowed and harmonized in perfect tune and perfect time. Gertrude kept a fixed smile on her face. Tizsa, usually difficult to read, looked rapt. Only Ralph, who had never been musical, seemed untouched by the performance.

As for Nicholas, the music plucked at his emotions, sending them into turmoil, and yet his heart soared with pride in her.

Pride and something else. But he would not think of that here and now. Something was changing, in him, in his life, and he could not stop it.

When their piece was finished, Alexandra stood immediately, smiling distantly and leaving Griz to take the applause, while she went at once to the tea tray which had just been brought in.

His heart warm, he ferried cups and saucers from Alexandra's hands to his guests. And then he sat in the vacant space beside her, half a foot away from touching her and yet glorying in her nearness like a schoolboy with his first love.

The children were fetched down from the schoolroom, all but the baby, who was apparently fast asleep with his nurse. The cousins appeared to be the best of friends, and Evelina ran excitedly from him to Alexandra, who murmured something to her that stopped her bouncing. Instead, she and her cousins retreated to a corner for a bit more chortling. And only a few minutes later, the guests departed.

For his brother and himself, it was, Nicholas supposed, a step in the right direction. They had grown so far apart they would never be friends, but they could be cordial, and he hoped they would look out for each other. For Evelina and her cousins, things seemed much more ecstatic. Alexandra was right. The child had been deprived of friends for too long. Perhaps there was a way to introduce her to the neighbors' children, invite them for a picnic in the garden, perhaps, with Alexandra and Anna to supervise.

"I'll take her up to bed," Alexandra murmured on the stairs. "It has been an exciting evening for her."

"Join me once she is settled," he said, strolling toward the drawing room. He didn't want to command her like an employer, but it was the only way he could be sure she would obey.

Of course, the drawing room was dangerous. This was where he had kissed her. Desire swept through him. Perhaps the library would be better. But that was where he had first seen her, where he had almost kissed her. More than once.

The room scarcely mattered. He would not kiss her tonight. But there were things he wanted to know. Or at least, so he told himself. He suspected he merely wanted another half hour, another few minutes, in her company.

He was standing by the window with the curtain pulled back, gazing out at nothing but darkness when she knocked at the door.

"Come in," he said impatiently. "You do not need to knock."

It was no way to begin a delicate interview. Nor was he even sure why her knock irritated him. She entered with her eyes cast down, understandably annoyed to be addressed in such a way but unable or unwilling to answer her employer back. Shame drowned his spurt of temper, and he raked his hand through his hair before striding to the brandy decanter.

"Actually, I wanted to thank you for being such an excellent hostess tonight. Would you care for a nightcap?"

When he glanced at her, her gaze was on him, wary but unafraid.

"Thank you," she said calmly.

Taking that for assent, he splashed brandy into two clean glasses and brought her one. She took it without touching his fingers and immediately stepped back. He waved her to a chair, unreasonably disappointed when she did not take the sofa.

"I hope I didn't make you too uncomfortable," he said, sitting on the edge of the sofa.

"No. At a family dinner, I'm sure everyone understood it to be a matter of convenience. In other situations, though, it would not be good for your reputation or mine. Let alone Evelina's."

He frowned. "You believe me such a careless friend that I would do such a thing to you?"

"You are not my friend at all," she said calmly. "You are my employer."

Stupidly, it felt like a blow in the gut. He managed a faint smile. "I hope I am both."

Her gaze fell. She said nothing. He had a feeling he was digging a hole for himself that had no bottom, so he changed tack.

"At any rate, I hope you at least enjoyed the evening."

"Actually, yes, I did. Thank you for letting me be there."

"Oh, for God's sake," he burst out. "When did Alexandra Battle become so damned humble?"

Her eyes flew up to his. "You are angry with me."

He drew in his breath. "No. No, of course, I am not. I seem to be on edge, but I should not be taking it out on you." He stretched his glass across to hers. "I apologize."

At least she did not hesitate before she clinked her glass against his and sat back. "Your brother upsets you."

"No. Well, perhaps. He disappointed me a long time ago. But I still remember the boy who I thought looked up to me. Perhaps I disappointed him when I left him in pursuit of love."

Although he spoke with deliberate lightness, her eyes told him she came close to understanding the unbearable hurts that had piled onto him then. He had never expected his father to forgive him, but Ralph's silence had hurt. Nora's spectacularly quick abandonment had shattered him. But it was so long ago, he had almost forgotten. And he didn't regret Nora, who, in the end, had turned into a good friend.

He drank from his glass, then waved it expansively, dismissing what had gone before. "Water under the bridge. Tell me instead about your day."

"It was quiet. Evelina worked well, and we walked to the Strand where she bought those ribbons she wore this evening and came home through the market for a change. She likes her cousins."

"Yes, I am glad." He waited, but she said nothing further. His heart twisted. Who was this man she chose to hide from him? "James told me you had a visitor. A cousin?"

"Oh! Yes, he dropped in for half an hour. He is just passing through London." Her fingers crossed over each other on the glass. Perhaps she thought he would not see.

He hoped *she* would not see the furious jealousy twisting through him in response.

"A pity. I would have liked to meet another member of your family. What is his name?"

She blinked. "I beg your pardon?"

"Your cousin's name. It is not a difficult question."

For the first time in this interview, her eyes flashed. He was relieved to glimpse the sign of spirit, like an old, missing friend.

"Not difficult," she retorted, "But not necessary either. I apologize for meeting family under your roof. It won't happen again."

"That isn't what I mean, and you know it."

"Then you are guilty of prying, and that is worse."

"Do you have a reason to keep him secret?"

"No, of course not. But I have a right to privacy."

"So you will not tell me?"

She lifted her chin. "I will not." As she met his gaze, her breath caught, and she looked more miserable than anything. "You have secrets, too!" she said defensively, uncannily like a child claiming she had not started the quarrel.

He laughed. "Hardly! I live openly with my sins and their results—Evelina and Lady Nora in this very house."

She blushed furiously, adorably. "I do not refer to the affairs of the heart, which are obviously no one else's business."

"Then what?" he asked, intrigued, and not a little relieved by the implication that she did not regard her mysterious visitor in such a light.

"The machinery in your cellar."

That wiped the smile from his face, and he saw by the flash of triumph in her eyes that she saw it. "The machinery in my cellar," he repeated. "Where did you get such an idea?"

"From my ears," she retorted. "I hear it, sometimes, a rhythmic clanking sound that almost sounded like rattling chains. I was looking for the source of it the first night I was here."

His smile came back quite naturally. "When you accosted me in the library, in your nightgown."

"*You* accosted *me*," she retorted, and his smile widened, causing her to drag her gaze free.

"I suppose I did," he admitted. "Did I ever apologize? I had one brandy too many, and, at the risk of sounding like a coxcomb, I am used to women trying to inveigle me into marriage—or less honorable unions—by fair means and foul. For Evelina's sake, I am glad you turned out to be such a straightlaced governess."

"That was your apology?" she asked politely.

"No, that was my excuse. But I *am* sorry, and I do apologize."

"Then what on earth is it you do in the cellar at night?" A challenge tilted her chin, and she blurted, "That you are afraid of Inspector Harris discovering?"

Et tu, Brute. His lips twisted. So did his heart. "Tying up small boys and watching their chains rattle. Of course." He dashed the remains of his brandy down his throat and almost threw the glass on the table as he surged to his feet. He could not bring himself to look at her expression as he snatched up her hand and pulled her up beside him. "Come then, learn my grizzly secret. I'm about to break it all up anyway. With Harris poking around and friends and employees denouncing me, I shall have to put an end to it."

Surprise got her across the room, all but trotting to keep up with his longer stride. At the door, she made one instinctive move to be free and, ashamed, he loosened his grip. But he didn't let her go, and she didn't resist again. Instead, she let him pull her on, running downstairs at his side, across the deserted hall to the back door that led to the garden. But in the wall perpendicular to that, stood another door that was not visible at all when the garden door was opened.

Releasing Alexandra, he took the key from his pocket, slid it into the almost-invisible door, unlocked it, and threw it wide.

"Well?" he threw at her. "Do you want to see my secret, evil lair?"

CHAPTER TWENTY

I F SHE HAD truly believed him to be a wicked man, she would have
fled as soon as he loosened his grip of her hand. As it was, though,
her heart thundered for a hundred different reasons, none of which she
could untangle right now. She followed him into the dark cellar,
waited while he lit the lantern, and then trailed after him down a set of
rough, stone steps, through a spacious, empty stone chamber, and
through another locked door.

He seemed to have lost interest in whether she followed him or
not. But in this final room, he stopped and raised his lantern. "I can
light the other lamps if you like, but you can probably see what it is."

In the faint glow, she saw a metal monster. *Part* of a metal monster
whose lines faded into darkness until the lantern followed them. A
table with a platform above, a cylinder behind. Stains of ink.

Her breath caught. "It's a printing press!"

The light moved as he walked to the side of the room and set the
lantern on a bench. Trays of letters sat there. A few things began to fall
into place in her mind.

"You printed these pamphlets, the ones Griz and Dragan had that
so annoyed her brother. I saw James bringing a sack upstairs the other
night, and in the morning, it was gone. It contained pamphlets, didn't
it?"

"Did you think it was the bodies of my victims? Those whose parents would not pay the ransom?"

"Of course not," she retorted. "I just could not understand why you were behaving so furtively. I *still* don't understand."

He sighed. "I don't trust the government not to shut me down. I have a perfectly legal and much more up-to-date press in the city where I print many works, including Tizsa's survey of the health and living conditions of the poor. With this one, though, I can be more political, more radical, raise more of a commotion."

"And so, you didn't want Inspector Harris to find it."

"I had a compositor working on the galleys. I couldn't risk the police finding him."

She gazed at the press, "And this is what I heard. You print them at night when the household is asleep upstairs, well away from the noise."

"Which still managed to disturb *you*."

"I am a light sleeper. Will you really break it up?"

"I'm risking too many people who help me with it."

She frowned. "But what you print is not against the law."

He shrugged. "It sails close, but I doubt that matters if the infamous Lord Horace takes notice. It might raise too much of a stink to arrest *me*, but he can arrest others, destroy my business on which many livelihoods depend."

"He would not, could not do such a thing!"

"Perhaps not. I discover I am not willing to take the chance. I think the very mystery of the pamphlets has helped raise awareness of the issues." He waved one hand toward the press. "Maybe it was the revolutionary in me. But perhaps I can do more in the light, as it were."

"Stand for Parliament," she blurted.

He smiled faintly. "Maybe." He swiped up the lantern again. "Come, it's cold and damp down here."

This time when he took her hand, it was only to guide her. But her skin still tingled. She liked his touch, his nearness, the idea of being alone with him in the dark. And because he had trusted her with his secret, warmth folded around her heart.

When he would have released her to lock the first cellar door, she retained his hand for a moment.

"I will not tell anyone. I would not. Not even Griz."

The lantern light flickered over his faint, sardonic smile. "Oh, I think the Tizsas already suspect."

She released his hand, and he locked the door, turning so quickly, she didn't have time to move away. He bumped into her and immediately flung up his arm to her back to prevent her stumbling.

"Sorry," he muttered.

The dancing lantern shot flashes of light over his harsh yet handsome face. His body touched hers, her skirts billowing around his legs. His arm was warm and strong at her waist, his palm flattened across her back. Bent over her in quick concern, his face was too close, the flickering light playing over his lips.

"Thank you," she whispered, "for showing me." She could not resist. Standing on tiptoe, she touched her lips to his, the lightest, briefest of kisses, and then, lest he be appalled, she tried to flit away.

But his arm tightened at her back. His breath caught. Very slowly, his arm fell away, but she did not move. She could not. She was lost in his eyes, in the thundering of her own heart. She had done something momentous, something which could not be undone, and the consequences…

She gasped as his fingers caressed her cheek, cupping her face as he bent his head and kissed her.

His previous kiss, in the drawing room, had been all instinctive passion inspired by the emotion of the music, raw and searing. This time, he seemed to have thought about it. It was soft, tender, exploring, and nothing in the world had ever been sweeter than his mouth moving on hers, his tongue stroking hers, tracing her lips, her teeth. A new wonder of sensation opened up, spreading unhurriedly from his mouth through her whole body.

She relaxed against him, holding his face between her hands, sliding her fingers into his hair as the kiss deepened naturally, enchanting and arousing. And when it ended, he began another. Her body seemed plastered to his, despite the thickness of her skirts. Her breasts ached deliciously, pressed to the hardness of his chest.

His lips began to smile against hers. "Perhaps it is not so cold down here."

When his hand slid down and took hers, she realized she was trembling, not with fear, but with need. She wanted more kisses, more closeness. But she had his hand as they walked, warm and strong, with its caressing fingers against her palm. In a daze, she accompanied him out of the cellars into the more normal light of the back hall.

As they approached the stairs, faint voices and laughter reached her from the kitchen, where the servants must still be clearing up or perhaps enjoying a few minutes of freedom together before bed.

Hand-in-hand, they walked upstairs, past the first-floor landing, and upward again. At the top of the stairs, they would part, he toward his rooms, she toward hers. But when they came to the landing, he turned left without pause, still drawing her by the hand away from her own room.

Did he even know where she slept?

Of course he does.

She halted, causing him to stop with her. "My chamber is the other way."

"Mine is this way." Still, he did not release her.

Her breath caught all over again as she understood him. Fresh heat surged through her, and he took her back into his arms. "Come with me," he whispered. "Come with me…"

If his last kisses had been seductive, this one was wicked. As if he had learned everything about her senses, her reactions, her yearnings. And she was lost.

"It will happen," he whispered against her lips with thrilling intensity. "Don't you think it might as well be now?" His hands slid down to her waist over her hips, then upward once more over her breasts. And when her lips parted in a silent moan of need, he covered them with his once more.

She was won, and they both knew it. She longed for him. She ached for him. She was so insanely in love with him, it would tear her apart.

His mouth left hers slowly. His eyes glowed, hot and exciting, as they stared down into her face, devouring her. And yet, he didn't move. He didn't tug her onward to his rooms, his bed.

His hands lifted to her face, not quite steady as they caressed her.

"It cannot be now, can it?" he said hoarsely.

"Yes," she gasped. "Don't you know that it can?"

His mouth took hers again, fierce and yet somehow regretful, as though he had already left her. He tore his lips free and pressed his cheek hard to hers. "Goodnight, Alexandra Battle. Sleep well. I certainly won't."

And then he was gone, and she was cold, staring after him as he strode along the passage.

Blindly, she turned the other way, almost stumbling back toward her room. What on earth just happened? She turned the handle of her bedchamber door and found it locked.

Of course. I locked my father in there.

Emotion caught in her throat. It might have been laughter or tears.

SHE WOKE DISORIENTED, with daylight streaming in through the bed curtains. She wore her nightgown, with her robe and a blanket pulled over her, and she lay across the bottom of the bed.

Of course. Her father had somehow managed to take up most of the rest of the bed. He hadn't wakened when she had come in last night, and so she had simply changed and curled up here.

She turned over to see if he was awake now. But the bed was empty. She sat up, pulling back the bed curtains, then stood and walked around the bed. He wasn't in the room. He must have gone early, before the servants were up.

In vain, she looked around for a note, for anything that might give a clue as to where he had gone, or even to find a word of thanks or affection. But there was nothing. With dread, she opened the drawer where she kept the purse with Nicholas's coins and breathed a sigh of relief to find it still there. He had not sunk quite that low.

Nicholas.

She sat on the bed once more. She had meant to tell him about her father last night when he had shown her his secret printing press. But all that had flown out of the window when he'd kissed her. When she had kissed him.

Desire flamed through her even at the memory of those kisses. *It will happen*, he had said fervently. And then it had not. An attack of gentlemanly conscience? An awareness of what a damaged reputation could mean for her?

Or a realization that she was not worth the hassle. Men desired easily and abandoned quickly.

He did not abandon Lady Nora…

And Alexandra was the governess. If he had made her his mistress, he would have replaced her with a new teacher for his daughter. And she had gone willingly, like a lamb to the slaughter. What had she been thinking of?

Love. Foolish, silly, unrequited love.

She covered her burning face with her hands, then abruptly stood and went to the washbowl. Ten minutes later, she was dressed and her hair pinned up. The perfect governess. Except for the turbulence roiling beneath the surface.

Surely no one could kiss as Nicholas had kissed her without *some* feeling. And he had been the strong one in the end, the one who had saved her from herself as well as from him. Tiny doubts and huge questions ate her up, and yet as she had breakfast with Evelina and listened to her chatter, she realized that beneath it all, she was wildly happy. Because there was something between her and Nicholas. Perhaps it hung by a hair, balanced on a knife-edge, but it was there. The very fact that he had, in the end, sent her away proved that he cared for her more than for his lust.

She hugged her feelings to herself as she went out into the garden with Evelina for a quick game before beginning lessons. She wished with all her heart that Nicholas would join them. If she saw him, she would know... How would he look at her? How could she bring herself to look at him with others present?

She needed to see him. She needed to take her courage in both hands and have a private interview with him. Not least because she needed to tell him about her father. He had trusted her with his secrets; it was only right she tell him hers. And from there...but she did not dare look ahead.

One day at a time. Alexandra. You are good at that.

The rain came on during the morning, so in the usual break between lessons, Alexandra left her pupil to play in her room for ten minutes while she went downstairs. On the landing below, she met Mrs. Dart bustling toward the library with what looked like a bundle of letters in her hand.

"Is Sir Nicholas at home this morning?" she asked the housekeeper as calmly as she could.

"He is indeed," Mrs. Dart replied, giving the letters a little flourish. "He's asked for these, though Lord knows why. He took no interest in them before. You are not leaving us, are you, Miss Battle?"

"Why no..." She frowned at the letters, a sudden unease clawing at her stomach. "What are they?"

"The letters of application we received for the governess's post."

Her world reeled. He was not simply checking on her credentials somewhat belatedly. He was checking on all of them, and there was no reason for that unless…

Unless he was replacing her.

She was being punished for his lust and her own…

Or, more likely, he had found out her father had stayed in her room last night. Perhaps he had even seen him leaving. Dear God, perhaps they had met. Lord knew what her father might have said at such an encounter. Sir Nicholas might not even have known it was her father. Either way, how dare he think the worst?

Because I lied to him. I told him my father was dead… Such an old, familiar lie, it had almost become truth.

Oh yes, they were both at fault. But surely, *surely*, he should speak to her before dismissing her? That he did not, made last night, made all their previous interactions worth nothing.

She could not bear *nothing*.

I should resign before he dismisses me.

"If you're going to see him, you can take these with you," Mrs. Dart said, holding out the letters.

"Oh, no. No, I was just going for a breath of fresh air." She almost bolted away down the stairs, her mind and heart both bursting with anger at the injustice, with anguish at such betrayal.

NICHOLAS COULD NOT concentrate on the books before him. His urgency, of mind and body, was all concentrated on Alexandra Battle. She was so new in his life, and yet he understood with certainty that she would not have tolerated, let alone returned, his kisses without feeling something in return. In fact, she had kissed him first, a quick, almost desperate brush of the lips that had moved him more than any of the blatant, deeper kisses of other women.

Dare he call her feeling love? Perhaps. If not, he was determined to make it so.

Rapt, he wondered if he imagined he heard her voice outside the library. And when a knock sounded on the door, his heart seemed to jolt against his ribs.

"Come in."

But it was not Alexandra, only Mrs. Dart who entered the room, rustling in with the pile of letters he asked for.

"Ah, thank you, Mrs. Dart." He took them from her and set them in front of him.

"What do you want them for anyway?" she asked with the impertinence of someone who had known him since he was in short coats. "You haven't frightened Miss Battle off, have you?"

"It would take a better—or worse!—man than I," he said sardonically, flicking through the letters. "Tell me, if you had not liked or approved Miss Battle for some reason, which of these would have you interviewed next?"

"There's a list at the front of my choices and why I made them."

He glanced up at her. "Now I remember why I wanted you to run my household. You are a wonder, Mrs. Dart."

"I am," she retorted and scowled at him. "And so is Miss Battle. I've seen a huge difference—for the better—in Evelina since she came. The girl loves her. It would be a mistake to part them. In my opinion," she added hastily.

"Which I value and heed. I have no intention of parting them. I'll explain in due course. Thank you, Mrs. Dart. You may go."

Mrs. Dart sniffed and departed, leaving him to plow through the letters and her notes. He smiled to himself as he read Alexandra's. He could see exactly why she had been chosen. And, in fact, none of the others really seemed to measure up as a replacement. He could do worse than discuss the matter with Alexandra herself, along with his bigger ideas for this house.

Of course, several matters had to be discussed with Alexandra herself, preferably somewhere he would not be tempted to touch her and ruin everything. In the circumstances, the schoolroom and his daughter's chaperonage seemed the safest place, so, when he could contain himself no longer, he made his way upstairs and along the passage to the schoolroom. His heart beat with anticipation, with ridiculous happiness, just because he would see her.

Chapter Twenty-One

H E CHOSE TO enter by the playroom door. From there, he could see into the larger schoolroom, where his daughter and her governess appeared to be enjoying their luncheon. Evelina was laughing, which did his heart good to see. Mrs. Dart was right. There was little sign now of the anxious, serious child who clung and threw tantrums for anyone's attention.

Alexandra was smiling faintly, her gaze on the child as she ate, and yet something about her seemed distracted. He hoped she thought of him.

"Papa!" Evelina, forgetting her table manners, leapt up and threw herself across the room in a tangle of English and Italian babble.

He gave her a hug and his attention for a few moments before he suggested she return to her seat and her manners. Giggling, she obeyed without fuss.

Although he had had no time to see Alexandra's reaction to his arrival, he had the impression she had gone very still. But when he finally plonked a chair between them and sat in it, he saw that she was not flushed, as he imagined she might be, but pale. Moreover, her attention was not on him but on Evelina.

"You are too late for luncheon with us," Evelina told him. "And now that the rain has gone off, we're going to the park to meet new friends. Will you come, Papa?"

That he was genuinely tempted surprised him. Looking after a gaggle of over-excited children in unenclosed surroundings was his definition of hell. But for some reason, he felt a powerful tug toward fun with his own little family.

He loved Evelina, and he would always protect her to the best of his ability, but he couldn't remember when this had changed from responsibility to fun. Probably round about the time Alexandra Battle had come into their lives.

But Miss Battle, it seemed, misunderstood his hesitation. "Your father is too busy today, Evelina. Another day would be better when you are not distracted by new friends."

Unused to being spoken for, Nicholas blinked. Alexandra glanced at him at last, and her gaze was cold, almost accusing. It shocked him, that look. He was used to her disapproval, her reluctant approval, even her anger. But she had never before looked at him with such ice in her eyes. It shocked him into silence.

Evelina, clearly itching to be up and moving, watched impatiently as Alexandra popped the last morsel into her mouth.

Nicholas said, "Evelina, why don't you go and wash and prepare for your outing, I would like a word with Miss Battle before you go out."

Evelina ran happily into the playroom. Alexandra rose and followed her. For a moment, he thought she was actually going to walk out, but she merely closed the door and returned to her chair at the table.

"You shall have it in writing by the end of the day," she said calmly. "But I wished to tell you in person that I am resigning my post. I shall serve the month's notice that was agreed, unless you would rather I did not."

If she had slapped his face, he would have been less astonished. As it was, he stared at her, searching her face for the joke and then for the reason. He learned nothing, for her expression was carefully blank, her eyes veiled. And yet, something about her straight, tense posture told him she was held together by a mere thread.

He sat back, giving himself time to think. "Is this because you feel insulted by my behavior last night? Or, worse, you feel unsafe?"

She waved that aside so impatiently it might have meant nothing. That chilled him more than her coldness, more than her promise of resignation. "We both know why I am doing it, but yes, I owe you the truth, and so I shall tell you everything."

"That sounds ominous," he observed, but no light of humor crept into her eyes or curved the lips that had kissed him so passionately.

"The man you asked about last night. The man who visited me."

"Your cousin," he prompted as she paused.

She dragged her gaze free of his. "He did not leave yesterday afternoon," she blurted. "I'm sure you know that, too. He stayed the night in my room. He is not my cousin."

The pain of jealousy, the fear of loss ripped through his stomach. He had thought she was different, thought he knew her. Damn it, he did *not* know her, and he would *not* lose her to some other betrayer.

"Then who?" He tried to keep his voice carefully neutral, years of habit causing him to hide his hurt. It came out somewhat flippantly, but it was better than whining.

And at least, she met his gaze once more, her chin lifting with that little hint of pride that he loved. "My father."

Relief swamped him like a tidal wave, so forceful that it was several moments before his brain could think beyond the joy that she had not gone straight from his arms to those of a lover.

And then it hit him. He frowned. "Your father is dead."

She shook her head. "No. We faked his death, his friend—a doctor—and me. In order to avoid the charges of fraud and theft that would have sent him to prison. I took his 'body' with me when I left Italy with the Laceys and helped him escape when the ship docked in Barcelona. I did not see him from that day until yesterday when he popped up in the market. He seemed well, said he had money but needed somewhere to stay for the night. I didn't ask why, didn't want to know, to be honest, so long as he promised to go away and not ruin my life again."

He searched her face, no longer quite veiled enough. "Your father hurt you."

She dashed her hand over her eyes. "My father always hurts me. And yet there I was, pleased to see him and sorry to see him go. Anyway, there you have my crime—less than you thought but no less worthy of dismissal, and so I save you the time. I am sorry, for Evelina's sake, but I no longer have your trust."

She sprang up, taking him by surprise once again, "As I said, my formal letter of resignation will be with you by the end of the day."

She would have bolted to the door, too, except he finally caught up and seized her arm. He stood, towering over her, saw the misery in her eyes, and the desperate warmth he had known was there all along.

"I do not accept your resignation," he said softly.

She didn't back down. She stared straight back, making no movement to be free. "Then why are you seeking another governess?"

His heart hurt because she didn't know. She really didn't know. "Guess," he challenged and tugged her hard against him—just as Evelina bounced into the room, and they sprang apart.

"I'll get my bonnet," she said shakily as she dashed away.

He wanted to laugh, except it wasn't quite funny.

GRIZ WOKE WHEN Dragan's hand closed around hers. That was not at all unusual. Nor was the spike of hot excitement as he pushed against her. So, it took an instant of complete disorientation before she realized their sitting position was wrong and far too hard and that there was nothing amorous in Dragan's hold. It was a warning.

Her eyes snapped open. Footsteps had entered the front door of

Ricco's dwelling. It could have been Inspector Harris, who knew they were there, watching from the inside, or one of his men who were supposed to be *discreetly* watching the outside. Or it could be Ricco himself.

Silently, Dragan flexed his fingers, arms, and legs and picked up the notebook and pencil beside him. They were hiding beneath the kitchen table, with a decent view of Ricco's hiding place. Early morning light shone somehow through the kitchen window.

The footsteps hurried up the narrow hall and into the bedroom. Griz heard the creak of the wardrobe opening, the swish of clothes hitting the bed. She exchanged excited looks with Dragan. He was packing.

This was borne out when he walked into the kitchen with an open carpetbag in his hand. Dragan gazed at him, unblinking, as his pencil began to move silently and at speed across the paper. Griz concentrated on not breathing.

Ricco, a tall man of distinguished features with black hair greying at the temples, dropped the bag on the floor near his hiding place and tossed his tall hat on the table above them. Griz started, but somehow managed not to nudge Dragan's sketching arm.

She didn't recognize Ricco, but she could understand why he had been mistaken for a gentleman. Perhaps he was, by birth. His clothing, too, was decent, the garb of a respectable, wealthy man, only somewhat crumpled and grubby, as though he had worn it for days on end. He had not stopped to change his clothes, so clearly, he was in a hurry. Perhaps he suspected, or even knew, he was being watched and hoped to get away by the surprise of getting in and out so quickly.

He knelt behind the door, by his hiding place, penknife in hand, and froze when he realized the nail he wished to pry up was not there. Cursing beneath his breath, he used the knife to lever up the floorboard instead and plunged both hands into the space, searching dementedly for his treasure.

He hurled himself upright, furiously kicking the removed board, which hurtled across the floor toward the table. Dragan shifted his foot to prevent injury, but Ricco was in no state to notice so faint a sound. He swore, and at length, both hands clutched in his hair.

Then he dropped his hands, glancing furtively toward the window before he bent and fastened the bag and snatched it up. He strode to the table once more, and Griz tensed. Dragan's pencil stilled.

But Ricco only grabbed his hat and strode out of the room and down the tiny hallway. The front door opened and closed quietly.

"I hope Harris's men are awake enough to arrest him," Griz whispered. "Should *we* go after him?"

Dragan regarded his drawing, which, although not finished, bore a clear resemblance to Mr. Ricco. Griz had known it would. "I think we have to leave the police to their business. Besides, if he somehow eludes them, we have *this* now to help track him down. Let me just finish a few more lines before they blur in my memory…"

The pencil flew over the paper again. The speed and accuracy of his sketches still fascinated Griz.

"And then?" she prompted, as he slowed.

"And then I think we should go home to bed," he said deliberately.

Griz warmed and leaned her head on his shoulder—not his drawing shoulder—and he smiled as he scribbled a last piece of shading and put the notebook and pencil away in his pocket.

They crawled out from under the table, and Dragan helped her to rise.

"If he escapes them," Griz said, "he will surely run to anyone else involved in this business, and Mr. Harris can arrest them all. If there *is* anyone else, of course. He may just find someone else to rob."

"As long as they don't lose him again."

"Perhaps we should just have arrested him here."

"Perhaps." The conversation had got them to the front door. Dragan paused, frowning, with his fingers grasping the handle. "The 'gentleman' thing bothers me. It's as if he has a double life."

"Well, at least we can prove to Mr. Harris that it is not Nicholas Swan."

"But it might be someone who knows him," Dragan opened the door and closed it again behind them before offering her his arm. "Did you not find something familiar about him?"

"About Ricco? Not really. Did you?"

"Yes, but exactly what eludes me."

Griz finished her careful quartering of the yards, middens, and outbuildings nearby. "There is no sign of him," Griz noticed with satisfaction. "And Harris's men have gone."

"Let's hope they're with Ricco and not their breakfast."

"Breakfast," Griz repeated happily. "Now there is a good idea."

"Better than bed?" he inquired.

"Well, no," Griz said, flushing and surreptitiously stroking the inside of his arm. "Obviously not better than *that*…"

ALEXANDRA WAS BOTH surprised and alarmed to receive an invitation to visit Lady Nora that morning. Usually, she only went to accompany Evelina, but this morning, her ladyship's maid brought the invitation to her in the schoolroom and then departed hastily, as if she could not bring herself to leave her mistress for any longer.

It worried Alexandra. Everything seemed to worry her now. That Sir Nicholas was looking for a new governess, that he claimed he would neither dismiss Alexandra nor accept her resignation, that he had kissed her two days ago, that he had not touched her since…except that almost embrace yesterday afternoon, interrupted by Evelina.

Her whole world seemed to be in turmoil. He had joined her and Evelina for dinner last night and had been good company, but afterward, he had made no effort to speak to her alone. She felt in limbo and unable to ask for clarity. What could she say? *What do you mean by kissing me? Are we pretending it didn't happen, or do you expect me to hang around in case you want to do it again?*

Even the questions didn't make sense to her. And on top of that, she was still expected to attend his brother's ball in Brook Street this evening. Where she would stand out like a sore thumb in her plain green evening gown. She would have to ignore supercilious, pitying, and contemptuous glances and probably blatant rudeness.

From one day at a time, she was down to dealing with one hour at a time.

Accordingly, when she let Evelina have a break that morning, she did not join her but walked around to Lady Nora's quarters.

The outer room was brighter than normal. Draped over a chair was a rather beautiful silk gown in a gorgeous shade of purple, both unusual and eye-catching. Once, probably not so long ago, Lady Nora would have looked stunning in it. Spencer came out of the inner bedchamber, smiled, and beckoned her inside.

She went, hoping she was not about to discover Lady Nora at death's door, no doubt with her hand in Sir Nicholas's, for he would not let her die alone.

But the sick woman was by herself, propped up on a myriad of pillows. She seemed no weaker than before. In fact, there was a sparkle in her eyes that Alexandra could not recall before.

"Lady Nora, how are you?" Alexandra curtseyed and took the proffered chair beside the bed.

"I am excited to hear you are going to the ball."

Alexandra wrinkled her nose.

"Don't you wish to go?" Lady Nora asked in surprise.

"To be ignored, save for a few looks of resentment, curiosity, and pity? No, I can't say I am looking forward to it. I am still hoping my invitation has been forgotten, and I can stay at home."

"No chance. And I see no reason you would be regarded with

pity."

"Lady Nora, you have seen my evening gown. It is the best I have."

"No, it isn't. Spencer, bring the gown," Lady Nora instructed and smiled at Alexandra's bewildered gaze. "We are of a similar height and build, I think. Spencer has updated it a little and can finish any minor alterations once you have tried it on."

Alexandra stared from her to the purple gown in Spencer's arms. "Oh, no. I couldn't. It's much too fine for…"

"For the governess?" Lady Nora said tartly. "Then wear the green. But if you do not wish to be pitied, you will do better in the purple."

Alexandra closed her mouth.

"At least try it," Lady Nora said, closing her eyes.

Alexandra glanced wildly at Spencer, who grinned conspiratorially, set the gown at the foot of the bed, and set about unfastening Alexandra's dull day gown.

Two minutes later, Spencer led her across the room to a full-length mirror, and she stared at herself in wonder. The gown was beautiful, shimmering, perfect in length. Her hair had escaped its pins and had tumbled around her face. She looked like some wealthy, decadent beauty. Spencer lifted her hair, rolling it into the softer, looser style Alexandra had used to favor. The decadence faded.

Alexandra swallowed.

Spencer smiled and led her back to the bed. "My lady."

Lady Nora opened her eyes, swept them up and down, and nodded once. As her eyelids fluttered closed again, she said, "You will do. You will draw all eyes and brazen it out in style. It can be fun, you know. Good luck, my dear."

"What if he does not want me there?" Alexandra blurted.

"He does," came the surprisingly strong response. "Why do you think he made sure you were invited? Why do you think he is looking for a replacement governess?"

Alexandra blinked. She knew a surprising amount for an isolated invalid. "Why?"

Lady Nora smiled without opening her eyes. "Because he has different plans for you. And I will be glad, when I die, to know that he has a friend as well..." Her voice died away into sleep.

"Perhaps the smallest tuck at the shoulders," Spencer commented. "The rest is fine. I'll bring it to you this afternoon."

⟫⟫⟪⟪

NICHOLAS WAS PLAYING hide-and-seek with his daughter in the garden and wishing Alexandra would join them when Dragan Tizsa strolled out of the house to join him.

He was still counting up to fifty while Evelina hid. "Tizsa," he interrupted himself. "You find me on important business."

"So I see."

"Has Harris come to arrest me?"

"No, because I've seen our Ricco, and he isn't you."

Nicholas glanced at him. "Is he arrested?"

"No," Tizsa said regretfully. "We let him leave the house. The police followed him, but before they could catch him up, he vanished. Griz and I are annoyed since we had left him for the police."

"Fifty!" Nicholas called randomly. "Here I come, ready or not!" He strolled forward. "Then what can I do for you?"

"Look at this?" Tizsa said, drawing the familiar, well-thumbed notebook from his pocket. He flipped quickly through it and showed him the pencil sketch of a middle-aged man. "Do you know him?"

"Is this Ricco?"

Tizsa nodded.

Nicholas halted to look at the picture more closely. Reluctantly, he shook his head and walked forward past the ever-watchful James. On impulse, he stopped again. "James, do you know this face?"

The man drew his gaze away, presumably from wherever Evelina was hiding, and glanced at the picture. His eyes widened, and he took the book from Tizsa, staring at it.

"Yes. Funnily enough, I do." He stabbed his beefy finger at the page. *"That* is Miss Battle's cousin."

CHAPTER TWENTY-TWO

O NCE DRESSED FOR the evening, Nicholas went to say goodnight to his daughter, who was in her nightclothes, having her hair brushed by Anna.

"You look very handsome, Papa," Evelina approved.

"Thank you," he said gravely.

"Will you dance all evening?"

"I might dance once or twice."

"Well, don't sit all night talking and being boring," his daughter scolded. "And you must make sure Miss Battle has fun because I don't think she really wants to go, and one *should* want to go to a ball, shouldn't one?"

He frowned. "Yes, I believe one should." So why didn't Alexandra? Had it something to do with him? Or with her father? When she had spoken of her parent the other night, he could have sworn the feelings were genuine. He could even relate to that conflicting mix of love, anger, and frustration which he had felt for his own father.

So it was possible she was still helping Alexander Battle escape the law. But he did not believe for a moment she had been part of the kidnapping plots. Quite aside from the fact that it was she who had pointed out the cloaked man—presumably Battle himself—it was just not in her nature.

But…was it possible she would refuse to dance with Nicholas?

He could not even laugh at himself for the anxiety. Instead, he thrust it aside and bade Evelina be good for Anna.

"I will," she assured him. "But will you come whisper goodnight when you are home?"

"Of course."

The door opened, and Alexandra entered. She wore a wide-skirted silk ball gown of the rarest shade of purple that somehow reflected her eyes. Her hair, elegantly styled for once and held in place by Spanish combs, highlighted the delicate beauty of her face. Although she wore no jewelry, she looked stunning. And he was not the only one who noticed.

Evelina and Anna were both staring at her. She stopped dead, a flush staining her cheeks, and Evelina ran to her and seized her hand.

"Why, Miss Battle, you are beautiful tonight!" she exclaimed. "Is she not, Papa?"

Nicholas was not a tongue-tied boy, however much he felt like one. "Miss Battle is always beautiful," he managed. "Although, tonight, I grant you, she is particularly lovely. Are you ready to go, Miss Battle?"

"Of course," she said, sounding uncharacteristically nervous. "I just came to show Evelina Lady Nora's gown."

"It does not look like Lady Nora's," Evelina observed. "It is perfect for you."

Evelina hugged her, and she did not complain as Eva had if Evelina had endangered her elegant toilette. Instead, she hugged her back, and Evelina whispered something in her ear that seemed to deepen her flush—although that might have been due simply to bending down.

Leaving Evelina, they walked downstairs to the waiting carriage.

"What did she say to you?" he murmured as they left the house.

"Oh, something about dancing," Alexandra replied, glancing around her.

"I hope you will heed her advice."

"As you do?" she retorted, accepting his hand to climb the steps into the carriage.

"On this occasion," he replied. Although tempted to sit beside her, he took the opposite bench with his back to the horses. At least that way, he could look at her more easily. "I'm sorry," he said abruptly as the carriage began to move forward. "I did not think of you having nothing suitable to wear."

Her breath caught. "I hope you do not mind me wearing Lady Nora's gown."

He frowned. "Mind? Lord no. I didn't realize she had such taste. Why would I mind."

"Because...because of your past relationship with her," she said carefully.

He smiled with genuine amusement. "I'm afraid the youthful torch I carried for Nora burned out a long, long time ago. I am glad to rediscover her as a friend." He paused, searching her face. "And now, you think me fickle."

"Are you?" She looked away, her mouth opening to apologize.

"I was at nineteen," he replied before she could speak. "Most young people are. Weren't you?"

She shook her head. "I am not given to romantic notions of the brief *or* lasting varieties."

"I don't believe that's true."

"Why not?" she challenged.

Because of the way you kiss. He didn't say it aloud. Not yet. She was much too skittish. "I'll tell you when you dance with me."

ALTHOUGH CURIOUSLY SOOTHED by Lady Nora's advice to brazen it out in her lovely silk ballgown, several other anxieties bombarded Alexandra during the drive to Brook Street. Not least of those was Sir Nicholas and what, if anything, he meant to do with her. And then there was the fact that as she had glanced out of her bedchamber window just before leaving, she had seen a figure moving along the mews, who bore a passing resemblance to her father.

Fearing he was back, she had looked very carefully around her before she climbed into the coach, and as they traveled toward Mayfair, she kept darting wary glances out of the window.

Fortunately, there was no sign of him as they paused in Half Moon Street to pick up Griz and Dragan. In fact, she began to think anxiety had been getting the better of her, and her father had, in fact, left the country by now. Or at least escaped whatever trouble had led him to her in the first place.

At least the presence of Griz and Dragan broke the tension of being alone with Nicholas and unable to share her feelings or gain a clue as to his own. In ball dress, Griz looked as carelessly charming as she always did, and Dragan even more handsome than usual.

"What news of our arch-villain?" Alexandra asked, making an effort.

"We saw him, and the police lost him," Dragan said wryly.

"But at least Inspector Harris now accepts Ricco is not Sir Nicholas," Griz added.

"Well, *that* is good news!" Alexandra said.

"I thought so," Nicholas murmured, which told her he already knew, an oddity she shoved to the back of her mind.

It was a long time since Alexandra had entered a formal ballroom as a guest, and there was no denying her confidence was boosted by Lady Nora's gown. Other guests might regard her as an upstart, but at least they would not pity her.

She entered by Lady Grizelda's side, to prevent any gossip, and when they were welcomed by their host and hostess, she rather enjoyed the flicker of surprise in their eyes. And when she followed Griz into the throng, she saw a good deal of attention on their little group. Of course, society knew all about the estrangement between the Swan brothers, following Nicholas's scandal. His attendance here as his brother's guest in what was his own house no doubt intrigued everyone. If they looked at her at all, they no doubt imagined her as some distant relation of Grizelda's.

Sir Nicholas accepted two glasses of champagne from the tray proffered by a liveried footman and presented them to the ladies before taking glasses for himself and Dragan.

He raised his glass with a sardonic smile. "To fun." Although his gaze swept around them all, Alexandra couldn't help believing he spoke particularly to her. And suddenly, with the music playing and the lights of the ballroom beckoning, her anxieties melted away. He was right. This *was* fun, and she would enjoy her evening.

She smiled and drank.

Griz, she noticed, raised her glass almost to her lips and hastily lowered it again to look about her. "It is a fine ballroom. With access to a terrace, too."

"Especially good for assignations," Nicholas murmured.

"And for hiding," Griz said, just as Mrs. Swan reached them, gushing.

"How delightful to see you! Lady Grizelda, perhaps I might introduce you to a few people since I doubt your particular friends are here…" She swept Griz off, and Alexandra, remembering she was meant to be chaperoned, followed her.

It was, clearly, an exercise in introducing the duke's daughter to Mrs. Swan's friends, a triumphant boost in the hostess's standing. Griz tolerated it with the barest hint of discomfort. To each introduced group, she presented "my friend, Miss Battle."

After the third, Mrs. Swan, fortunately, bustled off to her other duties, namely introducing partners for the first dance. With a polite nod and smile, Griz took Alexandra's arm and drifted away.

"It's quite a novelty for me," Griz confided, "to be used in this way. I'm not sure I like it. I think I prefer to be ignored."

"Then why come?" Alexandra asked. "You must have known she was like this."

"True. But you couldn't really have come without me. Not without causing scandal."

Alexandra stared at her. "You came because of *me*? Why?"

Grizelda's eyes twinkled. A smile lurked on her lips as she raised her glass, which seemed to distract her. She wrinkled her nose and hastily set the glass down on the nearest table. "I seem to have taken champagne in dislike. Is it good?"

Alexandra took another sip. "It's fine. Don't be angry, Griz. Start a new fashion by dancing with your husband."

Griz laughed as the orchestra finished its background piece and, after a brief pause, began a waltz introduction. "Perhaps I will. Or I could go and disrupt assignations on the terrace."

"Too early, surely."

Griz opened her mouth to make some humorous reply, then closed it again as she clearly saw someone approach them.

Alexandra twisted around to see who, and her heart turned over.

Nicholas bowed to them. "Miss Battle, may I have the honor of the first dance?"

She couldn't help the widening of her eyes. "Me?"

"If you would be so kind," Nicholas said gravely.

Silently, Griz took the glass from her hand and set it down beside her own. In something of a daze, Alexandra took Nicholas's arm.

"You look stunned," he observed as they walked onto the dance floor among the other couples.

"I am," she confessed.

He turned and took her in his arms so naturally that she might have waltzed with him a hundred times before. "Why?"

Why did their bodies fit together so perfectly? Why, when the dance began, did she know so clearly that he would step back and turn, that it would feel so good to follow every movement of his lean, muscular body…?

No, the question had been why was she stunned. And now, if ever, while they were so physically close and could not easily escape each other, was the time to answer it.

"Because I don't understand what is going on between us," she blurted.

"I know. And it is true, I have only recently worked it out myself."

"Then I beg you will enlighten me," she said, quite without sarcasm. "I thought we were friends. There have been some moments between us which…well, you know perfectly well what moments. But then you are cold and distant, you begin inquiries for another governess but will not accept my resignation or admit you are dismissing me. And after all that, in front of your family and a hundred friends for all I know, you ask me for the first dance? It makes no sense to me."

His dark gaze held hers, warm, oddly glittering, and yet he did not appear to be laughing at her. "That is because you do not have all the information," he said softly. "Which is odd for so clever and perceptive a person. If I told you that I have never met anyone like you, that you intrigue and fascinate, comfort and soothe me, that though I have barely touched you, you move me as no other woman ever has… Would that make things easier to understand?"

She stared up at him. Her feet did not stumble but continued to follow his as though someone else was controlling them. "No."

A breath of laughter caught in his throat. "Alexandra Battle, I love you. You cannot be both my wife and Evelina's governess."

Now, she did stumble. At once, his arm tightened at her waist, spinning her around, almost off the ground to cover the lapse, and then they were back in step.

"Wife?" she whispered. "Wife? When you know all about my origins, my father, my lies?"

"That is the point. We know each other's lies now because we trust each other. As for the rest, do you imagine I would ruin you and make you my mistress just because you were not born into my own social rank? My egalitarian principles are not so frail. All I want is your love. And if I don't have it, I shall court you tirelessly until I do. If it takes all my life."

Her mind and heart were whirling. For the first time, she allowed dangerous possibilities to enter her head—a future of love and happiness and safety. Nicholas. Evelina. Children of her own...

"You do not speak," he said softly. "I know you care, or you would not melt in my arms... Do you not love me a little?"

"A *little*? Dear God, Nicholas—" She broke off, unable to speak because she was spun quite suddenly into cool fresh air.

She appeared to be dancing on the empty terrace until he halted beyond the windows, where there was no danger of being seen. There was no decorous space between them now. He pressed her to him, thrilling her, exciting her, and somehow her hand had slid from his shoulder around to the back of his neck.

"Well?" he said urgently. "Do you love me?"

"Love you?" she repeated helplessly. "Nicholas, I adore you, I always h—" The rest was lost in his mouth, which devoured hers like a starved man.

After the first, shocked gasp, she kissed him back with equal passion, pushing her body against him, almost fighting with lips, tongue, and teeth for control of the amazing kiss. Though she didn't give up, his strength won out, and after her wild, blissful surrender, he gentled the embrace to one of slow, sensual tenderness that melted her bones.

"Then you will marry me?" he whispered against her lips. "Please say yes, or I will explode."

Laughter and tears caught her unawares. She seemed to be made entirely of emotion.

His eyes looked stricken as he brought up his fingers to wipe at the dampness on her face. "Tomorrow will do. No, take all the time you need, sweetheart, don't let me rush—"

"I don't need time," she interrupted, tightening her arms around his neck. "I will marry you now if you like."

He kissed her hair and pressed his warm, rough cheek to hers. "If I could, I would. But I'll settle for a month while the banns are read."

Her whole being sang with happiness. She wanted to run and laugh and play the piano with outrageous exuberance. Instead, she hugged him tight, and that felt even better.

At last, with reluctance, he raised his head, his hold loosening. "Then we have tonight to enjoy without anxiety."

"Nothing can stop that now," she said, smiling, and softly kissed his lips.

It seemed he had to return the favor, and then, with a catch in his breath that told her he wanted much, much more, he dropped his arms and stood back, inspecting her. "No one would know I almost ravished you. Apart from the soft, warm glow in your eyes that tempts me to much more wicked intimacies."

Her whole body glowed at that. A sweet, heavy yearning that could not be satisfied here and now. But soon...

He touched her cheek. "Even your tears have vanished in the breeze."

She turned into his hand to kiss it. A sense of wonder overlaid everything, even her own boldness, which felt so very natural.

He said, "The first dance has ended. If you wish to enjoy the rest of the evening without the drama of announcements, you should go back inside first. I'll follow shortly."

He caught her hand and kissed it, and, smiling, she left him. She seemed to be walking on air.

In the milling around following the end of the waltz, no one seemed to notice her re-entry. She didn't much care if they did, but in truth, he was right. There would be more fun in the evening without the drama.

A young man walking in a group at the side of the dance floor suddenly changed direction, veering purposefully toward her. Pulling her brain ruthlessly out of the clouds, she remembered he had been introduced to her by accident as part of Mrs. Swan's campaign to make Griz known.

"Miss Battle." He bowed to her, and she curtseyed in reply. "Would you grant me the pleasure of the next dance?"

"Thank you," she said. "I should be glad to."

And she was. The first dance with Nicholas had cleared everything for her, leaving only joy in the music, in dancing, and talking with pleasant people, while her heart soared. Because Nicholas loved her. Because she would be his wife and live her life with him. No more loneliness...

She knew she was smiling too much, but she didn't care. *Nicholas, Nicholas...*

She caught sight of him, dancing with his sister-in-law, and was glad. Griz, who had danced the first waltz with her host, was sitting this one out, surrounded by people all trying to talk to her at once.

In fact, as the dance came to an end and Alexandra curtseyed to her amiable partner, it came to her that Grizelda's smile was too fixed, her skin too pale.

Parting on the best of terms with the young man whose name she could not remember, Alexandra made her way through the throng toward Griz. And suddenly came face to face with another lady she knew. She would have nodded politely and passed on, but the other woman stayed her.

"Why, it *is* the governess, is it not?" she drawled in apparent amusement. Her eyes, however, were not amused. More...threatening.

Alexandra blinked. It was Mrs. Jenner, the widow who had called on Nicholas the day the piano had arrived. Whose soiree he had attended. Who had once inspired Alexandra with such painful, foolish jealousy.

"I am certainly *a* governess," Alexandra replied, refusing to be cowed.

To her surprise, Mrs. Jenner took her arm, walking with her as though exchanging confidences with a close friend. "Yes, you are, and you would do well to remember it."

"There is nothing wrong with my memory, ma'am," Alexandra said, trying to keep the tartness from her voice. Tonight, of all nights, she did not wish to quarrel.

But the other woman's contemptuous gaze swept down the length of her person. "I did not realize you had your admittedly puny claws into him to this degree, but it is quite ridiculous to suppose you can win him from me wearing a Paris gown that is two years old."

"Rather more than two," Alexandra said pleasantly. "And for what it is worth, what I or anyone else wears makes absolutely no difference to Sir Nicholas. Good evening."

Alexandra moved in the opposite direction, forcing Mrs. Jenner to either release her or appear to be desperately hanging onto her. Mrs. Jenner hastily chose the former, and Alexandra made it at last to Grizelda who, by then, had risen to her feet and was fanning herself.

"Excuse me," Griz murmured to those around her, her voice unusually shaky.

"Griz?" Alexandra took her arm in quick concern. "Do you need some fresh air?"

"Yes. Yes, I really think I do…"

As the next dance was forming, Alexandra fought their way around the edges of the dance floor to the terrace doors.

Since the ballroom was by now quite warm, more people had spilled outside into the cool of the evening. But Alexandra spotted steps leading down to a formal lawn and a wooden bench by a hedge of roses.

"Can you make it to the seat?" she murmured.

"Yes, of course, I just feel a little shaky. So silly. I am never ill."

When Griz was seated on the bench, Alexandra sat on the edge beside her. "Shall I fetch a glass of water? Or Dragan?"

"No, thanks, I feel better already, to be honest. It was just so hot and crowded in there I was afraid I would faint."

"Has this happened to you before?" Alexandra asked.

Griz shook her head. "No." She frowned. "Well, I suppose I felt a bit dizzy yesterday afternoon, but I was tired after being awake most of the night in Ricco's house. Oh, that reminds, me, Alex—"

"Griz, are you expecting a baby?"

Grizelda's jaw dropped. "Expecting a..." She stared at Alexandra. "Dear God, I hope not. Do I? Oh, God, Alex, what if I am?"

"Don't you want a child?" Alexandra asked gently.

Grizelda's eyes filled with unshed tears. "Oh, I do," she whispered. "I do. But not...not yet! How am I to have fun with Dragan when I have a baby?"

Alexandra refrained from pointing out that it was fun with Dragan that had got her to this place and then realized she hadn't meant that kind of fun. "You mean, climbing walls and chasing people across the city, hitting them with bags? That kind of thing?"

A smile flickered across Grizelda's face. "Yes, that kind of thing."

"I can't imagine even a whole gaggle of children slowing you two down for long. You will find a way, Griz. You always do."

"I do, don't I?" she said, thoughtfully. Her arm closed protectively across her belly, an expression of wonder suffusing her face. "Oh, my... this is huge, Alex."

"Huge, amazing, and wonderful. I am so glad for you."

"I shall be a terrible mother."

"You will be a delightful mother, caring and fun."

Griz dashed a hand across her eyes and laughed. "And what of you, Alexandra? I saw you vanish with Sir Nicholas. Have you reached an understanding?"

"I believe we have," Alexandra admitted, blushing, and Griz gave her a rare hug, which she returned.

They sat back quietly for a moment, each lost in their own thoughts until quick footsteps on the stone stairs behind made Alexandra turn.

It was Dragan. "What are you two plotting out here alone?"

Griz jumped to her feet. "I'll tell you if you dance with me."

"I'm happy to oblige," Dragan said promptly. "Miss Battle, will you accompany us?"

Smiling, she shook her head. "No, I shall sit here a moment longer."

They were, she thought, as they walked away hand-in-hand, very sweet. Ill-matched by conventional standards, perfectly so by their own. And hers. They were devoted to each other, and she looked forward to seeing them as parents.

And now it was possible she, too, would be a mother one day.

"Tell you what," a familiar voice said, as its owner eased himself onto the bench beside her, "You should be able to do better than making friends with courtesans."

She stared at her father in astonishment.

CHAPTER TWENTY-THREE

DURING HIS DANCE with his sister-in-law, Nicholas had exerted himself to be charming and put her at her ease. Now that she was no longer defensive of her children's home, she seemed to realize all the awkwardness of keeping it and making him, its owner, her guest. However, he paid her many compliments, and by the end of the dance, she seemed more at ease. When, in truth, more than half his mind and heart were not on her at all but were dwelling still on those moments with Alexandra.

His promised bride. His wife. The contentment of family life had never called to him before. In fact, to him it had seemed a contradiction of terms. Now, with Alexandra, he longed for it. As for the intimacies of marriage...he doubted he could wait. Fierce desire for her wracked him still, even dancing with another woman.

So all in all, he was relieved when the dance came to an end, and he could bow to his sister-in-law and move away in search of *her* once more...

"Sir." A footman waylaid him. "A Mr. Harris has asked to see you. He is in the front reception room, if you wish, or we can deny—"

"No, I'll see him. Thank you." Nicholas strode out of the ballroom, eager for good news. He didn't want to spoil Alexandra's happiness with this mess. Not tonight. Tomorrow was time enough.

He found Harris pacing the floor of the reception room with a face like thunder.

He closed the door. "Good news?" he asked hopefully.

"Not exactly," Harris snapped. "He didn't go into your house as we expected. We followed him here to Brook Street."

"*Here?*" Nicholas stared. "Where is he, in God's name?"

"In the garden at the back. My men are surrounding the place."

"Why don't you just seize him?" Nicholas demanded.

"Because he's here to speak to his daughter, and we're quite keen to hear that conversation."

Anger surged through Nicholas. His hands clenched, and he took an involuntary stride closer to Harris. "She has nothing to do with his crimes."

"Then she won't mind handing him over," Harris said, quite unintimidated.

"For God's sake, Harris, he's her father! Would you hand yours over to prison?"

"My father hasn't kidnapped children or extorted ransom for them. I'm telling you this as a courtesy, sir, but if you interfere, I will arrest you."

"Then arrest me," he flung over his shoulder. "For I won't let him go near her."

He was already out the door before he finished speaking, marching back to the ballroom.

His impatient gaze could not find her among the bright throng, though eventually, he located Lady Griz and Tizsa entering from the terrace door. He pushed his way toward them, forcing himself to smile and nod to acquaintances and excuse himself civilly to those he disturbed.

At one point, Caroline Jenner stood in front of him, smiling. "Nicholas, there you are. You have not yet asked me to dance."

"That is true, and I shall be happy to rectify the matter in just a little. Excuse me…" He caught her frown, the spit of temper from her eyes, but he didn't care.

At last, he reached the Tizsas, who, for some reason, looked dazed in a happy kind of a way. Perhaps they had enjoyed a moment in the garden.

"Where is Alexandra?" he asked without preamble. "Have you seen her?"

"She's still in the garden," Griz said in surprise. "Just below the terrace. Sir—"

"Ricco is here," he interrupted, making grimly for the terrace door.

Behind him, Tizsa spoke with uncharacteristic severity. "Stay here, Griz. I mean it."

⇢⇥⇤⇠

"COURTESANS?" ALEXANDRA REPEATED, outraged on behalf of her friend, the duke's daughter. "She is *not* a courtesan!"

"That's a polite word considering, but there, we won't quarrel over it."

"Papa, what the devil are you doing here?" She peered at him to make sure, for he sat in the shadows, but he was not wearing evening dress.

"I came to see you," he said easily. "We didn't get the chance to say goodbye before. And well, the thing is, turns out I need money after all."

"I told you the last time, I don't *have* any money," she said impatiently.

"Well, you looked mighty cozy with a man who does—he whom you call your employer."

Stung by his contemptuous tone, she snapped, "He is no longer my employer but my affianced husband."

Her father rubbed his hands together. "Even better. Get me a hundred, there's a good girl. You can send more later."

"Send it where?" she asked, bewildered. "Where are you going?"

He sighed. "Something came up. Well, something went wrong. I waited too long, and it all blew up in my face. Always quit while you're ahead, in life as in gaming."

She frowned at him, wondering yet again how this had happened to such a once-great musician. "Papa, when did you last play the piano? You can always make money that way. *Quick* money if you need it."

He put his hands behind his back, like a child hiding illicit sweet-meats. "Thing is, the old fingers don't work so well anymore."

"Perhaps they would if you eschewed the brandy."

"I did. But the wine isn't good for them either. No games, now, Lexie, and no scolds. Just get me the money."

"Don't be silly, Papa, even if I was prepared to ask him, which I'm not, he would have no reason to carry money to a ball."

"I'll wait until tonight. You can throw it over the garden wall if we time it right to avoid the policemen swarming all over the place."

"Police?" she said, startled. "Why are police swarming around Hungerford House?"

And like a sledgehammer pounding her head, she knew.

His comments about courtesans meant he had seen Griz dressed like Nell and her comrades the night they had chased the cloaked man and his underlings and rescued the kidnapped boys. He had been in London for months but only come to her when he was afraid to go home or to his usual haunts after the kidnappers were arrested. He had told her he had money when he stayed in her room. But since then, Griz and Dragan had found his hidden ransom money.

"Ricco," she whispered. "You are Ricco." She leapt to her feet, backing away from him in horror. "Papa, how could you? How could you take *children*—"

"I never hurt them," he said defensively. "Paid a fortune if you must know, just to have them looked after and kept happy."

"But you *abducted* them! You took them away from their homes, their parents! Do you have any idea of the damage that could do?"

"Oh, grow up, Alexandra, they were all pampered little—" He broke off, his gaze darting, and rose slowly to his feet.

No wonder. Dark figures were swarming across the garden from the back wall and from either side.

"Get me out of this, Lexie," her father said urgently. "Take me through the house to the front. There must be fewer Peelers there."

And she saw suddenly that this was her fault. If she had left him to be punished in Italy, surely, he would not have gone on getting worse, overstepping more and more boundaries until he was kidnapping children.

"Not this time, Papa," she said hoarsely. "Not for this."

Even in the gloom, she saw the anger and betrayal in his eyes. She had always been there, even as a child, to get him out of trouble. To help him find his way home when he was drunk, to hide from importuning women, to plead his ill-health to theatre managers when he was too drunk to play or had found a congenial gambling den instead. She had helped make him this.

"No matter," he said savagely. "I'll go myself."

He swung around toward the terrace and, like Alexandra, must have seen Nicholas and Dragan running purposefully down the steps. Shame and despair flooded her. He had ruined her life. Again.

He changed direction, bolting toward the little herb garden that led to the kitchen door. At once, Dragan ran to head him off, and in any case, policemen fanned out to block him.

A huge, ominous cloud descended on Alexandra, like a prophecy of imminent tragedy. Instinctively, she threw herself toward Nicholas, and indeed, his path blocked by Dragan and several policemen, her father doubled back toward the terrace steps with startling speed. And now, something in his hand glittered in the moonlight. A dagger? Certainly a blade of some kind. And Nicholas was striding purposefully to meet him.

Nicholas must have seen the blade, for his posture altered, ready to meet the threat. But Alexandra could not allow that. That he should face such a danger from her father.

"No!" she shouted and threw herself between them, her arms spread out. Nicholas bumped into her back. With sudden horror on his face, her father tried to slow his charge, to swerve. He even flung his hand up in the air to avoid hurting her. But he didn't drop the blade.

Nicholas's arm snaked around her waist, spinning her into the rough, terrace wall, which she grasped, gasping. Before her eyes, Nicholas and her father were grappling. Nicholas had seized the wrist that held the knife, but her father's free hand was at Nicholas's throat.

With a sob, she pushed off the wall, meaning to hurl herself into the fray once more. But it was too late.

The knife had already fallen to the ground. Nicholas's swift chop to her father's arm broke the hold on his throat, and faster than she could easily see, Nicholas had seized him, wrenching his arm up his back in a secure grip. Dragan was there, policemen were there, including Inspector Harris.

"Take him away," Harris ordered. "Quietly, by the back gate."

"Wait," her father said hoarsely, and for some reason, they did. Two burly policemen still held him captive, but the others stepped aside, clearing a path between him and Alexandra.

Their eyes met.

"I'm sorry, Papa," she whispered. "It was too much. Finally, it was too much."

He swallowed. Perhaps he was thinking of what might have been. Or what would be. "Will you come and see me? If I don't hang?"

Tears coursed down her cheeks. "Of course I will."

A ghost of the old devil-may-care smile curved his lips. "Then take me away, gentlemen. I don't believe I like this party."

"Only because you ruined it, you...you..." The tears came faster, but astonishingly a strong arm came around her shoulders, and she was held against a broad, hard chest.

Nicholas held her while she wept.

⟫⟫⟫⟪⟪⟪

MINGLED WITH THE grief and shame and guilt surrounding her father was wonder that Nicholas still sat at her side. Mrs. Swan, told something of the arrest made in her back garden, had obligingly made a small parlor available to them, while she and Griz recovered.

Not that there appeared to be anything wrong with Griz now. Beneath her frown of worry over Alexandra, she was radiant, and, of course, she had not even been in the garden during the capture. But she had clearly decided Mrs. Swan's kindness would be more easily elicited for her than for Nicholas's upstart governess.

Alexandra's tears had dried. She had almost stopped shaking. Dragan thrust a glass of brandy into her hand, and she drank gratefully.

"When did you know?" she asked him.

"This afternoon, when I showed James my drawing of Ricco."

She closed her eyes. "Why didn't you say something to me?" She knew the answer, of course. Because they didn't know that she wasn't helping her father.

"For one thing, Harris wanted to be sure neither you nor Sir Nicholas was involved. For another, Sir Nicholas wanted it all settled and Ricco arrested while you were out of the house."

Sir Nicholas's arm tightened. "I didn't want you upset. It never entered my head that he would come here, even if he did spot the watching police at Hungerford."

She opened her eyes and stared at him. "But you left Evelina alone at home, knowing he would come there to get to me?"

"Not alone, no," Nicholas said. "Apart from the police outside the house, there should be one inside, along with James, one footman, and two brawny stable boys."

MARY LANCASTER

She accepted that. "But how did he know I was here in Brook Street? Did he see us leave?"

"Perhaps," Nicholas said, "Or he may have been speaking to the stable staff, who let drop the direction for the carriage this evening. They would not tell me that, but they did admit to seeing him in the mews."

"My father is very plausible," she said anxiously, in case he planned to turn off the too-talkative grooms.

"I might shout at them," Nicholas said flippantly, "but I usually give a man two chances."

What about governesses? Or brides? "I thought you would hate me," she whispered.

"Oh, why?" Griz said, kneeling in front of her. "None of us can help our families. And yet blood is thicker than water. I once tried to protect my own father when I thought he might have murdered someone. He didn't," she added hastily.

"He was captured trying to avoid hurting me," Alexandra said.

"In his own way, he looked after you," Nicholas said. "It is just a way that should never have been. Do you hate me for being responsible for his arrest?"

She jerked to face him, staring. "Of course, I do not!" And then she saw what he meant. That her father's behavior, her father's crimes, made no difference to his feelings either. She became fascinated by the reflection of a candle flame in his dark, warm eyes. Eyes that often hid the deep kindness and compassion of the man.

"We'll just go back to the ball," Griz murmured, allowing her husband to help her to her feet.

The closing door echoed in the room. Nicholas's arm lay warm at her waist, his shoulder almost touching her cheek. She took his other hand, large, capable, and just a little rough for a gentleman's, and held it between both of her own in her lap.

"Tell me honestly," she pleaded. "Do you still wish to marry me?"

For answer, he leaned over and kissed her, a tender yet thorough kiss.

"Even if the scandal of my father's crimes breaks over our heads?"

"Especially then."

Her fingers tightened on his. "Did you ever doubt me?"

"No."

This time, she kissed him and laid her head on his shoulder. It was sweet and peaceful.

"Tell me," he said at last. "Would you care to dance?"

And quite suddenly, that was exactly what she wanted to do. She smiled into his shoulder, then released his hand. They rose together and walked back to the ball.

CHAPTER TWENTY-FOUR

A LAMP BURNED low in Evelina's bedroom, as it did every night. In its pale glow, she looked angelic and peaceful, her beauty and innocence so intense it made Nicholas's heart ache.

"Sweet dreams, little one," he murmured, touching only her hair so as not to wake her.

Unexpectedly, her eyes opened, and she smiled sleepily. "You're both here."

Beside him, Alexandra smiled back.

"We'll both always be here," Nicholas said. "Miss Battle is going to marry me."

"I know *that*," Evelina said scornfully and went back to sleep.

Clearly trying not to laugh, Alexandra rose and tiptoed from the room. Nicholas followed her.

"I think she knew before I did," he said wryly.

"Certainly before I did." Alexandra's hand crept into his as they walked along the passage. He liked the feel of it there, warm, soft, loving. "You know that...that if we have—if *I* have children with you, it will never make any difference between them and Evelina. I will love her just as much."

"I know." He stroked her palm with his fingertips. "I will enjoy having more children. With you."

Ahead of them, her bedchamber door seemed to be lit up like a beacon, at least in his mind. Perhaps she imagined it, too, for he heard the change in her breathing. Desire, powerful and overwhelming, fought with gentlemanly instincts and common decency, and yet he needed her to know how he felt. She needed to know.

"I want you," he murmured, almost conversationally. "More intensely than I have ever wanted any woman in my life."

"That is good," she said, not quite steadily.

"It is also mightily inconvenient when you are under my roof, alone with me in the dark of the night, only hours after you watched me disarm your father before the police hauled him off to gaol."

He meant to break the mood, give her a reason as well as the will to make him wait. But she did not drop his hand.

"My father will go to prison, and rightly so, for what he has done. I will not desert him. But more than ever, you and my love for you are all that I have. I want you to frighten the dark away, to show me the goodness, the joy in life. In making life. Please don't leave me."

He halted by her bedchamber door, his heart thundering. Surely no one had ever borne tension like this, conflict like this. His breath came too fast, but he could not slow it as he raised his not quite steady hand to her cheek.

"Do you want me to hold you?" he whispered.

She turned the handle and pushed open the door before wrapping both arms around his neck. "I want you to love me."

He dropped his head in massive relief, finding and devouring her urgent mouth. They almost fell into the room, and he kicked the door shut with his heel. He swept both hands through her hair, sending pins and combs flying in all directions. But this was how he had first seen her with her hair tumbled about her face and shoulders, beautiful, alluring, devastating…

And wearing a lot less clothes. The fastenings were the work of mere moments before the gown fell around her elbows, and he could push it to the ground and lift her out of it. Of course, there were still a ridiculous number of petticoats to deal with, but at least that slowed him down, reminded him of his manners, of her virginity, and of the pleasures of unwrapping so wonderful a gift.

He gentled his kisses, forced his hands to sensual rather than demanding caresses as he undressed her. Her eagerness delighted him as with trembling hands, she pushed at his coat and pulled up his shirt.

And then she was naked in his arms, and his mouth went dry all over again.

"I have no words for your beauty," he whispered, crushing her in his arms once more. "But I worship it. I worship you…"

Her eyes seemed to sparkle with enchantment beneath the mists of desire. She clung to him, and when he lifted her, carrying her to the bed, they seemed welded together, skin to skin *almost* close enough.

He laid her beneath him, sweeping his hand down the length of her body to rest between her legs, and watched her fall apart in wonder from his touch.

"What…what…" she gasped, reaching for his mouth. He gave it and slid inside her at last, like coming home. And then, though he sometimes shook with the effort of restraint, he loved her with gentle, adoring passion until they gave each other the ultimate physical joy.

⸎⸎⸎❮❮❮

WHEN ALEXANDRA WOKE, it was light. He had left her at dawn to preserve her reputation, and returned to his own room. She longed for the day he didn't need to, but that only strengthened her happiness in the new day.

The wonders of last night still astonished her. She had wanted his closeness, to bask in his happiness, but she had never expected to feel anything so intensely sensual, so uniquely joyful. And this would be hers again when they were married.

No wonder people kept having more babies.

She giggled at the thought and threw off the covers. There was sadness in every life, including her own. There were responsibilities, pleasant and unpleasant, and she accepted those, too. But she would not let them spoil her happiness. This was her new life.

A life full of love and wonder, but also full of purpose. As they had lain together in a quiet moment, his head on her breast, he had told her his idea of taking another house in a better area and turning this house into a school that would accept children from all walks of life. The wealthy would pay for the poor, and so education and care could be provided for families like the one Evelina had discovered in Covent Garden. Children did not regard wealth or class, and so he hoped they would grow up understanding each other, with more and different opportunities.

"Would you object to that?" he had asked her sleepily. "Evelina would go, too."

"Of course, I would not. I would like to help."

"It will take time... And maybe you are right, and I should look into politics, too." He had raised himself up on his elbow, tousled and devastating. "I feel we can do anything now we are together."

"So do I," she had whispered, and then the hot desire had closed in again, spinning her off into new, heady pleasures that made her tingle just to remember.

Singing to herself, she washed and dressed and pinned her hair in the new, loose style that suited her best. Then she threw the curtains wide and went downstairs to greet her family.

About Mary Lancaster

Mary Lancaster lives in Scotland with her husband, three mostly grown-up kids and a small, crazy dog.

Her first literary love was historical fiction, a genre which she relishes mixing up with romance and adventure in her own writing. Her most recent books are light, fun Regency romances written for Dragonblade Publishing: *The Imperial Season* series set at the Congress of Vienna; and the popular *Blackhaven Brides* series, which is set in a fashionable English spa town frequented by the great and the bad of Regency society.

Connect with Mary on-line – she loves to hear from readers:

Email Mary: Mary@MaryLancaster.com

Website: www.MaryLancaster.com

Newsletter sign-up: http://eepurl.com/b4Xoif

Facebook: facebook.com/mary.lancaster.1656

Facebook Author Page: facebook.com/MaryLancasterNovelist

Twitter: @MaryLancNovels

Amazon Author Page: amazon.com/Mary-Lancaster/e/B00DJ5IACI

Bookbub: bookbub.com/profile/mary-lancaster